FLORIDA FABLES

The Story of

WHISKEY CORNERS

A Novel

TONY DUNBAR

Also by Tony Dunbar:

The Florida Fables

The Story of The Sarasota Assassination Society

The Story of The Sarasota Celery Fields & Other Mysteries

The Story of Whiskey Corners

The Tubby Dubonnet Mystery Series

Crooked Man

City of Beads

Trick Question

Shelter From the Storm

Crime Czar

Lucky Man

Tubby Meets Katrina

Night Watchman

Fat Man Blues

Flag Boy

Other Books by Tony Dunbar

Our Land Too

Hard Traveling: Migrant Farm Workers in America

Against the Grain: Southern Radicals and Prophets, 1929–1959

Delta Time

Where We Stand: Voices of Southern Dissent

American Crisis, Southern Solutions: Promise and Peril

The Battle of New Orleans: Mysterious Tales

FLORIDA FABLES

The Story of

WHISKEY CORNERS

TONY DUNBAR

Blind Pass Publications
Florida

ISBN : 979-8-218-07565-1

Blind Pass Publications, LLC
Post Office Box 1096
Englewood, FL 34295

Many thanks to Ben Hecht for his outlandish stories about Charles Ort in A Child of the Century (New York, 1954).

Credit for the photograph above: State Archives of Florida, Florida Memory, Image N033465.

Credit for the photograph on page 61: "Cigar Factory Lector," Burgert Brothers, State Archives of Florida, Florida Memory, Image RC03558.

Credit for the photograph on page 262: "Airfield," Ray K. Williams, State Archives of Florida, Florida Memory, Image PR76017.

PROMISE

This story is about fifty percent true.

DEDICATION

I thought upon the banks o' Coil,

I thought upon my Nancy,

I thought upon the witching smile

That caught my youthful fancy.

- Robert Burns

The Story of
WHISKEY CORNERS

A NOVEL

Looking back on it now, I see many things I wish I could have done differently, but the world was changing so fast that hold tight and hang on was about the best anybody could do. You all probably know that the great Florida land bubble blew up in 1926, and everybody watched the paper fortunes they had made selling sand dunes and swamps to tourists turn into . . . paper. Temporarily purged of pitchmen and con artists, people in Florida got by okay - eating the fish we could catch, the beans we could grow, and cabbage palm hearts we could turn into stew. This was before the big Crash sent the rest of America into the breadlines. We had a head start.

There's a whole lot you don't know, a lot of unwritten history, about those days. I'll try to catch you up on some of it, at least the part I know, the part that concerns our sunny little town of Sarasota and those sinful big cities nearby, Tampa and St. Petersburg. I had better warn you that a lot of bad people travel through this story: union busters, mobsters, crooked cops and even the Ku Klux Klan. Sorry to say, but that's the way things happened.

So the splash, slap and dance of our Florida came tumbling down in 1926, but believe me, buddy - up, down and sideways, before and after that crash, it was quite a ride!

TABLE OF CONTENTS

CHAPTER ONE
MY REUNION

In the sunny 1920's, Sarasota was realizing its dream of becoming a real metropolis by the Bay, a booming and glamorous destination where big money could be made just as fast as people could grab their own juicy piece of the pie. I capped my career as City Marshal and Deputy Sheriff by solving the murder of Harry Higel, who maybe you never heard of, but he was quite the man around this town, being our three-time mayor and developer of Siesta Key. Figuring out who laid him in his grave did not bring me any public acclaim, but it did give me a lot of personal satisfaction. On the other hand, my domestic life took a turn for the worse.

Clarinda, my wife, right out and left me. She left our house, our farm, our dog and her horse. She even left me with the Dodge, her book of birds, and most of her clothes. And I didn't really know why. I mean, I eventually learned that she had gone to rejoin the mother who had abandoned her when she was only sixteen. Yet, I had always been led to believe that my wife hated that woman, whose sweet name was Lovelady Barlow. And I knew that Clarinda had every right to be disappointed with me about my very brief affair with Estelle Braxton, but that had ended five years before Clarinda left me. Nothing else stands out in my mind. I just came home one night and Clarinda wasn't there.

I'm not as young as I once was, but don't try me. I've been in law enforcement all my life, and I still think I'm as tough as I ever was, even without the gun I carry. Objectively, I believe it's true. But Clarinda knocked me off my little grandstand.

By and by, my close friend Reuben Ephram made inquiries and informed me that Clarinda was in St. Petersburg. I was slow about it, but I finally decided to search her out.

I found my wife, but this is the way it went.

They called the bustling, blazing city of St. Petersburg the Sunshine City. Sunny and hot, was what it was, but it had its own airport, real sky-scrapers, traffic jams and tin-can tourists. It was an exciting place.

But Clarinda, I learned, had settled into a sleepy little community north of town known as Seminole. It was beside a lake of the same name. On a paved Seminole street with sandy sidewalks I located her mother, Mrs. Barlow's, quaint "Needles and Threads." That would be Lovelady's shop for ladies. Reuben had told me that Clarinda and her mom lived together in the apartment above the store. He hadn't actually seen them, but he had talked to a lady customer who had.

I made the three-hour drive and parked in the shade of a tall coconut palm, got out and stretched the kinks out of my legs from my road-trip up the new Tamiami Trail. Taking a deep breath, I walked resolutely toward the door. A little bell tinkled to announce me. It was cool inside, thanks to a pair of ceiling fans, and the air smelled like what I think of as lilac.

"Just a minute," a woman called from the back, and I knew Clarinda's voice. I didn't say anything at the moment. I just waited, absorbing the atmosphere of the place. Bolts of colorful fabric were stacked neatly on the walls, and a glass display case ran down one side of the room showing off spools of thread, scissors, needles, and a great many other items I didn't know the use of. There was a small poster on the wall for the National American Women's Suffrage Association.

"Can I help you, sir?" she said brightly as she came through an archway, and then, "Oh, my, my," when she recognized me.

"Hello, Clarinda," I said. "You're looking mighty good." It was true. Her blonde hair might have faded a bit, but she has the kind of high cheekbones, full lips, and fierce blue eyes that keep a woman's face nice looking no matter how old she is. Of course, she wasn't exactly old, maybe 52 by my calculation. She still looked to be as light as a feather – her arms were still white as cream. And I was still in love.

"Hello, Gawain," she managed to reply, using my full name, and spread her hands out on the top of the glass case to steady herself. "It's been nearly a year."

"Yes it has been, Clarinda. I think it's time we should talk about this and try to work something out." I had rehearsed that in the car coming up.

"Work it out how, exactly?" She was blushing.

"I don't know." I stepped forward. "Would you want to go someplace? If you're busy I could come by later. Maybe go out for supper?"

I heard a chair scraping the floor above me, the sound of footsteps on the stairs in the back, and another woman appeared under the arch. She could have been Clarinda, only fifteen or twenty years older, and she had a pile of white hair tied up in a bun atop her head by a purple scarf. And she gave me a big smile, like she'd known me her whole life.

"You must be Lovelady," I said. I had never met the woman before, since she had deserted both Clarinda and her husband, Pa Barlow, before I ever entered their lives.

"And you must be Gawain MacFarlane." She hurried forward to clasp my hand warmly in hers. "It is so nice to see you, honey."

This was the reception I had hoped to get from Clarinda, and I was a little confused by it all.

"Mother, please," Clarinda said. "Get acquainted with the man before you propose to him."

"You hush, Clarinda," Lovelady said. "You know I've always wanted to meet my grandson's father."

I should say that Clarinda's and my son, Wallace MacFarland, or Mack as we called him, had grown up, gone to the Great War, come back as a pilot, and now had a flying job in Tampa – just across the bay.

So Clarinda hadn't deserted him – just me. "Are you going to stay long, Mister MacFarlane?" Mrs. Barlow let go of my hand to touch her hair.

"I don't know for sure ma'am. I was just saying to your daughter that she and I ought to have a private talk."

"Well, of course you should," Lovelady chirped. "Clarinda, why don't y'all go for a walk down by the lake, and I'll mind the store."

Clarinda shrugged. "All right," she said with some reluctance. After all, it wasn't her who had agreed to this meeting. "I'll just get on a pair of walking shoes."

I listened to her going up those stairs while I had to parry a series of questions from Mrs. Barlow about my health, my farm, and the well-being of her grandson Mack. Finally I heard Clarinda coming back down. She had changed her shoes, but she had also put on a fresh turquoise blouse, the loose sort that women wear at the beach.

We got out the door, with Lovelady still going on about how nice it was to meet me and she hoped to see me again. Clarinda pointed us toward the lake, a block away. We kept a couple of feet between us, and she led me into a grassy park under live oak trees. It was nice there in the shade, and we just strolled along for a minute in silence before we came upon an empty bench and sat down.

"So, how have you been?" I asked. I hadn't really worked out the way this part of our conversation was supposed to go. It's funny. Thirty years of marriage and you don't know what to say.

"I'm okay, Gabe," she said, using my other name, my professional name.

"What would you think about the two of us getting back together, and you coming home?" I asked, getting to the point.

"I can't, honey," she said and took my hand in both of hers. She caught my stare and held it. "My mama needs me."

"Your mama didn't need you for thirty years," I objected, "and it looks to me like she can take care of herself."

Clarinda shook her head and turned to look out over the dark green water. "I've been seeing someone," she said.

That sat me back like I'd been sucker punched, and I reclaimed my hand.

"It just happened," she went on. "I've been so bored for so long, with the god damn country life and everything else, and raising oranges, and dealing with church ladies, and kicking dirt off my boots, and. . . ." She stopped for breath and gave a big exhale.

"Yeah, I know all about that," I broke in. "That's why I'm here. Times are changing fast in Sarasota. We can, too. But you say you're seeing someone?"

"Yes, Gabe, I am." She faced me again. "He has a department store, or at least his father does, but he runs it. He has a car that starts every time. He plays golf. He can make a martini . . ."

"A martini? And he likes you?" I interrupted loudly. She hopped to her feet.

"Indeed! Why wouldn't he fancy me? He says he loves me."

I stood up, too. "What does your mother think?" I asked lamely.

"What does that matter? She thinks he's too fat. That's why she's so nice to you."

"He's fat?" I shouted.

"He's not that fat," she said, retreating, "and he's very kind and generous."

I couldn't even look at her. "Well, ain't that something!" I said, disgusted.

"You never showed up!" she complained.

"You left me, Clarinda!" I could insist on that point all I wanted, but we were back where we started, only in a worse place since now she had a boyfriend. "I guess you can find your own way back," I said, and tramped to my car, bristling sparks I imagine.

She didn't try to stop me, and I didn't hear any crying.

A poem came to mind. It was from a book of "songs" by Robert Burns, a keepsake from my father:

> *Her eyes, sae bonnie blue, betray*
> *How she repays my passion;*
> *But prudence is always her reply,*
> *She talks of rank and fashion.*

O why should Fate such pleasure have,

Life's dearest bands untwining?

Or why sae sweet a flower as love

Depend on Fortune's shining?

CLARINDA BARLOW MACFARLANE'S STORY

I felt bad for letting Gawain down. I believe he really did want me to come home, to get us back to the way we were. However, the time when that way was satisfying to me had come and gone.

Growing up, I had made do with a hard-working, lovable drunk father and no mother, since she had bailed out, and none of that was a bit of fun. Now here I was married to a retired lawman who had too much time on his hands, since the orchards paid for themselves, but he was still used to me doing the cooking and cleaning. Tired of Catfish Creek? You bet! Wanting to see more of the world? Yes, indeed.

We'd done the family thing, and Mack was all grown up and moved on. And I was supposed to sit out there in the country knitting my life away on the farm?

I guess Gawain may have had some of the same problems or he never would have had that affair with Estelle Braxton.

I joined with our missionary ladies to support Prohibition, and, along with the younger ones, to demand the right to vote. But I got tired of them, too. They all seemed to have futures I could only dream about.

Seeing my mother again, and her inviting me to run away and live with her, opened up some kind of door, and I'm real happy I went through it.

There's nothing wrong with Gawain. In the old days, he and I fought outlaws together, guns loaded. Now all that's over, and Sarasota has become civilized. But I haven't seen much of a reward in it for me. I'd say that, without the fireworks it took to settle the country, the town is boring.

Nobody really knows who I am or what I might think of to do. Clarinda Barlow MacFarlane is not one-dimensional, to use a big word that Gawain taught me. And, yes, I do love Gawain.

Selling bolts of cloth and pretty ribbons may not be the most exciting thing in the world either, but being here in this little town of Seminole has given me the chance to know my mother again, and to take walks, by myself, around the lake, down at the beach, wherever I like.

I didn't expect to meet men and didn't want to, but Alf took a fancy to me and won't seem to quit. I don't think he's as rich as my mother believes he is, and we both agree he is stout. But what I like best about him, and what makes me overlook his faults, is he says he wants to take me to France.

LOVELADY BARLOW'S PRAYER

Whatever have I done, Lord, to deserve the charity you have shown me? I left my husband in the wilderness because I couldn't stand being poor anymore. I abandoned my baby when she needed me the most. You know all about that. I stole my daughter away from her husband. Now I'm trying to run off her stupid boyfriend who wants to take her to France.

But I'm happy, dear God. I'm happy, for the first time in my life. Thank you. Thank you. I feel like there's a purpose in my life.

CHAPTER TWO

STEPPING OUT

I left Clarinda and her mother and drove directly toward downtown St. Petersburg. I had no particular destination in my mind, or anything else for that matter. I was just numb and wanted to see what else the screwy world had in store for me. Before long I was in the city, wedged into a heavy stream of cars moving at a crawl down a busy street. The sidewalks were packed with strolling tourists and rows of those unusual green benches which were occupied by the whole spectrum of rambling Americans, all just watching the world go by.

It occurred to me that I'd just spend a few dollars and get a hotel room, stretch out, shake off the road weariness, shake off life's pointlessness. My dog back home would be fine, right? A car backing out of its parking space caught my eye, and I slid in. Right in front of me was the Hotel Detroit and my feet carried me past a smiling doorman into the lobby. The carpet was thick. The paintings on the wall were modern. The desk was mahogany, and the agreeable attendant offered me a room up the stairs on the third floor. I said I needed a bell boy, which I didn't. When a lad rushed up in his red suit I took him aside, slipped him five dollars and told him just what I wanted and when I wanted it. Now.

The room upstairs was better than I was used to. A window overlooked Central Avenue and from it I could watch my car. There was a fire escape down the hall. Hot and cold running water, my own bathroom, a settee and a big bed. I sat on that bed and stared out my window, doing just what all those people on their green benches were doing: watching our old world turn. It wasn't long before my entertainment arrived. A brown bottle of Canadian Club. I gave the bell boy another tip for that, not even caring if it was the real thing or an artful imitation so long as it did the trick.

"Let me know if there is anything else you need, sir. My name is Jerry."

"Thanks, Jerry. How late do you work?"

"Midnight, sir."

"Is there any ice in this place?"

"I can bring you a little bucket."

"Do that. Just knock and leave it outside the door."

I used my Case Double X pocket knife to cut through the seal and poured myself a glass, thoughtfully provided by the management. It smelled like whiskey.

I went back to sit on my bed, looked down at all the people, and drank. A radio was on the night strand. I twirled the dial and found Ted Lewis playing, "When My Baby Smiles on Me." I wished my baby had.

Well, I had done without Clarinda for almost a year and survived, okay. It's just I hadn't expected to get kicked in the gut the moment I tried to get her back. I hated to admit it, but I'd had enough of being alone.

Whiskey is a funny thing. Sometimes it makes you want to dance. Sometimes it makes you gloomy. Sometimes whiskey fills you up and puts you to sleep. And sometimes it makes you want to go out and get something to eat. And that's what it did on this strange spring evening sitting in this strange room in a strange city.

Down in the lobby there was a nice restaurant with white tablecloths and candles, but I had in mind some place a little more down home. Two blocks away on 4th Street was the Sunshine City Diner. I had been there once before. The establishment featured booths with red upholstery and good peach pie. That's where I wanted to go, as the afternoon got cooler and the shadows from the buildings got longer.

When I pushed open the door to the restaurant I found what I hadn't acknowledged to myself I was looking for – a pretty waitress named Germaine. She cocked her head when I walked in, sort of recognizing me. After all, it had been several months, but it turned out I had made an impression on her.

Pointing a finger at me she asked, "Aren't you the lawman who stole my silverware?" She had a crooked smile and a nice figure and was wearing a white apron and a candy-striped dress that didn't cover her knees. There were quite a few customers in the place, and at a table in the back one was waving at her.

"I didn't steal it, ma'am. I paid you good money for that knife, and I needed it for evidence." It was true. I had needed it to get the fingerprints of Billy Neal, the man I then suspected of murdering Harry Higel, the beloved three-time mayor of Sarasota. Later on, I convicted Billy and carried out his sentence.

"Did you catch the guy?" she wanted to know.

"In a manner of speaking, yes," I told her. I had indeed caught Billy Neal, and he now lay buried in the sand somewhere on Siesta Key as a result.

"Did you come to eat or just to make eyes at me?" she asked.

"Both, if that's okay." I gave her a big smile.

"Well, grab a booth. I'll be back with a menu in just a minute." And she was off to see what her other customers wanted.

The menu arrived, and a handful of silverware. She asked what I wanted to drink, and I told her sweet tea.

I liked the place, and the couple of belts of Canadian I'd tossed off at the hotel had me feeling relaxed and brave.

"Have you decided what to order?" she asked, coming back.

"What do you recommend, Germaine? And what time do you get off work?"

"Naughty boy," she said, and waved that finger at me again, but I think she liked the fact that I'd recalled her name. "Turkey and gravy is good, and the meatloaf ain't bad, but if I was you I'd stay away from the spaghetti."

"Turkey and gravy will be fine, but you didn't answer my second question about getting off of work."

"That comes with mashed potatoes, green beans and a house salad, and you're mighty fresh. This place closes at nine." She turned and went off with my order, and I thought she gave me a toss of her hips.

"She seems like an intelligent woman," I said, not realizing that I was talking out loud. The man at the booth behind me laughed, but fortunately he was leaving.

My meal came back quick, and it was hot. Germaine passed by every few minutes, and we chatted a bit here and there. I learned that she'd worked at the diner for two years, but her real devotion was making seashell jewelry. Several shops on the beach were carrying her earrings and bracelets, she said, and they were selling like hotcakes. She lifted her yellow hair to show me a pair of spiral bangles. "I cut these with a little saw," she said. "The shell is from some sort of mussel, a white one."

When I was done and she was clearing the plates, she asked if I wanted another slice of peach pie. She had remembered that from the other time I was in the place.

"That'll be just fine, ma'am," I told her. I was feeling quite frisky. "And a cup of coffee, black."

"Just what do you have in mind, should we go out at nine?" she asked.

"I don't know, this is your town. We could take a walk, I guess. See the sights?"

"There aren't many sights to see here at that hour," she laughed. "These old folks roll up the sidewalk after dark."

"In that case, we could go over to the Hotel Detroit and have a couple of drinks."

Germaine frowned. "What kind of drinks do they serve?"

"Canadian Club, sweetheart. There's a bottle in my room."

"That sounds appealing, but dangerous."

"Not at all. I'm a virtuous soul." This was me, being a new single man, I guess.

But that got another laugh. "There's no such thing," she declared. "Do you have a car?"

"Yes, I do."

"Then there's two ideas? One is go have a drink in your room and the other is take a ride in your car?"

"That's right. Let's do them both, in that order."

There was that twitch of the hips again when she went off to get my pie.

As it turned out, we went back to my hotel room and had our party there. Jerry the bellhop earned another five dollars and left a paper bag with a bottle in it outside my door, alongside another bucket of ice.

Germaine showed herself to be as hungry for love as I was, and since her roommate would probably feed the cat she said, her night belonged to her.

I sent for Jerry in the morning and ordered up some toothpaste and a couple of toothbrushes. He grinned broadly when I said bring two, but the look in my eyes wiped the smile off his face. After that, he took our room service order – biscuits, bacon, eggs, and lots of strong coffee.

It all had a bracing effect, and after Germaine and I showered off we went back to it in bed. She was a fine feeling woman who cared about making me happy. She wanted me to care about her pleasure, too, and I tried my hardest to oblige.

It was Sunday, her day off, and we enjoyed each other all the way till check-out time. Then we picked up on the second idea and took a drive in my car.

I had never seen the beach at St Petersburg, so that's where we went. You had to pay a toll to get across the bridge, and that made the trip more of a special treat to Germaine who, as she explained in some detail, watched her pretty pennies.

The little town across the bridge is called Pass-a-Grille, which has narrow brick streets and quaint places to shop. Germaine wanted a sun hat, and while she was trying on dozens of them, I grabbed a change of underwear and some other necessities that I had not thought to bring along on my drive from Sarasota. Then she helped me pick out a couple of white cotton shirts from Cuba and a pair of sunglasses, like the tourists wore.

Better dressed, we took a stroll on the beach. It was a breezy day and the waves were quite high. Plenty of kids were battling with the surf, and bathing beauties were showing off their legs as they ran among the dozens of blue-striped umbrellas set up in the sand. I told Germaine more about my life, and the adventures I had had, and that I had a son who flew airplanes. I clarified what might be any misconceptions she might have gotten the night before. I was not exactly single, but I had a wife who had left me. That freed her up to tell me that she'd been married herself, but that her husband had been killed in our war with the Kaiser. And, she'd recently broken up with a boyfriend because "he just got too rough."

Across the bridge, driving back, she directed me though complicated streets to her place, which was a small house off of Euclid Boulevard, on a small sandy lot with one lone palm tree. She made it clear that I wasn't invited in, adding, "I don't think my roommate would be pleased with any company."

"So, what are your plans?" she asked from the passenger seat.

"I think I'd like to stay around this area for a while," I replied. Why did I say that? My real objective on this trip had been to reunite with Clarinda. Clearly I was off to a bad start, but this was just a fling – the second one I'd had in thirty years. I should have been trying to get myself back on track.

"I'd like to see you again," she said.

"Well, don't you think we both ought to take a little time for sober reflection," I replied, more soberly than I felt. It was undeniable that my prospects for companionship sitting right besides me in the car were a whole lot more promising than with my wife.

"I don't know what sober reflection means," she said, "but whatever. Where will you stay?"

I had no firm plan. The idea of lingering around St. Pete had simply popped into my mind unbidden. Clarinda was here. And now Germaine. My son lived in close proximity. I'd tossed in my badge as a Sarasota County Deputy Sheriff, and I had resigned as Chief of Security for Palmer Farms. So you might say I was temporarily retired.

"As much as I know of my future, Germaine," I told her, "after I drop you off I'm going to drive over to Tampa and track down my son. Maybe he'll have some ideas, and I'll take it from there."

Germaine had ideas of her own.

"Hmmm. Tampa's okay," she said, "but if you like St. Petersburg, I know a place you might be able to rent for cheaps. And it's close by here." She paused and watched me sort of nod. "The cook at my restaurant has a little rental cottage out in back of his house. He was telling me just yesterday that he's kicking out the guy who's staying there. We could drive by and look at it if you like."

"We could," I agreed, still cautious, but not nearly cautious enough.

"Only problem is," Germaine added, "he drinks a lot."

I shrugged that off and turned the steering wheel as directed.

The cook's name was Sammy Flanigan, and his flat stucco house looked a lot like Germaine's except that it had a Ford jalopy parked in the front yard and two palm trees instead of one. We knocked on the door and a big stocky fellow with a face full of white whiskers and smelling of gin opened up to see who we were. He recognized me.

"You're the guy who likes peach pie!" he yelled. "And Germaine, too! Come on in and get out of the sun!"

His front room was dark and pretty much of a wreck. On the table facing his ragged green sofa was a chunk of dry yellow cheese on a platter and an open bottle of clear booze.

"Want a drink?" he shouted.

I was about to say no, but Germain said yes. In time I would find out that she liked to drink, too.

Larry got out a couple of glasses and poured us all a shot. "No ice," he reported sadly, but got right down to it anyway.

We sat and drank. The liquor from his bottle went down hot, and it kicked the whole way. Larry explained that he couldn't show me the little room out back because his renter wasn't clearing out until the morning and, at the moment, the two were not on the best of terms. "But it's clean, and bug free, and it's got a toilet that works," he assured me.

I told him I'd think seriously about it and would come back in a day or two to look the proposition over. That much settled, he slapped my shoulder and gave it a good squeeze. I didn't see the handshake coming and I thought he might have crushed a bone or two.

Germaine was happy on the way back to her house and hummed a little "Cuban Moon."

"Sammy's all right," she told me when she got out of the car.

"You're all right, too, Germaine, but let's go slow."

"I get even better over time," she said. The way she sashayed her way into her house reminded me of how she had felt the night before.

Catch the moments as they fly, said the Ploughman's Poet
And use them as ye ought, man:
Believe me, happiness is shy,
And comes not aye when sought, man.

CHAPTER THREE
MACK'S HOUSE

My son is Wallace MacFarlane, but we always called him Mack. He trained as a flyer in the War, and he wanted to keep at it after he got home. Sarasota didn't have much to offer in that line, but Tampa and St. Petersburg did. In fact, I've been told that the first scheduled airplane flight in the entire United States was made by a Benoist hydro-plane, going from St. Pete to Tampa, and you can just guess who paid big money to be on the first trip. A showman and real estate peddler named Noel A. Mitchell! He was once the mayor of St. Petersburg, but he lost his job for hosting drinking parties at City Hall. I had interviewed him in connection with the murder of Harry Higel, but whatever part he may have played in that callous and brutal crime, he got away with it.

The seaplane business didn't last, mostly due to mishaps such as structural malfunctions in the planes and collisions with submerged objects, but from Mack's time in the Army he knew some other airmen who had settled around Tampa. As a group they had bought a pair of war surplus Curtiss Jenny training biplanes. I knew this because Mack needed to borrow a few dollars from me to get started. Their business was flying stunts at fairs and circuses and taking passengers up for thrill-rides. Their airfield was a cow pasture on the north side of the city near the Hillsborough River. I had been there once to see the planes, but I had never been to Mack's apartment. I knew his address though.

Leaving Germaine and St. Pete, it took a while to find where my son lived. Like an old man – strike that - I circled around dusty streets bordered by wooded lots, tire shops, citrus groves and bungalows needing paint, until at last, as the moon was starting to rise, I found what looked like an Army compound but the sign said "Happy Acres." A gentleman walking his dog pointed me to the "hut" where "the flying ace" bunked. I was getting it now. These were converted soldiers' barracks.

Mack's "hut," which looked like a big storage shed to me, had flowers planted out front next to the "Keep Out" sign. There were lights on inside and a couple of motorcycles in the yard.

I beat on the door, and a pretty young woman answered. Laughter and loud voices came from behind her.

"Is Mack home?" I asked.

She let the door swing open, and I saw my son and another couple sitting around a table in a big front room peeling shrimp. "Mack!" she yelled. "You got company!"

My son saw me and jumped up. "Hey, Dad!" he exclaimed. "Come on in! Is everything alright?"

"Everything is fine," I assured him as he hurried to greet me. "I'm just passing through."

"Great to see you!" he pumped my hand and circled my shoulders with his big arms. He had grown larger than me and had a clean-shaven chiseled jaw to go with his rusty slicked-back hair, a little scraggly for my taste. "Have some boiled shrimp! Meet my friends!"

Did I say Mack was a good looking guy, more than six feet and skin as brown as saddle leather from being in the sun? He introduced his friends as Eugene Pull-knot (which I later learned was spelled Poulnot) and Eugene's girlfriend, whose name I didn't catch. The woman who had answered the door introduced herself as Christy, which had a nice sound to it I thought, and she was evidently Mack's girlfriend. Her last name was Barlow. That grabbed my attention since it was also my wife's maiden name.

They had a big bowl of shrimp, and big bowl of empty shells, and they were drinking beer. They made me a place, and I sat right down.

"My father's a retired sheriff," Mack explained to the group.

"Deputy," I corrected him. Eugene didn't blink at that though we were all drinking illegal booze. This beer came from a big bucket. It had brown foam on top and it smelled like hard cider, so it had to be home-brew from somewhere close by.

"Eugene and I were buddies in the Army, but now he's a printer by trade, looking for work like the rest of us."

"I thought you had a job, Mack?" I inquired.

"It's hard to call flying a job, Dad, it's so much fun, but, yessir, I'm making ends meet." He smiled at me, and also at Christy, the young lady who was peeling shrimp beside him.

"I'm studying to get into the union," Eugene said. "My father's helping me. He works at the Tampa Tribune."

"And I'm a house painter, thank you very much," Christy chimed in.

"That's right," Mack agreed. "She's got a job working for me painting the outside of this old place."

"Not just that. The fellow down the road wants to hire me, too."

"You better stay away from him," Mack told her. "He's not to be trusted around good-looking women."

"And you are?" She poked him. This banter continued.

"What brings you to Tampa?" Mack finally asked me.

"I went to see your mother," I said, "and she's fine."

"And?" he asked, without a pause.

"We can talk about that later, son. Anyhow, have you got any place I can sleep?"

"Sure, you can have my bed," Mack offered with enthusiasm.

"I'd rather sleep in my car," I told him.

"I could make you a nice soft bedroll in here on the sofa," Christy offered sweetly, which sounded so comfortable I just grinned and nodded. I liked this girl.

It was a nice evening, but the party broke up soon after we finished off the bucket of beer. After his guests left and Christy went to gather some bedding for me, Mack repeated his question about his mother.

"There's no big story to it," I said. "She's happy in Seminole. I invited her, but she doesn't want to come back to the farm. So, we're not very likely to get back together."

"Sorry to hear that, Dad," he said.

"I'm sorry, too, but that's the way it is."

"At least for now."

"Right." I shrugged. I didn't tell him that his mother had a boyfriend named Alf.

Christy made my bed and disappeared again somewhere toward the back of the house. Mack patted me on the shoulder and wished me good night. He switched off the lamp. I never did hear Christy leave the premises, but then I was out like a light.

Mack was up early, frying eggs on the stove behind the very couch where I was trying to sleep. As I yawned and got up, he explained that he had a package to deliver down in Fort Myers. It would take two hours and a full tank of fuel to get there.

I knew this had to be a fairly small package if it was to fit into the front cockpit. Those planes are small, as I could attest from my one airborne adventure, with Mack piloting from the seat behind me, but perhaps there was cargo space on this aircraft that I didn't know about. Mack didn't say what was in the package.

But he told me a little about his work over a quick mug of coffee. He did simple stunts, nothing too dangerous, he said, at county fairs. "I don't want to get myself killed," he said. "I'm starting to think about having a family."

He also carried people who wanted a thrill up for short flights. But during the week, he picked up real paying jobs ferrying important people ("You know, gangsters and politicians," he laughed, making light of it) around to some destination they wanted to arrive at in a hurry, or unseen. Or, like this morning, he was going to ferry a package for just such an "important person."

"Private 'taxi'," he said. "That's the best way to describe it, and the best way to make a living in the flying game. You know fuel ain't free. Are you headed back to Sarasota right away?"

"Not sure if I will," I said. "I'm thinking about staying around over in St. Pete for a while and getting a change of scenery."

"And see Mom?"

I looked at him and shrugged.

"Anyway, Dad. We can spend more time together."

"Let's do that," I said. He was ready to go, and so was I.

I followed his motorcycle over to the airfield where he kept his plane, parked in a barn. It had a fresh coat of bright silver paint that would reflect sunlight. Together we pushed it outside, and it cranked right up. Watching him take off was an emotional experience, but not for the reason you might think. I was proud of him, yes, but I was also feeling sorry for myself because of how strong Mack seemed and how much he had to look forward to as compared to me, who had no irons in the fire and nobody who cared where I went.

Except for Germaine, I thought. She seemed to care.

Feeling low makes some people want to curl up and cry. But it makes me want to cause trouble. As in, make another pass at Clarinda.

CHAPTER FOUR

THE BANK ROBBERY

Two men, nicely dressed in suits and wearing very similar gray newsboy hats, walked together into the Dryades Street Branch of the Canal Bank & Trust, right downtown in New Orleans, on a Friday in February, at the lunch hour. It was the last Friday of that month, which meant payday for regular working folk and the day that the branch's business customers deposited their receipts. The men got into line, sized up the marble-columned atmosphere of the place, and then, out of their coats came a pair of revolvers and a sawed-off shotgun. The robbers knocked over the ropes and started yelling at everyone to get down on the floor. The tallest of them kicked open a swinging door, splintering the carved walnut, and forced his way behind the tellers' cages. "This is a bank robbery!" he told those who might fail to understand, and ordered up all their cash. He had a black bag in one hand and his gun in the other.

Quickly, he worked down the row.

Guarding the bronze doors on the street outside were two other robbers, handguns at the ready but discreetly behind their backs. In their car by the curb, motor running, was a woman with swept-back black hair, witnesses said later, two hands on the wheel and a cigarette stuck in her lips.

29

The crew in the bank had their bag of money and screamed at everyone to, "Stay where you are!" almost in unison. They ran for the doors. One of the robbers tripped over the ankle of a lady sprawled out on the floor, clutching her purse, and apologized as he hastened away. They had been in the bank for only five minutes.

All the crooks piled into their get-away car, and the driver forced her way into traffic. They made a quick left onto Common Street. A squad of patrolmen, only a block away, was radioed to engage the bandits in hot pursuit. They hit the sirens and tried to track the criminals, careening in and out of intersections crowded with pedestrians, calling on other cars to assist, but all to no avail. The robbers all got away.

I took a quick trip back to Sarasota to make arrangements with a neighborhood kid to look after Nero, my dog, and to grab some gear. Then back to St. Pete to put some of my stuff into the cottage behind Sammy Flannigan's house – Sammy, the Sunshine Diner's cook. I wasn't really sure what I was doing there, but right away I drove up to Seminole to see Clarinda, unannounced. That was a mistake. Mrs. Barlow hemmed and hawed about where her daughter, my wife, was. She may have gone shopping somewhere, maybe, but while trying to explain this, Lovelady confessed that the transportation for the shopping trip may have been provided by Alf. So that was two big strikes on Clarinda!

After that missed connection I took up with Germaine more seriously but in a carousing way. We went out regularly. She finally told me her last name, which was Doré. I had a little more money than I needed in my pockets, having sold two of the lots I owned in Sarasota. I had paid $200 apiece for them in 1917 and sold them in 1923 for $2,000 apiece. The boom was in full swing. The man who bought those lots sold them for $3,000. I bought three more lots south of town near Osprey for $1,200 each, and sold them for $2,500. Others were getting more. I hired men as I needed them to work my citrus groves and paid Reuben, my childhood buddy, to oversee the labor for a piece of the proceeds, and I still made money. Without lifting a finger to earn it.

This may sound like I was a busy man, but, not true. I drove back to Sarasota no more than once a week on the average just to tend to business and see my banker. To make this trip easier, Mister Gandy built a bridge from St. Petersburg to Tampa, which cut my trip home by half. I traded in the old Dodge for a 1925 Chrysler Phaeton, a sweet car for a sort-of bachelor, and I used it to drive Germaine out to the dog track that opened in St. Pete, where we could watch the greyhounds run, bet to our hearts' content, and sip from a flask of good Canadian. It was all illegal, but nobody cared!

Sarasota opened its dog track, too. It even had fifty slot machines. They were illegal. And nobody cared!

You could get even wilder and drive south on the new Tamiami Trail to Englewood with its Royal Casino, sitting out on piers in Lemon Bay. It was a family restaurant with a wonderful view of the sunset and the moon. But you could get booze after hours and on Saturday nights they'd open up the room with the card tables and slots. And nobody cared!

Get drunk enough, you could drive on down south to Whiskey Corners, a roadhouse way out in the country where big, respectable-size, mixed drinks were the specialty. People there were dancing and playing cards and having a good time. This was during Prohibition, and nobody said boo!

When I was the law down in Sarasota this didn't go on, at least not with such popularity. But now nobody, law included, seemed inclined to stop it. The money was rolling in.

Back in Tampa, Mack was doing well, but it became obvious to me that his income depended on being cozy with a lot of the rich criminal element that was busy opening nightclubs and organizing Bolita rackets for the Cubans who hand-rolled fat prime cigars. Cigar-making was taking over from fishing as Tampa's biggest industry. Or second biggest industry, I should say, since the biggest was tourists and building banks to finance all the real estate tycoons so that they could buy more land. We thought it would never stop.

GERMAINE DORÉ'S STORY

I'm the one they're talking about when they say, "if it wasn't for bad luck I wouldn't have no luck at all." My bad luck has always had to do with money or men – not enough of the one and too much of the other. My father was Davey Doré, and he played the mandolin in a vaudeville troupe. He was celebrated and traveled all over. One day he just kept on traveling, and I never saw him again after that. My mother, who was a Jarvis, was good at keeping time with a tambourine, but there wasn't much money in it since, to be honest, tambourine playing isn't that much of a skill and getting a job mainly depended on a woman's good looks. Which she had back then, and I have, too.

We weren't poor exactly, but everything always seemed to depend on when "Mister Johnny," or "Mister Winter" would come around and offer her a gig. When that happened, mama and me would go out to eat and I'd get a new dress. My brother, Whitey, took my mother's maiden name because he couldn't forgive our dad for leaving us like he did. Wasn't long and Whitey began running with a rough crowd.

Enough of my troubles? Well, they didn't end. I dropped out of high school in St. Petersburg to marry "Squad" Murphy, hero of our football team, who had advanced to be a bench-warmer at Florida State. I had a baby we named Kate. Squad hurt his knee, and dropped out to get a job at a car lot. We all tried hard to be a family, I think, and might have made it if Squad hadn't been so good looking and successful with his female customers. I ended up leaving him which provoked him into showing a mean streak I didn't know about. He came around and beat the shit out of me one night in plain view of Kate. After that, I bought a pistol which I swore I'd use if he or anybody else tried to hurt us again. I sent Kate off for her own safety to live with my mother, who passed her along to my aunt, and now the girl doesn't want to see me much. I tell people my husband died in the war, which simplifies things. This is all background of how I ended up waiting tables. I needed to make a living.

I've met a few boyfriends that way, but nothing that lasted long. Maybe I don't really want a full-time man in my life anymore. The Sunshine City Diner is the best of the places I've worked, particularly because the owner, who happens to be the cook, only had to see my pistol once before he quit hitting on me.

Gabe? We make love. But more like friends, which is very unusual but not too bad for where I am at this time.

While I was busy being irresponsible, Mack went the other way and got married. To Christy. They had a nice wedding in a Tampa

Presbyterian Church and about fifty people came. Mack's buddy Eugene Poulnot was his best man. Christy's dad was there to give her away, despite the fact that she was swelling around the waist. In talking to him beforehand, I established that his branch of the Barlows was not related anywhere close to my wife's branch, which was a relief. This gentleman bred cattle in Arcadia and said their family hailed from England. Clarinda showed up, and brought along her boyfriend, Alf. He was as large as advertised. I didn't talk to him or shake his hand. Clarinda gave me what I'd call a pained smile. I'd had better manners than to bring Germaine with me.

But I was very proud of my boy, and prouder still when Christy gave birth, not very long thereafter, to my only grandchild. He was a scrawny little lad they named Gordon for some reason, perhaps to go with the Barlow side of the family. That didn't bother me. I've done a bit of research into Scottish names, like my own "Gawain," which I'd like to point out means "White Hawk," and I'm of the belief that Gordon is as much a Scottish name as it is an English one.

"Anyway," Mack assured me, "we'll call him Gordy. Isn't Gordy MacFarlane a grand name?"

"Yes, indeed, son," I said, and gave him a slap on the back. I probably toasted him, too, since I was drinking a lot at the time. Drinking. Cavorting with women. This was the life of the new head of Clan MacFarlane.

CHRISTY'S STORY

Mack MacFarlane was the guy for me the first time I saw him. Tall, good looking, a fly-boy from the Army, and he rode a motorcycle. Of course I picked him. I saw him at a county fair in Arcadia, my home town. He was smoke-writing in the air and offering people "adventures of a lifetime, in the clouds" for three dollars. I didn't have that kind of money, nor did the boy I was with, but Mack spotted me and later, when the show was about to close, he beckoned me over.

"Want to go up?" he asked.

I was a sharp cookie then, and I knew he thought so, too.

"Sure," I told him. "Let's see how high we can go." I handed my cotton candy to my date and ran to that plane. Arcadia, fare-thee-well.

The "live and let live" attitude on the west coast of Florida had its limits. Get past those limits and you could be in real trouble. I'll just tell this story because it illustrates what was hiding behind our blinding sunlight. It's a gruesome tale I heard at the diner from my landlord, Germaine's boss, Sammy Flanigan, and I saw two-inch articles about in the St. Pete newspapers. It could have been a warning about the times to come, about some of the things Mack and his buddy Eugene

Poulnot would witness later. I'll describe those for you, too, if I get that far, because they hit close to home. But first, this bit of truth:

The paper had a picture of a slight young man with a wide open countenance, wire-rimmed spectacles and blond hair carefully combed back. He worked the desk at his mother's hotel in St. Petersburg. His name was Robert, and he was just a few years out of the University of Florida. He had actually practiced law for a time in Clearwater, but he preferred the hotel work. The pay was steady, and he got to meet lots of people.

"He got to meet lots of men," Sammy informed me with an eye-roll.

It was a Wednesday in March, and a husky fellow of this desk clerk's acquaintance came in. Robert enjoyed his conversations with this visitor, who delivered a mix of biting comments about society and ribald jokes. They met for coffee a few times at the restaurant next door. His name was Dulaney.

This Dulaney had an idea. He invited Robert to join him and meet two "girls" at nine o'clock that night in a nearby city park.

"Well, alright," Robert said, according to Sammy, who pantomimed Robert blinking and cleaning his glasses on a handkerchief, "I could do that."

The young man walked over to the park after dark, but found it deserted. So, he started home.

As reported in the newspapers, a figure stepped out of a parked car and asked, "Say, where's the dog track?"

Just as Robert raised his arm to point, he was stunned by a blow from behind and thrown into the car. A canvass sack was thrown over his head and the beatings began as the car sped away.

"Bob, you've been running around with the wrong ladies," one of the men said. Robert believed he knew the voice, a cop named Peacock whom he'd once had an unpleasant encounter with.

The men – and through a rip in the sack Robert believed there were five – drove him to a deserted place near the Safety Harbor community on Old Tampa Bay. They dragged him from the car, punching him all the while, and then stripped off his pants and unmanned him. The assailants left him on the ground bleeding and drove off. Eventually Robert regained enough of his senses to pull up his pants and limp to the first house he found. On his knees at the door, he begged for help, and the kind souls took him to the hospital.

"Do you think that boy was looking for girls? I'd say he was sprinkling fairy dust!" Sammy proclaimed happily and loudly.

"I don't care what he was doing," I said, "They shouldn't have. . ."

"No, of course not," Sammy interrupted. "I'm just saying."

"Saying what?" I asked, but Sammy was off to pour some paying customer a cup of coffee and, no doubt, to repeat his gory speculations.

Saying what? I knew a place where men met sometimes on a lonely lane in Sarasota. I'd passed by there a number of times in my official capacity. I didn't see any laws being broken, so I left it alone. It didn't matter what I thought about it. That just didn't count. I didn't see any violent activity, and it's the violent and cruel side of human behavior that I was paid to attend to. And it's the violent and cruel side of human nature that offends me personally, not what peaceable people do to satisfy their needs. That's not my business, and I don't think it's anyone's.

I do know that this boy Robert reported the crime to the Clearwater police, and a warrant was issued for Mr. Dulaney, the hotel visitor, charging him with engaging the five thugs to mark the young man for life. Dulaney was duly arrested, and two men showed up from Tampa to post his $5,000 bond. One of these, I'm told, was the holder of a Tampa post office box where applications for Klan membership were to be mailed. A Grand Jury was summoned. It reported a "no bill," and Dulaney was released. It didn't end there.

Robert went over to Tampa and brought charges against this Luther Peacock, who had been a county deputy sheriff and a Tampa policeman, fingering him as the leader of the gang. I'd heard about Peacock in the old days. They'd said he was a head-buster. Peacock turned himself in, accompanied by a lawyer, and he was shortly released in his counsel's custody.

Six days later, Peacock died. A doctor said it was apoplexy, a stroke from nowhere. They didn't do an autopsy.

I don't believe anyone was ever prosecuted for the crime against the young man, and as far as I know Robert just faded from view.

This is the kind of thing that was happening in Tampa – the big city.

If you could ignore events like this, you could have a good time there.

Looking for those good times, Germaine and I sometimes hit the Tampa clubs. Did I mention Bolita? This was the game of games! A customer buys a number, could be ten numbers, and then goes to the El Dorado or the Lincoln Club, whichever one is announced to hold the contest that night, and they all drink and laugh and party. At the appointed time, out comes a beautiful woman in a sequined dress holding the Bolita bag with a hundred little balls in it, all numbered. She struts and sings and prances and poses and gets the crowd standing up and clapping, and then she pitches her bag into the air. Whoever comes up with it gets a drum roll and cymbals, and then, with all watching, the lucky guest can reach in and pull one little ball out of the bag.

On occasion, when the crowd is too rowdy for the throw, the beautiful lady might have to call some eager man onstage to pluck the winning ball from her bag. Whatever comes out is the winning number, and that's the winning ticket. Of course, more than one person may have bought that number, so they divide the prize. However you work the math, the house wins.

You didn't even have to go to a nightclub to play. Gas stations sold the tickets. It was all completely illegal, but . . .

There were also moonlit nights when Germaine and I would just stroll around the neighborhood, or drive out to the beach to enjoy the black white-capped waves, with the palm trees behind us waving and the clouds above drifting across the stars. All in all, you'd have to say it was a pretty good life. But I was never satisfied with it. I missed Clarinda.

I didn't waste any more time trying to make up with my wife, however. Let bygones be bygones, that's what I'd say, and tip a glass.

Then one day, seems like the summer of 1926, all the air went out of the balloon. I don't know what started it, maybe some honest newspaper reporting, but suddenly everybody started questioning the value of all our plentiful sunbaked Florida real estate. A panic set in. Buyers from "Up North" who were sinking their life's savings into vacant lots, based on circulars they saw posted on telephone poles, all at once got wise. Real hysteria exploded among the guys with the straw hats and the clipboards hawking, "Last Chance! Choice Land for Sale" on every street corner, and they went scurrying for cover one step ahead of their bankers and angry customers. It all came crashing down in one loud roar.

I was left in a better place than many. I had the three buildable parcels in Sarasota I had paid too much for and couldn't sell, but I had pocketed a few bucks along the way, and I wasn't in debt. Some of my cash was in a strong box, which was lucky because the banks all failed. Nevertheless, by the end of the year, paying rent for my digs in St. Petersburg began to seem like a luxury I couldn't afford. It was time to move myself back to the farm on Catfish Creek.

Germaine didn't take it so well. She had enjoyed the high times as much as I had. And I guess you might say we had gotten attached to each other. But when Mack took me aside and offered to slip me a few bucks "just to help you get by, Dad," my mind was made up in a hurry.

I went to say goodbye to Clarinda. She couldn't talk. She was in the middle of teaching a sewing class. I thought she was as pretty as ever, but what did that matter? I gave her my message. I was leaving town. She chewed her lip and nodded. And she looked sad. That made two of us.

When a man is in his 50's, he generally thinks that his table has just about been set. What's ahead of him is going to be a lot like what's behind him, only not as much fun. But that moment, moving back home and living through the "Panic in Paradise" of 1926, I'd say kicked off a brand new phase of my life. Three things happened.

First, I got connected to the Ringling Brothers' Circus. Second - and maybe we in Florida set it off - the whole world started to collapse into the Depression. And third, I finally got a letter from my wife. This might take some time to tell.

CHAPTER FIVE

THE RINGLING CIRCUS COMES TO TOWN

Now for the first thing that happened. My old Sarasota "cow town" had always aspired to be a rich man's paradise. To be correct, a rich woman's paradise, since Mrs. Bertha Palmer had started it all rolling. She saw the value of the location and the weather, the ways you could exploit the unsettled natural terrain, and settle it, and she brought progressive cattle raising to Florida. And she could pay for it all. The massive project to create the celery fields, which hired me for its law enforcement, was all due to her and her kids.

But she made her biggest impact by bringing us class. Her home in Osprey was immense, artistic, tropical and elegant. She brought in the Vanderbilts and the Morgans and built a train depot in Venice so that the millionaires could arrive by private rail cars and attend her parties. She died at War's end, but there were others to pick up her torch, the Gillespies and Selbys and Fields.

But best of all, there was John Ringling. His circus came to town and my life entered a new phase.

The great ringmaster had fallen in love with Sarasota on a winter visit, and he commenced construction of a magnificent three-story mansion, a work of art he called Ca' d'Zan, complete with gardens and fountains on the Bayfront. That wasn't enough splendor, so he bought a little island out in the bay known as Bird Key, then another one further out called Coon Island, and then he paid to have a long wooden bridge built over Sarasota Bay (we already had one from the town to Siesta Key, but that's another story) so he could develop home sites on these islands for the very prosperous capitalists who craved incredible sunsets and limitless fishing. At the very end of his causeway he laid out a circle for shops, and he changed the name from Coon Island to St. Armands Key in honor of the old Frenchman who had once claimed to own this spit of sand and all the impenetrable mangroves and palmettos that went with it.

But how Mr. Ringling figures into my life is that he moved his spectacular circus, the winter-time home base of it, to Sarasota - just when everything else was going to hell in a handbasket. Can you imagine how amazing a sight it was, that first November, when the Ringling Circus rolled into town by train and by truckload, with all manner of caged animals and beautiful women?

Sure, we had had circuses before. The Ku Klux Klan brought in the Bob Morton Circus annually up until the real estate bust. It always did well. They even crowned the "Klan's Miss Sarasota." I'll have more to say about the Klan as we go along, I'm afraid. Its tentacles had reached throughout our society and was strong among insurance salesmen, shoe store owners, stock brokers, that sort. But Bob Morton's show, as popular as it was, was nothing compared to the Ringling Brothers & Barnum & Bailey extravaganza!

The Big Show unloaded all their lions and tigers, huge snakes, trapeze artists, the sword swallower and the fat lady, all the clowns and flags and sparkling costumes, put them behind a loud band and marched them from the rail yard to their winter quarters at the Fairgrounds, which Mr. Ringling had bought from the city. The elephants led the parade – right up Main Street!

Talk about a new class of people moving to town. These were carny people, Yankee hucksters, Siamese twins, fat men, tattooed women and dwarfs. The human cannonball took up winter residence, as well as the Giant Samoan.

And this is how I became a private detective. My childhood friend and farm manager, Reuben, who also had law enforcement experience furnishing security for the Palmers at Celery Fields, got a job with the Ringling Circus. Actually, with the Pinkerton National Detective Agency, the outfit that Ringling used. Reuben told me it was interesting work, very easy, and he thought they would hire a retired professional like me.

Due to my financial reverses I needed a job, so I went in and applied to a Mr. Charlie Siringo. He found out that I had been the Sarasota City Marshal and a County Deputy Sheriff. I talked a good talk, and he said, "You're hired as soon as you fill out this form and take the oath." I filled out the form, which asked about my experience and my record, and also whether I was a Socialist, a Communist, a subversive, or a member of any labor union. I checked all the right boxes. If I had been a Communist I would have checked the right box, too. He administered the oath, in which I swore to respect the Constitution and laws of the state, to live upright, and to follow the rules of the Agency.

"Congratulations," he said. "You are now a Pinkerton detective."

I informed him that I'd never been trained, licensed or referred to as a detective before, and he said it didn't matter. I got a silver badge with an eagle and the Pinkerton name embossed in raised blue letters.

As a private detective, I was required to dress like a regular working stiff and circulate through the crowds that came to the shows Mr. Ringling was constantly presenting. It was Ringling's idea that he could make good money from our bountiful Florida winter tourists by presenting his aerial acts and lion-tamers during the off-months, before he took his Big Show back on the road. I was told to wander the grounds when the Circus was open for business and look for pickpockets and purse snatchers, and I was given some good pointers on how to spot them. This was the most interesting part of the work, since real detectives showed me how easy it was to grab my wallet, to the point of stealing a money belt right off my pants. In time, I got to where I could be a pretty good sneak thief, too, were I so inclined. I wasn't, of course, but it was useful education. And I learned how to spot the "grifters" who prey on the "yokels." That's how Pinkertons talk.

I was also supposed to keep my ears open around the lunch counters and the bars where the employees hung out and report any grumbling or talk of organized labor.

This part wasn't well thought-out, since it's hard to keep up a serious conversation - over a ham sandwich with a complete stranger- without telling him what part of the enterprise you worked for. I couldn't say I was the boss's spy.

I went in search of a better position. Reuben had an "undercover" assignment, too, working as a dishwasher in the canteen at the Fairgrounds where employees got their grub, and he turned me onto Mr. Charles Ort who ran the "concession department" and was possibly in need of some detecting.

Charles was one of the more fantastic people you'd ever chance to meet, and I say this with the backdrop of the Ringling Bothers' Circus with its Human Moths, the Lizard Lady and the Thin Man. Charlie, I came to call him, didn't want to meet me at the Fairgrounds because that's not where he spent his office hours. No, he held court at the Corner Cigar Store at the corner of Main and Lemon in Sarasota, soon to be renamed the Gator Bar & Grill when Prohibition ended. Walking in for our meet-and-greet was like dropping a pig in a barbeque pit; I mean it was smokey.

Charlie had a group at the bar buying him drinks, and they were all puffing cigars. He was, maybe still is, a big well-fed man with a round face and curly blond hair. His lips are made for smiling and his eyes for laughing. In a voice loud as a trumpet, he was spinning some yarn. I came along just in time to hear him say, "…the deal of a lifetime," before he focused on me as fresh meat and flashed a radiant smile.

"Brother, who are you?" His warmth seemed to welcome me into his church.

I told him who I was, Gabe MacFarlane, and that I'd heard he might want to hire some "talent."

His eyes squinted as he studied me, stood up laughing all the while, drink in hand, and slapped the back of everybody he could reach, and guided me to a table in the corner.

He waved for the barmaid and ordered me a drink. "Whatcha got Gabe MacFarlane?" he asked. "Whatcha got for me?" His eyes twinkled merrily.

I told him I was a Pinkerton Detective referred for an undercover assignment, which he laughed at. I laughed, too. "Actually, this is my home town," I explained. "I like working. I'm an old cop. And I'm flexible about what I do."

Charlie lit up. "And I'm an old hustler, and flexible as a Perfolastic girdle! Let's hoist a few."

We did, and I found him to be a fine and likable fellow.

For the Ringlings, he managed all their money-handling operations, other than the ticket booths and the Big Show itself. His realm included all the candy stands, custard trucks, hot dog vendors, and even some of the sideshow attractions, everything they called "concessions." The business arrangements for all of these "concessions" were referred to as the "privileges," which independent operators paid Ort for. I guess he then paid Ringling. Charlie Ort said he could use some help getting free-lance pickpockets and petty thieves and swindlers away from these "concessions." I thought the expression "free-lance" sounded odd at the time, but Ort travelled on to other topics.

What he was really interested in was my knowledge of the Sarasota real estate market. We talked about everything I owned in the county, and I thought maybe he wanted to buy something, but it turned out that he was interested in being my broker to sell them. And to impress me with his smarts, and because he was drinking heavily, he shared a wild tale.

"Key Largo, that's where a fortune may be made," he said in a whisper loud enough for the surrounding tables to hear. "I know. I know. I tried!"

In a lower voice, which some of the other carny characters strained to pick up, he murmured, "We promoted it with buried treasure!"

Men of means, "men with vision," he said, had invested with him and together they acquired most of the beach and jungle that existed on that first key past Miami. Key Largo it was called, and it was nothing then but palmetto, hermit crabs, seashells, and oak jungle, to hear Charlie tell it. Hot, smelly and full of bugs. His eyes bulged while describing its jungle-like condition.

But backed by Yankee money, he set out to change that rugged and natural state of affairs, and he put men to work with bulldozer and dredge to clear and expand a beach and rough-in a grid of streets through the tangled brush. He drew up plans for a "King of the Keys" subdivision. Then up came the For Sale signs.

We ordered more drinks, and Charlie went on. To put across the project, he rented an office for the Key Largo Corporation, now supposedly a ninety-million-dollar group of pioneers, Charles Ort,

President, in the Flagler Arcade in Miami. Sales were brisk, but there was a lot of competition. Real estate men held forth on all the street corners hawking their own choice lots, sure ways to triple your money overnight. But one day, says Charlie, into the office came this handsome young novelist named Ben Hecht with a strategy to push Key Largo out in front of all the competition and "way over the top."

And here Charlie's story got even more fantastic and, had I been sober, I would have questioned it on the spot. Hecht, it seems, came highly recommended as being a rising literary figure with connections to all the papers and New York society. He also had a larcenous streak "wider than a whorehouse shill," and that appealed to Ort. Hecht laid out a plot to plant a pirate's treasure in the sands of Key Largo and entice a bevy of New York socialites to board the ex-German-Kaiser's black yacht, which happened then to be berthed on Long Island, and sail down to Florida to look for this buried gold. "The publicity alone, can you imagine?" Hecht asked. Ort repeated this to me, eyes aglow. "I loved it!" He was shouting now.

Charlie agreed to Hecht's terms - $5,000 a week plus expenses for twelve weeks! That figure would have made my head spin if it wasn't already.

So a press release was issued to papers nationwide and Hecht went off to recruit his socialites. To his dismay, none could be enticed to participate, so he and Ort "came up with a better plan."

"Among my investors," Charlie went on, "was a man rather active in the Ku Klux Klan who happened to be well connected with gamblers and politicians in Cuba." At this point I almost stopped Ort to ask whether he was also a Klan member, but I hesitated. I didn't want to know. His story continued:

"Through that man's influence we got the loan of a satchel of authentic Spanish doubloons belonging to President Machado himself! Next, Ben Hecht located two Old-Spain-looking amphoras, you know, big clay jars, in a Miami antique shop," Charlie continued, "and we sailed Hecht and the pots over to Largo where we filled our amphoras with the doubloons and buried them in the sand not a hundred yards from the beach."

Since no socialites were coming to make a search, Hecht hired a local conch who lived in a shack down by the water to claim he found the treasure. Well!

"True to his word, he usually was, Ben Hecht got the story out all over America, and, Lord, here came the newspapermen! Our old fisherman earned his pay and told the story of finding his great fortune just the way he was supposed to. And did the buyers love it? Yes, they did! They all hoped that there were more jugs to be found on these little pieces of land they could own for just a hundred dollars down and twenty a month." Charlie had a dreamy look. "They came! They came! And did they buy!

"And then, WHAM!" Charlie slapped the table, rattling our glasses and making me reach for the bottle. "The CRASH!" he shouted. "Before you know it, a mob was beating down the door at the Flagler building and people were demanding their money back, and Ben Hecht hopped a train north with about $10,000, the best money any of us made. But

I don't begrudge him a bit! It was part of the times! And man, what times they were!"

Charlie stopped to catch his breath and mop his brow with a red handkerchief. We each took a drink.

"So, here you are," I said to keep the story going.

"I've told this tale before," he confessed, but then resumed. "It was no picnic there for a while. My wife and I spent our nights sleeping in the car. I was soured on Miami and all those shenanigans. But, I just happened to know Mister Ringling, and he knows my talents, and, yessir, here I am," Charlie recovered. "It's all about the show, you know? It's a con, true, but people love it. Don't we all love a show?"

I was hired. The job Charlie gave me was to pick up the cash from the concession vendors on a regular basis and run it back to Ort's "office" at the cigar store tavern. It wasn't advertised that I was a Pinkerton man, and before long I wasn't. Charlie said he'd rather just pay me than pay the detective agency my salary plus a fee, so I turned in my silver eagle badge. Though I quit the agency, I still considered myself a private detective, just like the tough guys in Crimson Crime magazine. The only thing I lacked was clients.

CHAPTER SIX

THE GREAT DEPRESSION HITS

The hard times spread all over Florida. My little farm was hurt in 1926, but kept limping along. The local men picking my oranges were happy to have a job, even at reduced wages. I couldn't complain about the work I was getting from the Circus. There was no need for me to beat anyone up, or even to arrest anyone for that matter. The "yokels," the "yahoos," sometimes went wild and crazy, staggering out of the freak show, and there were the fathers who may have tippled too much while sitting in the grandstands with the kids, under that great big tent, but at closing time, when the mosquitoes sound louder than the sirens from the Roller Coaster, the crowd always seemed to get out of the gate peacefully.

I had been staying in touch with Germaine and Mrs. Barlow, Clarinda's mother, mainly through letters. Sarasota had a Ringling Circus, a Palmer National Bank, and a radio station, but for a long time we didn't have much in the way of phone service out in the country. There was always talk of running a line out to us on Catfish Creek, but early on there wasn't much enthusiasm for it in the neighborhood, the reason being that we were being offered a party line where about twenty subscribers and the exchange operator could all listen to what you had to say. My neighbors value their privacy.

If I needed to use the phone I'd drive down to Harvey's Texaco on McIntosh Road. He'd charge a nickel, but anything "long distance" cost an arm and a leg. All of this is to say that Germaine and I were not communicating on a daily basis, and Clarinda never responded to my letters.

If I planned to be in St. Pete, I'd let them both know by mail ahead of time. So far, Germaine always said she'd be happy to see me. From the Barlow residence, nothing.

Thanks to the Circus I came out of the Bust of 1926 with a few greenbacks. I should have kept them in the strongbox – since I had an idea to get a better car - but the banks were opening back up, and we all had faith in a recovery. But not for long. The bottom dropped out in 1929! Again!

This was the second big thing that happened. Not just to me, or to Florida, but to everyone.

The stock market crash and the Depression hit us down here a little later than it did the rest of the country. After all, we had a cushion: tourists. Flocks of people from all over America drove their jalopies down south to see our tropics, our Spanish moss and alligators, to sample our bizarre roadside attractions and to wander our beaches under the stars. In Sarasota, travelers still loved to see our Circus, and the Tin Can Tourists, official now, still wanted to assemble for their cookouts and conventions in Payne Park. Most people in Florida didn't even know what the New York Stock Exchange was.

We limped along for a while. But then the Bank of Sarasota failed, again, and depositors like me lined up to learn how badly we were going to get screwed, again. It took a long time to get my payout of 18 cents on the dollar. You can imagine that tempers were high!

All the news on the radio was bad unless you believed President Hoover who was saying that recovery was just around the corner. Like everybody else, I lost any idea that I was in control of my destiny, but I knew I was lucky to have a job with a going concern.

Germaine was still waiting tables at the Sunshine City Diner, and when I'd drive up there we'd drown our sorrows at one of the Tampa clubs. I've mentioned that Bolita, once the high-class rage, had spread from the speakeasies to the streets, where at any filling station you could buy numbers. Everybody did, hoping to get lucky when they threw the bag at Club El Dorado and the pretty lady pulled out the special ball. It was a Cuban import, and Tampa was full of Cubans. They were settled in the south side of town, in Ybor City, and the premier employment was rolling high class cigars in the big warehouses that had sprung up. A lot of them spoke English, and I got to know a few of these skilled people just wandering around town. I learned some of the history.

An unhappy workforce on their home island had convinced a number of rich Cuban cigar makers to set up shop in Tampa, and behind them came thousands of workers, who may or may not have been happy. As described to me, these factories were unusual in that there were no machines. The workers were the machines. They hand-rolled cigars, and got paid per each. Their products, *Flor De Martinez Ybor* and *El Principe De Gales*, were top of the line and sold well all across the United States and Europe. The Cubans had a tradition that seemed especially wonderful to me, a regular man aspiring to be literate.

In their factories, an "intelligent man" would sit on a raised platform and read to the craftmen while they worked. The information, usually from a Spanish-language newspaper, could be about sporting events and celebrities, but was most often about politics. I liked their idea of worker education. Myself, I'd never had much schooling, but I've stuck to a habit of trying to learn those three new words a day, and I was and am a believer in self-education.

That Spanish news must have been pretty "red" because the cigar rollers kept forming unions and meeting at their labor halls. These cigar rollers were proud professionals, sitting every day at the same table and churning out these perfect cigars, but their emigrated Cuban overlords got it into their heads to find a way to stop the spread of any Red-Russian propaganda. Times were rough and getting rougher, but it was the owners who precipitated all the social disruptions I'm about to tell you about. Stop reading if you don't want to know about it.

All the newspapers and newsreels reported huge street protests all across the nation, and even more all around the world. There were Nazis rising in Germany and Mussolini Fascists taking over Italy; textile workers were being machine-gunned to death in strikes in Massachusetts and armed banana pickers were rebelling against United Fruit in Central America. Stalin was collectivizing the Soviet Union, and Herbert Hoover was beating Al Smith and keeping the country dry. All the causes were unrelated, but they had a common message. The world was in a sorry shape!

We all read the headlines in our newspapers every morning and listened to Lowell Thomas on our radios every night, looking for some direction, some glimmer of hope. People everywhere were angry, hungry, and in a state of unrest. Not so much with us in Florida, I suppose. Fortune might cast laboring people here into a turpentine camp, a sawmill, or a phosphate mine, where they were kept too dirt-poor and under-the-gun to put up much of a struggle, but by and large nobody worked in an actual factory. Except in Tampa. None of our other Florida communities, to my knowledge, had any big industries other than tourists, whiskey smuggling, and fish.

St. Pete, my personal vacation spot, had all three of those things. The town was all about trying to have a good time, or trying to show paying customers a good time. But across the bay in Tampa, my son Mack knew from personal experience that things were very different. When he was flying big shots around, he got to hear what they thought about the Cubans, the Blacks, the unions, and working people in general.

Organized labor was a real threat to the muck-a-mucks. It mattered to their pocketbooks, Mack said, and the cigar industry with its 40,000 employees had become the lead money-maker for the whole town. After all, Tampa didn't have a beach, and nobody ever said it was a beautiful city.

"We're in a class war," Mack informed me one afternoon when I was buying him a grouper sandwich at the St. Pete beach.

"Who says?"

"That's what my wife says. She gets that from her brother." Mack's wife Christy's brother was a car mechanic. He worked at Fred Ferman's Chevrolet, and I'd never heard him say one single word about politics.

"Really?"

"And so does Eugene. He preaches stuff about the class war all the time."

"I thought he was a printer at the newspaper."

"He is, and it's a good union job," Mack explained. "The dues are rough on him, but he says paying dues is worth it because he's well paid."

"That's important," I agreed.

"He says he's thinking of being a socialist." Mack tossed it out like it didn't matter much, and maybe it didn't. Up north the Communists and Socialists were running their people for office. But down in Florida the only Communists and Socialists I had heard about were in Russia, unless you believed what they said about the Cuban cigar workers in Tampa.

"There's a lot of dangerous people down here, and they don't go for that Socialist, Communist stuff," I reminded Mack, thinking about the Klan. "You'll get burned if you get too close to that mess."

"Not to worry, Dad. I steer clear of the rednecks. Controlling them is your department." He was making a joke. "The dangerous people I deal with are into gambling and whiskey, and I'm just a simple airplane jockey, part of the background."

I didn't like what he said about me controlling the rednecks and told him so. Certain people would take a look at me, especially back when I was wearing a badge and a gun belt, and consider me a redneck. But they can stick that wherever. I was born in the country and worked the land for a living and rambled through God-knows how many blazing-hot miles of Florida underbrush to bring the law to this place and make way for civilization - pardon me for going on – and yes, I might be a redneck. But I don't like the meaning people give to that word. I don't wear a white sheet and a pointy hat, and most of my neighbors don't either. So don't talk about me controlling rednecks.

But I could support Mack's chosen line of work – in a way. The nightclub and casino owners who had made their money on illegal booze and gambling, who break the law every night, didn't really bother me. They supply people with entertainment they like. My main issue with them is the grip they have on every police chief and sheriff around here - who they pay off so that they can merrily go about their illegal businesses.

Back when I was the law in my town, Sarasota, if I wanted to turn a blind eye, I did. But I didn't charge anybody for it.

CHAPTER SEVEN

THE SINKING OF THE ZALOPHUS

Then, after getting involved with the Circus and then the Depression hitting, here came the third big thing that happened to me, the letter. One Friday after work at the Circus, I picked up a bundle of mail at the Sarasota post office. Among all the circulars for farm equipment and lots-for-sale was a week-old letter addressed to me in a handwriting I knew well.

Dear Gawain,

I have been thinking a lot about us and the way things have turned out. We have both been caring too much about ourselves and not about the other person. Maybe that's not the right way to put it down. I think we had a good marriage, better than most. I'm sorry about last time. If you want to try again to talk to me, you know where I am.

Love,

Clarinda

I stared at that piece of paper for quite a while. Could she not have figured out that I had been sleeping with Germaine? Maybe, but were we going to forget about her "dating" Alf, the boyfriend? This letter is what I had wanted and hoped for from Clarinda months past, but now I had rearranged my life. It was stressful, getting her mail now. I slid the letter into a Bible we kept in a bookcase beside the front door. Clarinda's Bible.

I'd just have to think about this for a few days.

The Bible is a place for treasures. I noticed a poem I'd once given to Clarinda folded up and nestled among the Proverbs. And a leaf I believed she'd kept from our wedding night, a leaf she picked up from the ground where we slept. It was in Ephesians, and it was too frail and dry to be touched. For no particular reason I remembered a statement a former preacher at our Catfish Creek Oak Grove Church once said. His name was Derksy Winston. I haven't been to that church in a long time. But I recall the preacher, who was an older guy with silver whiskers and a tight ring of shiny gray hair around his bald head, like the bristles of a brush, saying: "To be a practicing Christian you need two simple things. You need to believe that Christ can help you find your chosen path through your life, and you need to be a part of the community, the loving community."

Whether God or me had chosen my path, I was on it, and I was part of the community, no doubt about that. But in what sense was it loving? I guess I wasn't seeing that one yet.

As I've related, I was gainfully employed by Charlie Ort at the Ringling Circus at that time. It was a wonderful job. I didn't travel with the show when it left Sarasota every March for its grand tour across America. I was just hired to work the Sarasota shift, when all the clowns and the elephants came home.

One interesting thing did happen a few weeks into my job with Ort. I was riding the Merry Go Round, mentally doing a head-count of how many customers were reaching for the gold ring to be sure the concessionaire was honest, and I saw a nice looking lad with a blond crew-cut slide his hand into the hip pocket of a dad hanging onto his five-year old daughter. Slick as butter the thief lifted a wallet, which quickly disappeared into the crew-cut's trousers. When he jumped off the ride, so did I. Well, we had words, and I strong-armed the wallet away from the kid. He bolted and ran. I gave the poke back to its rightful owner, who fell to his knees blessing me, he was so happy. His daughter hugged my leg and got my pants sticky with cotton candy. I thought I'd done good, but when I got back to the "office," Charlie frowned and took me aside.

"It's all about the 'privileges'," he reminded me. It seems I had rousted one of his "privileges" whom I had not heard about. Believe it or not, crooks paid a "license fee" to Charlie for the pickpocket "concession" at the Merry Go Round, and at three other rides. I was "not to see them."

Blow me away! I didn't feel good about it, how could I? Turning my head while innocent people got robbed? I stated my position to Charlie, who sighed and then told me which rides I was to skip on my patrols. They were removed from my "jurisdiction." I accepted that as a compromise. Not that it was to my credit.

About that time, Charlie assigned me a position on the Zalophus. This was the $200,000 yacht John Ringling had bought to wine and dine the rich and famous on luxurious boating adventures across the Bay to St. Armands and Bird Key, where he hoped they would all build mansions. Ringling was almost as much interested in developing Sarasota real estate as he was in running his circus. This "houseboat" was actually 125 feet from bow to stern and claimed a fuel range of 4,000 nautical miles. Ringling piloted it - when he usurped the wheel from the captain - up and down the coast from Cedar Key to St. Pete, from Sarasota to Useppa Island.

It was quite an enormous boat for our harbor in Sarasota, the biggest most people had ever seen, and it was set up to accommodate overnight guests in its six staterooms with private baths. I'd heard they even had brass bathtubs, but I had never been aboard until Charlie Ort got the concession to manage its galley and salon. For this assignment, there were to be no pickpockets with "privileges," but there was to be one private detective, me, to make sure that neither the staff nor the guests pinched the silver. I wasn't undercover. I was officially security.

It was a cushy job. If the boat made an overnight trip, I slept in one of the empty rooms or one of the quarters set aside for maids and valets. Valuables were everywhere. Ringling's wife, Mable, packed the boat with fine China, oriental porcelain, Tiffany tea sets, Stieff silverware, marble sculptures, bronze busts and many other precious possessions.

A watch, framed like a picture on a stateroom wall, caught my eye, and Charlie Ort explained that Mr. Ringling was known to have collected rare "timepieces from the Renaissance," purchased from a Vanderbilt. There was art on the walls that I couldn't appreciate but knew must be worth a fortune. All the bathrooms had fourteen carat gold plated fixtures. I noticed that there was a wall safe in the master bedroom when Ort took me on a tour.

"What's kept in there?" I asked. He just shrugged. I'm sure he hadn't a clue, since Charlie was the last man you'd let have the combination to your strongbox.

We took a beautiful evening cruise to Useppa Island on one fine day in February over serene seas. Mr. Ringling wasn't with us, but aboard were Sam Gumpertz, whom I was told was the circus showman who'd managed Dreamland Park at Coney Island. I'd never heard of Dreamland, but everybody had heard about Coney Island. He'd brought along some friends, including one who the staff whispered was "The Mayor." I didn't know what he was the mayor of, but he sure had good taste in women since he was escorting a shapely brunette with a soft chin and great big eyes that stared right through you.

I did my best to be professional and manly, and I asked them to, "Let me know if there's anything you need."

The guests spent their time on the journey enjoying cocktails in the carpeted salon, and walking the deck to look at the moon until, as we were returning around Lido Key at about three in the morning, our giant yacht abruptly rammed into something huge and metallic hidden under the surface. Cocktails crashed to the deck.

We began taking on water fast. There was quite a panic. The captain's mate rushed the Gumpertz party down steps and onto our motorized skiff, and Ort yelled at me to go with them and be sure to get them safely ashore. I was surprised that Charlie did not personally want to be among the first to go, but he, the captain, and the remaining crew stayed behind with the intention of saving what they could carry and rowing ashore by lifeboat. In their rush to board the skiff, the Gumpertz party had little chance to retrieve jewelry and other personal belongings. As soon we were underway, it came to me that Ort, and possibly the crew, wanted a chance to clean out whatever valuables they could safely steal.

Running the skiff back over to the dock at John Ringling's compound, we watched in amazement the lights of the Zalophus blinking off as the proud yacht went under. A quick disembarkation was achieved and Mr. Gumpertz, The Mayor, his date, and I, were directed into a sedan chauffeured by a man I knew to be a tough hombre since I'd once arrested him from brawling on Main Street. We had both been a lot younger then.

I didn't know where the sedan was taking us, but we were going there fast. As soon as we cleared downtown and got onto Fruitville, I guessed it was to the new airfield the city had built.

A plane was waiting. It was a souped up Tin Goose, a Ford Tri-Motor, with room for passengers, and the pilot who met us at the steps was none other than my son, Mack.

"First I get ship-wrecked, then kidnapped in a sedan, just to find my son appearing out of nowhere to fly the survivors out of Sarasota in the dark. What's going on?"

"I don't ask too many questions, Dad. Just doing my job."

"We ought to have a talk."

He nodded. "Let's wait until everybody is safe and sound back home."

"Where's their home?"

"I don't know, but this plane is chartered to Tallahassee."

I let it go. I had to because Mack got his passengers aboard fast, fired up his three engines, and he was off in a high arc through the Milky Way.

My driver carried me back to the marina in Sarasota where I'd parked my car the day before. "You remember me?" he finally asked. His name was Duck Bewley.

"Yes, I do."

"You pack quite a wallop," he said with a chuckle.

"That was then." I didn't mention that I had cracked a knuckle on his boney forehead. "We were in the flower of our youth, I guess one could say."

He laughed, and we traded some good memories.

When the next afternoon I got reunited with Charlie Ort at the Cigar Store, he assured me that everyone had gotten away safely from the wreck.

"Who was that 'mayor' my son flew out of here?" I inquired.

"You didn't know? Why that was Jimmy Walker, the Mayor of New York City, and that girl with him was Betty Compton, the famous actress."

"His wife?"

"Hell, no. She's quite the looker, huh? And he's quite the dude."

"It's a good thing we didn't drown them both."

"Aw, no chance of drowning in the calm seas of Sarasota Bay. Do you know what my good friend Ben Hecht said about Mayor Walker?" Here he was talking about his fellow Key Largo con artist again, promoted now to "my good friend."

"Hecht says, 'Walker is a troubadour headed for Wagnerian dramas. No man could hold life so carelessly without falling down a manhole before he is done.' Now ain't that a magnificent line?"

It was indeed.

Later on we found out that the Zalophus had rammed into one of John Ringling's own barges, which had intentionally been sunk to serve as a mooring anchor for one of his beach-building dredges. The curious public never did find out what became of all the expensive artwork and jewels sprinkled about the yacht's furnished suites, or what was in that safe. And neither did I. But I would have bet that Charlie Ort might have had a pretty good idea.

Apparently Mack's flying service was going well. He got back from his flight to Tallahassee, where he deposited Mayor Walker and Miss Compton, who were met on the tarmac by a chauffeured Packard. Mack's understanding was that the car that met the plane went straight to the train station, and the prominent lovers caught the afternoon 1 o'clock Seaboard Air-Line to New York City, booked into separate compartments.

About a week after it all happened, my son and I shared our stories about that night, with plenty of laughter and beer. Mack was still living in the same "pad," as he and Christy called their Quonset hut, even though they were now properly married and had a loud baby named Gordy. His wails echoed throughout the former Army barracks. Christy welcomed me, and put a jazz record on the Victrola she'd gotten as a wedding present. She flipped the cap off a bottle of beer and took up breast-feeding her baby, waved goodbye and carried young Gordy into the back room.

Mack and I just looked at each other.

"Women …," he began, and quit.

No comment from me.

"Looks like you're happy, son," I said.

"I guess, yeah. I'm making a living. She's a good mom. She may be smarter than me, but no real complaints."

That's about as far as father and son can get on a good day. We enjoyed our beer; it was a hot afternoon. I thought about passing over to Seminole Lake and seeing Clarinda, but I decided I wasn't ready yet. I drove half-way back to Sarasota before I changed my mind.

THE LID BLOWS OFF IN TAMPA

 I stopped at a gas station on the Trail, got a handful of dimes and dialed her number from a phone booth. Clarinda answered the call at the shop she ran with her mother. She took a few breaths after I said "Hello, Clarinda" before asking where I was calling from. I told her. "I got your letter," I said.

"You did?" she asked.

"Yeah. I thought maybe we could talk again."

She said she'd meet me, at the same spot by Seminole Lake where we had had our last conversation.

She got there before I did and had left a space for me beside her on the park bench. She was wearing blue jeans and a fresh yellow blouse, and she had the same worried eyes I'd known most of my life. I won't go into all the details, but she knew a little about Germaine, probably from gossiping with our son. As for her suitor, it "isn't serious." She volunteered some bits of information about him which I didn't ask for and which didn't make me like him any more. At one point she laid her hand on my knee. I stared at it for a moment and then put mine on top.

"I got my land back," Clarinda said proudly. She was referring to her father's small farm in DeSoto County that had gone for taxes after his mysterious death. Clarinda had hired a lawyer to establish her title to these ancestral acres. Getting them back probably meant more to her than getting me back.

Anyway, we decided we'd give it another go. We didn't exactly say how or when. The idea was to take it slow. We both had to tidy up our personal affairs first.

CLARINDA'S STORY (CONTINUED)

I go back and forth about Alf. I know I told Gawain that it wasn't a serious affair, but that's not quite true. Alf has been romantic, in his way, and I have given him encouragement. He hasn't proposed, but he did ask if I were "free," meaning divorced. I told him I had spoken to a lawyer. The truth was I had spoken to a lawyer about my property rights, not about getting a divorce, but it wasn't quite a lie. A life with Alf would certainly be comfortable. He lives with his parents in a big house. I haven't been introduced to them yet, but I have been inside their home when they were vacationing – in EUROPE! They went by ship! Alf showed me his gun collection. He says we have to be prepared for a revolution in this country, and we must defend our property. His guns were fine. I didn't tell him that I could shoot, I don't know why. Not lady-like? As a matter of fact, I believe I could part his hair at fifty feet with a .45 and not scratch his scalp. I kept that to myself.

I also believe in defending my property – no joke about that, but I'm more worried about the rich getting richer than the poor rising up. I raised this subject with Alf, but he said we'd just have to disagree about that one thing.

The trouble is, the most exciting thing about Alf is he's rich. He's begging me to go travelling with him. And Gawain is begging me to go back to Catfish Creek in Sarasota. Ha, ha. But I don't particularly like or respect Alf. There, I've said it. One thing Gawain deserves is respect. So, I'm of two minds.

Tidying up our personal affairs didn't happen overnight. All of a sudden Charlie Ort got downgraded at the Circus. Instead of running all the concessions, he was reduced to overseeing the cotton candy stands and the Show of Living Curiosities, which included the world's smallest perfect man, the Wild Woman of Borneo, and Zip the "What is It?" I was put on part-time.

Things weren't perfect in the Ringling Empire. Even though people loved the lions and the tigers and the trapeze artists, the fountain of money must have dried up somewhere in Hooverville. The city fathers of Sarasota had to close the admirable John Ringling Bridge that went over the Bay to St. Armands because the timbers were starting to rot and Mr. Ringling didn't offer to pony up any money to replace them. The City itself was broke.

The Depression was affecting everybody but most dramatically the cigar factories in Tampa, where the lid blew off. Almost overnight the market for luxury cigars disappeared. I never could afford them anyway. But the factories laid off about a third of their workers. A new machine had also been introduced which could roll cigars automatically. Naturally, this made for a cheaper product. Like the vice-president said, what this country needed is a good five cent cigar. Well, now we had one, and it wasn't a joke. Cuban workers got kicked out of the warehouses and evicted from their homes.

I tried to follow all of this in the newspapers, which took the slant that everything was Communist, including the cigar workers' union that was leading street marches. This union also promoted race equality, which was more controversial than Bolshevism.

A house-painter named Frederick Crawford, a union supporter, was kidnapped by a squad of Tampa policemen who claimed to be executing a warrant. But there wasn't a warrant, and they didn't take him to jail. Instead the cops blindfolded Crawford and dumped him in a car. Mack heard all about this from his best man Eugene Poulnot, who knew the inside scoop and maintained that Crawford wasn't a Communist – he was a Socialist. This distinction didn't mean a thing to me, and apparently not to the kidnappers either.

Out in the woods they flogged this man Crawford with leather straps until they got tired of it. And for what? Taking part, they said, in "red meetings." When they were through and went away, Crawford limped to a farmhouse for help. He had recognized the cops but he wouldn't say who they were. "Are you crazy?" he demanded. "Once was enough for me!" Out of town he went.

There apparently were Communists in Tampa because they made news in November by holding a parade to mark the anniversary of the Russian revolution. The Cuban cigar-rollers had built a "Labor Temple" in Ybor City, and these marchers filled the hall and spilled over the sidewalks outside. The police attacked them and chased the people through the streets, arresting dozens. The officers of the force had a photograph taken of themselves displaying a confiscated Soviet Union flag. In response, workers at one of the factories went on strike; and, punching back, the cigar manufacturers removed the "intelligent readers" from all of the factories. This was an insult to the whole cigar-rolling tradition. As readers' platforms were dismantled, about 7,000 workers went on a three-day strike. In retaliation for that, they were all locked out.

Mack called and told me to stay clear of Tampa. The leaders of the city's business community had created a Citizens Committee of twenty-five "outstanding" but unidentified men to help the cigar manufacturers "wash the red out of their factories."

Well, I knew who one of the members of the Citizen's Committee was: Alf, the pompous boyfriend of my wife Clarinda. She had admitted to me that he was also a member of the St. Petersburg Klan. Their chapter, or Klavern, was "Olustee No. 20," named in honor of one of only two Civil War battles fought in Florida. Other than laying waste to 3,000 men on a single day sixty years ago, the only consequence of that engagement was that the Yankees withdrew from the field, so it made sense for the Klan to celebrate the occasion as a Confederate victory. It was also said that the Federal Colored Infantry protected the Yankee retreat, and that any of the wounded they left on the battlefield were slain by pursuing rebels. True? I don't know. In any case, I had no use for Alf or any of those people.

I'm making myself angry just talking about these bad times, but let me try to finish it up here.

This "Committee" and Tampa's Police Chief, Amazon C. Logan, organized another raid on the Labor Temple, and the police carted off enough records to identify 5,000 local cigar workers as union members and thus Communists. A federal judge enjoined the union from interfering with the peaceful operation of the cigar industry, meaning going on strike. With the weight of the courts behind them, the factories began reopening on a basis of open-shop Americanism, as approved by the Citizen's Committee. The judge rejoiced that, "the paid agitators began to leave Tampa like rats deserting a sinking ship. I can in mind's eye see that big, bold Negro in a red Packard with an Illinois tag, exceeding the speed limit on his way back to Chicago."

Mack reassured me that he was trying to keep his head down, but he confided that Eugene had gone to one of the strike meetings to voice his support. That was a mistake, Mack thought, because Eugene needed to protect his job at the Tribune. Like my son, Poulnot had a wife and family at home who depended on his wages. Eugene's typesetter union happened to be anti-Communist, and the shop steward came to talk to him so he kind of backed off of radical politics.

"But he has joined the Socialist Party," Mack confided in me. "I'm thinking about it myself."

That startled me. "What the hell for?" I asked. For me it was no big stretch to be a Democrat, but a Socialist? I didn't actually know what that was. In Germany, Adolph Hitler was saying he was a Socialist.

"There's people starving in breadlines, Dad," he told me, disturbed by the injustice of things, "and here I am ferrying all of these tycoons and mobsters, and you wouldn't believe the way they talk about, 'jungle bunnies' and …"

"You'd better not go there, son."

"Well, I know, but…"

"You can't say that about the people who raised me."

"I don't say that! They say that! And the fat cats from New York and the goombahs from Chicago…"

"The what?"

"Mobsters, Pop. Who do you think is running these clubs?"

"Call them mobsters, if that's what they are. 'Goombah' – that makes you sound low class."

"And that's what I am. I'm in the lowest class compared to them, and they'd call me cracker trash if I wasn't a war veteran, grinning like a monkey in the pilot's seat. These times have got to change."

This conversation with Mack brought to mind a visit I had recently paid to the Ephrams, the family of whom I have spoken, who fed me and looked after my welfare in my young years when we all lived on Sheriff Sandy Watson's farm near Bradenton. They were black as coal. Mr. Ephram had since died, but his wife Cordelia, who could have been a hundred, still lived with her eldest son Jake on the "Watson Farm." It was always called that even though Sheriff Watson had passed away. If he was my natural father, as I was led to believe, he took that secret to the grave with him.

And I'll take my anger toward him to the grave with me.

(Captain Duff, the last of my old guideposts is gone, too. I suppose this happens to all of us if you live long enough, and then you're on your own. But I still speak with him, spiritually, when in need of spiritual guidance.)

Jake Ephram managed the Watson Farm, but when I dropped by to see him and his mother one Sunday he was skittish. The Ephrams were far more aware about the way things were than I was.

"They watch us you know," Jake told me.

"They?"

"The Kluxers. Every time Reuben comes out here to visit there will be a car comes out here the next day. The skinny redneck who lives down the road or one of his cousins will want to know what we're up to. They think Reuben is some kind of mixed breed. I don't know. With Mister Watson gone, we don't have much protection any more. Now I hear his boys are talking about selling my place."

"I don't know anything about selling the place," I told Jake, "but if anybody bothers you or your mother, I believe I can take care of it."

"Can you?" he challenged me. "The white people know you tried to get special treatment for Seth when he was sent down to the turpentine labor camp. They don't like any of us getting special treatment."

"Would you rather I not visit?"

"No!" a shout came from the back bedroom where I thought Mrs. Cordelia was sleeping. "You come around here anytime, Gawain. We always got a home for you here."

Jake looked doubtful. He was wise enough to be worried.

Eugene Poulnot didn't get fired, and my son didn't join the Socialist Party as far as I know. And I do believe every one of us voted for Franklin D. Roosevelt. And that's all I want to say about my personal politics.

LOVELADY BARLOW EXPLAINS THINGS TO HER GRANDSON

The reason we left Georgia, Mack, was because we were run out. It was only recently that I told this story to your mother. I may have explained our departure differently in the past, but I'm tired of keeping quiet about what really happened to us.

Your granddad, Pa, was manager of a sawmill way out in the pine forests west of Valdosta and he was making pretty good money. All his crew were colored men. There was one named Bones who was a particularly good worker, and Pa gave him the job of foreman when some white boy wanted it. Bones' wife liked Pa, and maybe there was gossip about that. There were even stories made up about Bones and me.

The white boy had words with Pa, but there was no backing down. One night the Klan in their sheets, most of them, paid us a visit and dragged Pa out in the yard and thrashed him pretty good. They held me with my arms pinned behind my back, and when they was done they threw all our clothes and other belongings out of our little company house. They called me a slut and a whore and pushed me to the ground! Me – whose daddy owned a big peach farm!

Without so much as a "Kiss my Ass" they put us on the road with nothing but what we could carry. I was banished like Amos, holding only baby Clarinda wrapped in a blanket. Those demons – I won't even call them men – set fire to the pile of our possessions – everything we had to leave behind. I expect they did even worse to Bones, but we never did find out. We just went, and we kept on going until we ran out of road way down here in Florida on Horse Creek.

So Mack, you be careful in how you conduct yourself. Those fools are crazy, and now anyone they believe is too "red" or not "white" enough is liable to suffer. They have their spies everywhere.

CHAPTER NINE

THE MURDER OF
THE TWO COQUETTES

We finally got telephones out on Catfish Creek, and I used mine to call Germaine and arrange a visit. I used as few words as possible because the operator was probably listening in. But at our meeting I intended to deliver the news that Clarinda and I were going to try being married again. Germaine said she had something important to tell me, too, so I expected this to be quite a conversation.

Perhaps I should explain my relationship with Germaine. She is a very warm person and good company, definitely one of the best looking woman in her age group. We had a lot of fun when the candle blew out. But she didn't cook for me, clean for me, or ask a lot of questions about the state of my health or my hopes for the future. She could get hotheaded, especially after a few drinks, and carry on about some customer who had pissed her off, her boss, or local politicians who didn't tip. She kept a loaded chrome Smith and Wesson .32 with pearl handles in the drawer of her bedside table, and had threatened to shoot me with it, more or less playfully, on at least two occasions. Germaine had been married before – but not, she admitted, to a man who'd died in the War - and she viewed the institution with suspicion, which was fine with me. At the same time, however, I was nearly certain that during my absences she sometimes entertained other men, maybe even the ex-husband himself. I didn't complain about that. After all, I was at all times technically married myself. Despite all that, Germaine and I were good friends. We all need friends.

So, as soon as I got to her apartment and she leaned in to kiss me I broke the news that our affair was over. She stepped back in shock, I thought, and then she laughed.

"That's okay, Gabe," she said. "I knew it wouldn't last. This comes at a bad time though."

"I'm sorry about . . ." I didn't get to finish.

"It's a bad time, sweetheart, because I was just about to ask you for a great big favor."

I was relieved that there wasn't going to be a huge scene, though I had prepared myself for a few sobs and angry remarks. Yet, there was serious trouble in Germaine's family. I hardly recalled hearing her ever mention having a brother, but now he had apparently gotten himself in some serious trouble. His name was Whitey. He was the youngest of her disorganized relations and was a "good kid" though he was always in some kind of inconvenient difficulty and needing money.

"But he has a way of making people like him," Germaine explained, "and he's fun to be with. The problem is Whitey makes things up, about himself, and he has all these schemes about how he's going to shake dollars out of the trees. They never work out, you know, and lending him money is just like pouring it down the sink, honey."

The latest was he got in some mess over in Tampa about rigging slot machines, and he had to leave the state to "cool off." Probably he had gone to New Orleans.

Wherever Whitey had gone, now he was back in Florida and locked up - for murder! She showed me the letter she had just received:

Dear Sis,

I hope this finds you well. Not so good for me. I'm bum rapped here in the Sarasota jail. They say I killed two women at a house of ill repute. I swear I didn't do it. I could sure use some help. I'm not asking for money. They won't set any bail for me. I just need someone to help prove I'm innocent. Like Will Rogers says, it's bacon, it's beans or it's limousines. I guess it's just beans for me now.

Your loving brother,
Whitey

I was stunned. "Do you mean to tell me that your brother is the one they tracked down for shooting those two sisters on 24th street?" Of course I had heard about this shooting! It had been the biggest story in the Sarasota newspapers for the previous three weeks! "That's the most famous murder we've had in Sarasota since Mayor Higel was killed."

She closed her eyes and nodded sadly.

I shook my head in disbelief. I had a new level of appreciation for the Doré family. "What is it you want me to do, Germaine?" I asked.

"Can't you just investigate, Gabe? Can't you go see my brother in jail and find out what really happened? There has to be something we can do."

I must have looked hesitant, because she pleaded, "Gabe, you've got to. You're the only honest policeman I know!"

However hesitant I may have looked, I was really chomping at the bit to get involved. It was a big case. After she called me an honest policeman, I had trouble hiding my enthusiasm. This was taking the sting out of the way she had reacted, or not reacted, to the ending of our love affair.

"I guess I could go down to the jail," I said slowly, "and see if they'll let me talk to him."

"Ooh, thank you! Thank you!" Germaine jumped into my lap, ran her fingers through my hair and gave me a big kiss. I had to push her away and remind her that we were breaking up.

In leaving I told her, "There's only so much investigating I'll be able to do for your brother without getting paid, Germaine. That's just the way it is these days. My time's been cut at the Circus." It sounds funny now, but I was taking my budding career as a private sleuth seriously.

"I'm sorry to hear that, Gabe. I know you like that job. But you tell Whitey about the money, when you see him," she said. "My brother always has some cash hidden away somewhere."

I called Clarinda when I got back to Sarasota. Considering that I was on a party line at the farm, we had to watch what we said. "I had my talk with Germaine," I told her.

"That's good," she said and hesitated. "But I haven't had my talk with

Alf yet."

I was certainly angry and disappointed to hear that, and cut our conversation short.

CLARINDA'S STORY (CONTINUED)

Gawain thinks he's got me wrapped up now that he's had "his talk" with Germaine. Did he apologize for the whole thing? I'm sure he's gone a lot further with that floozy than I've gone with Alf. It's wonderful that he's had "his talk," but does he expect me to just come running back? And I really don't know why he's starting to call himself Gabe.

The following morning, I drove into town. It was about eleven o'clock when I parked at the courthouse. The county sheriff at that time was C.B. Pearson, and the Chief of Police was one Tilden S. Davis. I didn't know much about Pearson except that he had beaten out Bixby Hodges in the last election, which I thought was a fine thing. Tilden Davis I knew from experience to be a half-way intelligent cop, and fortunately, it happened to be Chief Davis who I found making a cup of coffee at the lock-up.

"Howdy, T.D.," I said. "Remember me?"

"Sure, MacFarlane," he said, stirring in half a pound of sugar. "How's the Circus?"

"I don't work there much anymore. Seems they couldn't sell enough peanuts to pay my salary."

"That's too bad." The chief cop rolled up a chair and sat behind his small cluttered desk. He didn't invite me to sit, but I did anyway, facing him. "What are you up to these days?" he asked me.

"Trying to put food on the table like everybody else. I'm a private detective, you might say. I pick up a little work here and there."

"Private detective?" Davis grinned. He had a narrow face and a clipped tan mustache. "I didn't know we had one of those here in Sarasota. Is there a lot of money in it?"

"Sometimes," I lied. "I've been asked to look into a matter that you're involved with."

"What's that?"

"The homicide of those two women, the Bell sisters."

"Really?" Davis rested his coffee cup carefully. He wiped a napkin over his mustache. "Who would hire you for that? Or is this where you say 'I'm not free to divulge my client's name'?" He grinned again.

"I don't mind saying. The guy you arrested for it, Whitey Jarvis, his sister asked me to investigate the circumstances."

That got a chuckle. "What circumstances? Jarvis was at the house; he fired the gun; we have his .38. And he ran off to Louisiana with the other hood who was there at the scene. We chased them down, the Sheriff and me. Quite a road trip. I'd never been as far as Pensacola, much less all the way to Louisiana. When they were cornered, in this hick-town Slidell, this other crook came out shooting, and we took him down. I was there MacFarlane. Your man Whitey had better sense than his buddy did. He walked out with his hands held high, and now we've got him locked up right where he should be and awaiting trial."

"Yeah. I read all that in the papers," I said. "Sounds open-and-shut. Still, I'd like to talk to him."

Davis thought about it.

"You'll have to surrender any weapons your carrying, and I'll have to pat you down."

"That's okay. I'm not armed." At the moment, my Colt .45 Government Model automatic was locked outside in my car.

Davis gave me a professional search and said, "You're clean I guess," and led me back to the row of ten cells. Three might have been occupied; it was hard to tell, the hallway being unlit except for the stray sunrays that penetrated the tiny slits of windows high on the walls. Yet, it was a lot nicer layout than the fetid two-cell holding tank in the old jail Sarasota had when I was the marshal.

Davis stopped at the end of the row and rattled the iron door. "Wake up, Whitey. You've got company." Within, a short man badly in need of a shave, who was wearing a baggy white outfit with horizontal black stripes, sat up on his steel bunk and rubbed his eyes. He focused on us and beamed as if happy. True to his name, he had a full head of shaggy blond hair. He was probably in his late 30s and had quite a wide and engaging smile.

"It's a great pleasure," he said. "Come on in, my good sirs."

"He ain't coming in," the Chief said. "You can talk through the bars." He turned to me. "Here's your man. If you need me, you know where I am." He went back down the hall, dragging his nightstick, a sound like a snare drum, along the bars as he went. The door to his office closed, and I heard the lock click in.

"Just you and me, Whitey," I said, not actually realizing I was speaking out loud.

"Who are you, sir?" he asked. "Doesn't matter. I'm glad for any diversion."

"My name is Gabe MacFarlane," I told him. "Your sister asked me to come see how you're doing."

Whitey put his palms together as if in prayer and went down on one knee. "Hosanna!" he exclaimed, and popped up beaming joyfully.

"Not like that. No hosannas. I probably can't stay long. Just tell me what happened." The whole place smelled like years of men's crud mopped over with Pine-Sol. The aroma was very familiar to me.

Whitey drew closer. "Me and Juanita, that's my girlfriend, Juanita Ropollo, we were having a few drinks at this bar," he confided. "She got preoccupied some way. We were there with this fellow from New Orleans, Donny, who Juanita was acquainted with. I was a little pasted, you know?" He raised his eyebrows and shrugged. "It was real noisy in the bar. Someone said there was a house down the block where we could have a quiet drink with a couple of Florida girls, all nice and elegant. Okay, that sounded right. Juanita wasn't in view at that moment. She was busy. So down the street Donny and I went, just enjoying the sweet breeze. And to the house we go."

"Okay. And then what?"

"There was some buzzer to get in, and Donny knew how to do it. And this broad, Lacey was her name I remember, she showed us into the front room. A very young lady, very pretty. So we all sat down for drinks. Again, all polite.

"It was suggested that there was some other man in the back of the house, with Lacey's sister, but that didn't bother us one bit. Then just as we were all getting cozy, the buzzer rings and in comes these other two gentlemen, and they are invited to sit down and join us. Then this other broad, Lacey's sister I guess, runs in from the back room, and this man she was with, he rushes in waving a gun and cursing at the top of his lungs. Lacey jumped up, but before she could say anything these two new fellows both pulled out a piece, and suddenly everybody is shooting. The guy from the back room took a hit and jumped out the window. My pal Donny was quick on the draw, and he joined in, shooting at everyone. And these other guys bolted!"

"And you did…"

"I crawled on the floor to the front door. God blessed me! I was lucky to get out of there alive! Donny found me in the yard, and we ran as fast as we could away from that place. Good riddance!"

"Your gun? Your gun was there."

"Sure, I fired my gun to defend myself. And I hope I hit them. I sure do. Anybody with balls would do his job, wouldn't he? But there were bullets flying everywhere, and I dropped my gun on the way out the door."

"Who were the guys who entered the house," I asked, "the ones who started the shooting?"

Whitey was absolutely mystified. "I have no clue," he said. "Complete strangers to me. When the shooting was over, they scattered out of there, bleeding like pigs. And I was right behind them, but they had disappeared."

"Pigs at slaughter?"

"That's right."

"Did you know you left the two sisters dying on the floor?"

"No, sir. I was not aware." His face was all dumb innocence.

"So, if you were the victim, Whitey, why did you flee from the home, leaving those two women, and drive all the way to Louisiana?"

"What would you do?" he asked waving his hands "Two women coughing up blood! One bloke crawling out the window bleating like a goat, leaking the whole way! And Donny, my ride, was getting the hell out and gone! I had to run for my life!"

"And drove…"

"Donny drove. He had a cousin living in some fish camp on Lake Pontchartrain. He traps crabs and lives in a damn shack. We drove all night. Me and Donny. Or at least Donny did. I slept. When we got to his cousin's house we were invited in and told we could stay till all our troubles blew over. After all, we wasn't the ones started it."

"And that's where you got caught? At the fishing camp?"

"Right. And Donny tried to shoot it out like a dope. Now he's paid the price."

"He's dead if that's what you mean. But if he was innocent, why'd he come out of the fish camp shooting?"

"Search me." Whitey scratched his head. "Very perplexing." I was almost starting to enjoy this guy. His words flowed out like soda fountain syrup. "All I can figure," he went on, "is Donny had a record and was a marked man. He said that several times to me while we were driving. I guess he decided he had no future either way. Me, I hid behind a chair. I wasn't armed, believe you me."

"You weren't armed because you lost your gun here in the whore house?"

"That's absolutely true. But, God's truth, I didn't know it was a whore house."

"That's bull?"

"Two sisters? I don't call that a whore house. To me, that's just an inviting locale to have a few drinks and listen to some jazz on the radio."

"That's your story?"

"Yeah." He smiled at me. "What's wrong with it?'

"Plenty. Where does your girlfriend, Juanita, fit in?"

"Nowhere, sir. When I first left Florida two years ago, I went to New Orleans, just bumming around. That's where I met Juanita. She's a good girl, but was down on her luck. I'm handy with cards, and so is she. We ran a poker game out of a little apartment in the French Quarter making a few dollars off the tourists who like to gamble. I don't claim that either one of us goes to church on Sunday."

"But then you came back to Florida, and Juanita came with you. Why was that?"

"She loves me," Whitey said, eyes wide open and soft.

"Yeah? I'm getting tired of standing out here."

"But it's true."

"Okay. Why did you come back to Florida if you were making money in New Orleans?"

"To be honest, I missed the Florida weather. New Orleans is certainly hot enough for my tastes, but it doesn't have enough fresh air for me. And there were some complaints about my card-playing practices. I would have come back here on my own, but it was great to have Juanita along. I try never to stay in one place too long. Trouble seems to latch onto me."

"It sure does. When did this Donny fellow enter the picture?"

"I met him in New Orleans. He wanted a change of pace and came along for the ride to Florida. He had enough dough for the gas money, so we let him come along."

"So, the three of you arrive in Sarasota, and now there's two dead women and one shot-up 'john' - some individual named Ricky Weed according to the papers - who limped away to Rouse's Roadhouse Tavern on Cocoanut Avenue where he got a ride with a friend. They found a police car at Five Points, and the cops got Weed to the hospital. He told the police he didn't know who the intruders were. And Lacey Bell, before she died, said she never saw who shot her."

"There you have it. That's life I guess. Except this Ricky Weed was firing away."

"And then you and Donny fled back to Louisiana, leaving Juanita behind."

"Right."

"What happened to you after Donny was shot at the fishing camp, after the police arrested you?"

"First the cops took me to New Orleans and tried to pin a bank robbery on me."

"You robbed a bank in New Orleans?"

"No, of course not. But I pled guilty just as fast as I could. I'd rather do time in Louisiana for bank robbery than face a murder charge in Florida."

"Whitey, I hate to say this, but I'm impressed. I had no idea that you were involved in so many spheres of criminal activity. You've really been around the world."

"Thank you. But I'm not too pleased to hear you put it like that. I am innocent of all those crimes."

"It sounds to me like you fled from Louisiana because you'd robbed a bank and came to Sarasota to hole up, not to enjoy our fresh Florida breezes. And then you ran back to Louisiana because you were wanted for murder here."

"I can see why you'd think that. It is actually what the judge believed. He sentenced me to five years for bank robbery, which suited me. But then he sent me back to Florida to be hung for murder."

"They use the chair now, Whitey, not the noose."

"Oh, God. Well, here I am, then." He used all his fingertips to mop his eyes.

"And your girl, Juanita?"

"She's even more innocent than me." Whitey stared at me sadly. Slow tears slid down his cheeks.

"That's great, Whitey. As I said before, I'm only here because your sister Germaine asked me to come. But I'm a private investigator. That means I need to be paid if I'm to get into this."

"Of course. That goes without saying," Whitey assured me. "You need to talk to Juanita. I think she can help us both out."

"Your sister Germaine told me to talk to you."

"Well, Juanita is out in the free world, and I'm in the slammer. So, she's the one to go to."

"Okay. Where is she now?"

"Why, Gabe, she's right here. Right here in Sarasota. She never left. Juanita's still in town to see what becomes of me. She's not a woman of any influence, but she cares about poor Whitey."

"Because it's love?'

"I'd say so." He bowed his head, again in prayer. I got to stare at his pink bald spot, until he sat upright. His eyes glistened.

"No one else has ever cared about me," he said. "She's all that a man could hope for."

"That's quite a testament. Where do you think Juanita would be found now?"

"I don't know!" the imprisoned cried in anguish. Down went the head again. "God, I wish I knew! But my guess is that later tonight she'll be at the place where all this started. The Roadhouse Tavern."

That gave me some time to kill so I bought a newspaper and a Coke at the five and dime. Then I ambled down to the waterfront to sit under a palm tree and catch up on the news.

Magically, Franklin Roosevelt, my preferred candidate, had gotten elected President and Prohibition had been repealed. So now all the full-page ads were for cabarets and cocktail dresses. And the liquor stores had suddenly come into the light and now sported neon signs. But the news itself was sobering – a mineworkers' strike was in full swing up north in the mountains, and the National Socialists were "Seig Heiling" through Germany. I dozed off, and dreamed about moonshine stills and jail cells.

I MEET JUANITA ROPOLLO

I'm told those fancy neon signs were invented in Lake Worth, Florida, but wherever they came from, neon glory blazed into Sarasota in a matter of weeks after Prohibition was repealed. In no time at all Whitey's quiet little bar on 24th Street was no longer the Roadhouse Tavern but had been rechristened as "Coquettes' Lounge" in homage to the slain sisters. The lounge now boasted a flashing red and blue sign you could see from all over the neighborhood, which was at the lower-class end of what Sarasota had to offer. But while the lots surrounding the bar might be overgrown and littered with junk cars, not far down the street was a scattering of houses decorated with flowers and hedges, like normal people might also live there.

Halfway between the Lounge and those normal people was a shabby stucco cottage shrouded by untidy cabbage palms, their fallen brown fronds piled up on the grounds. This was where the shooting – the murder of the two Bell sisters Bertie and Lacey - had taken place.

After the troubling experience of interviewing Whitey Jarvis, Coquettes' Lounge seemed just the right place to improve my mood.

The tavern had a solid oak door, painted brown, with a spy window near the top so that the doorman could check who was outside before admitting a customer. This was a vestige of Prohibition. Now the door swung open easily.

The scene inside was bright and noisy. Loud scratchy tunes came from a record player set on one end of the bar and a radio blared from the wall behind the pool table where six or so people all seemed to be involved in the same game of Eight Ball. A row of men and three women filled the barstools. The counter space along the wall was all occupied, and some children were eating smoked mullet and drinking Cokes at a card table. It took only a second to absorb all that. In my professional judgment, the atmosphere wasn't unsavory, but there was a lot of drinking going on. I went up to the bar and gently elbowed my way in between a couple of gents who seemed lost in their own quiet enjoyments. They both were wearing wide-brimmed black felt hats.

I smiled at one and turned to smile at the other, who ignored me. The bar maid took notice and worked her way along to take my order. "Canadian Club, if you've got the real thing. Otherwise rye. On the rocks, with a splash."

"Rye it is," she said. "Single or double?"

"Single, I guess." After all, I was on a murder case.

"Coming up. You look familiar." It was just a comment. She had close cropped brown hair and broad shoulders and went off to fix my drink without a smile. I couldn't place her, and must have turned to my neighbor with a puzzled expression because he said, "Maybe she knows you from working at Ringling."

I gave the man a closer look. "Are you one of W.E. Lawson's crew who put up the Big Top?"

"Yeah, that's me. Pete Noski. Sixteen years. But I heard you quit."

"No, I was put on part-time. Weekends only. I think I'm almost laid off. And I don't travel North. I'm just local. My boss got demoted."

"Charlie Ort?"

"You know him?'

Pete Noski chuckled but did not elaborate. "What was you?" he asked. "Some kind of security?"

"You could say that. You're still with the Circus?"

"Sure." He took a long drink from a big mug full of dark beer.

"You're in with a rough gang."

"I guess," he shrugged. "It's definitely physical. You have to step lively and know what you're doing. If you don't, something, or somebody, is definitely gonna come down hard on your ass."

My glass came, and I swiveled to look around the room. There was a couple necking in a corner, pressed up against the wall. The kids had been taken home.

I came back around to Pete. "Did you ever know a guy named Whitey Jarvis?" I asked.

"The one in jail for murder? Yeah, I seen him in here, as a matter of fact. Everybody saw him, or says they did. He's notorious in this neighborhood. He plugged the two Bell sisters down the street."

"Right, I guess so. That's what they say. Do you know a lady he hung out with named Juanita? Juanita Ropollo?"

He gave me a look, like: you're stupid. "She's right down there." He lifted his finger off the bar a quarter inch and pointed. "The one with the long black hair."

A glance told me that the lady in question was enthralling two sharp looking gentlemen seated on either side of her. They had open-necked blue shirts and nicely barbered hair, almost identical twins. The woman was wearing a light pink sweater that showed a modest amount of cleavage. She had a healthy tan and a gay laugh. She didn't appear to be in terrible mourning about Whitey's incarceration.

I signaled the bar maid and ordered another drink. "And one for the lady in pink," I said, nodding toward Juanita.

The drinks were served, and Juanita looked over at me in surprise. So did the two guys she was with. Or was she with them? One of them stood up, which he had a hard time doing, and took a few unsteady steps toward me to introduce himself. He looked like a petty crook who should be sticking up something easy, like a popcorn stand, but he wasn't packing so far as I could tell.

"I haven't seen you before, grandpa," he said. His handsome face registered somewhere between a dumb grin and an evil eye. He was drunk and young, and I didn't like him. I offered him my hand, which surprised him but he took it. Then I reached over with my other hand and broke his finger. That surprised him even more, and before he could scream I walked him to the door and pushed him out. "See a doctor, brother," I told him. "And leave me alone."

I went back inside and took back my stool. Conversations in the place had died down. Pete Noski looked over at me. He grinned. The barmaid changed the record and turned up the volume.

Okay, so far. I carried my drink down to the vacated stool beside Juanita and took a seat. Through dark eyelashes she looked at me suspiciously. The man on the other side of her straightened up. He laid some coins on the bar top, gave Juanita an angry glare, and made his departure.

"I'm Gabe MacFarlane. Whitey Jarvis' sister asked me to investigate the shooting of those women and see if I could help him."

Her eyes softened. "So, how could you possibly help?" she asked. Her voice was husky and had an accent I could only identify as New York Yankee.

"I don't know. Whitey tells a funny story."

"Funny, like ha-ha?"

"Not really. He says he didn't know either of the two men who showed up at the house. Or the man who came out of the back room. That doesn't make much sense, since they all started shooting at each other right away. Of course, it doesn't seem that any of the gunmen were killed. Only the two women were, and they lived there. The man from the back room was wounded and ran away. He could probably identify Whitey, but he won't have to since Whitey admits he was there. The two men who showed up last ran away, too. And you were sitting right here in this bar the whole time it happened?"

She nodded.

"My question then would be, how can you help, Juanita?"

"I can't," she said. "That's just it. I was having a good time right in this spot. And Whitey goes out to visit a couple of whores." She sipped at the drink I had bought her. It was something dark and fizzy.

"Who were the guys who came in and started shooting?"

"Maybe the shadow knows," Juanita said quietly. "Listen, I got to go to the ladies." She disembarked with poise and walked toward the back where the restrooms were located. I looked over and Pete smiled at me again. And he hoisted his mug.

After five minutes I realized I was being scammed. Down the hall, I knocked first then pushed open the door marked "Gulls." It smelled sweet inside, but there was nobody there. The door at the end of the hall to the backyard was unlocked. The mullet cooks had shut down their smoker and the yard was empty and quiet. The wood smoke was blowing away, and the air was filling with the smell of jasmine and rotting oak leaves.

On my way back through the bar, Pete Noski waved me over. I passed him by and looked out the front door. Just the sounds of a side street in a little city where the wind blew through the trees and bright stars came out at night. A car passed by slowly, crunching gravel, but there was no sign of Juanita.

Disgusted with myself, I went back to see what Noski had to say.

He had ordered me a drink and wanted some of my time, so I sat down again.

"She's your flapper, big man. Beauty and brains in a cute package, looking for trouble," he opined.

"That's very profound, Pete. Where'd she go?"

"Hell, if I know. If I did I might go there myself, except I'm married. She likes fun. The late night action is way down the road and out of town where the law is scarce."

I tried my drink, and it seemed to me that a cheaper brand of liquor had been supplied. "There are a lot of casinos and bars 'down the road'."

"I've heard her mention Whiskey Corners, once upon a time."

"Whoa, that's an hour's drive."

"But the people there are happy and free of care, so I've heard." Noski chuckled and put away his beer.

"I doubt there is any such a place." I knew Whiskey Corners, but I didn't say that to Pete.

"Whitey and his friend Donny. . ." Pete began, took a breath and resumed, "They had a lot of cash on them."

"That's interesting." So, maybe I would get paid after all.

"Donny was paying for their drinks out of a wad he pulled from his pants. Whitey had a canvas duffle, like a sailor, and he kept it between his feet. They looked like a couple of traveling salesmen."

"What was in the duffle?"

"I really couldn't say. Could have been his luggage or his laundry. But Whitey kept that bag close at hand. Both guys were acting like heavyweights. Paying for drinks. Losing money at pool. Juanita asked for Champagne. Can you imagine? They don't have Champagne in here."

"What did she get instead?"

"I don't know. Rum and Coke, I think."

"Did she ask for a 'Cuba Libre'?"

"That's it. Whitey sat right where you are, and he offered me a job."

"Yeah? Doing what?"

"He said they needed a driver. Someone who could stay sober and drive fast. He said it was a dangerous job but paid well."

"And you said?"

"I didn't say anything. He was drunk on his ass."

"That was it?"

"Yep. Donny came over and wanted to go down the street to Bertie and Lacey Bell's. Whitey was game. He asked me did I want to go along. I had no interest in bullshit like that. And, I didn't really know the lads. So, out they went, Whitey carrying his grip. Juanita saw them leave. She seemed happy they were going somewhere. There were plenty of men wanting to buy her a drink."

"Did you hear the gunfire?"

"Everybody in the bar heard it, and this place cleared out fast. I didn't wait around. I live in the next block, and I ran home in a hurry. Some cars drove past at high speed, and cops were all over the neighborhood in twenty minutes. By then I was watching all this from my own front steps."

"Quite a night."

"You bet, man. And nothing to do with me. I have a job and an ol' lady, and I plan to keep 'em both."

I tossed a couple of bucks on the bar for a tip and went out into the night. Whiskey Corners was quite a haul, but my house on Catfish Creek was a third of the way there. That would give me a few miles to gauge how the drinking and driving was going to go.

I went home first to think about it and give the booze some time to mellow. But it was lonesome there looking at the walls, and I got back in the car and pointed it south.

Whiskey Corners is called that because it sells liquor and sits at a crossroads with a four-way stop sign. One of the roads travels northward toward Sarasota and southward down the peninsula to Gasparilla Island; the other road goes east toward El Jobean and west to Englewood beach. Great pine forests cover the area, with rude houses and fishing camps scattered at the edges, but out by Lemon Bay there are also two or three new resort hotels catering to well-heeled fishermen. This makes for different sorts of people in the vicinity, but those who share the simple idea of getting away for a couple of drinks in a tavern come to Whiskey Corners. It's the only watering hole for miles.

The bar has another advantage. It's in Charlotte County, which is even more law-avoiding than Sarasota.

It was after ten when I drove into the shell parking lot, illuminated by its own bright blue flashing sign, an oasis of adult pleasures in a sprawling wild of scrub prairie inhabited by nature's creatures and cattle.

Cigarettes glowed in one of the parked cars, but the real action was inside, so that's where I went. Whiskey Corners wasn't much like the Coquettes' Club back in Sarasota. It was airier, bigger, and had a band. And a liquor store with its own entrance, separated from the long bar by a fence of chicken wire. I suppose that met some legal requirement. I could see a small window at the very back. Black customers, according to the law, would need to stand outside that window to buy their booze.

Clouds of smoke aside, the place was inviting and full. The only young kids still around belonged to the staff, and they were quietly playing checkers in a corner. Lots of grownups, in small groups, were partying and laughing, all reflected in the long mirror behind the bar, so I could survey the crowd. It was just like any other last-chance-for-a-drink saloon, but in this one I saw Juanita. She came from somewhere in the back and joined a couple of guys at the bar. Nothing new about that. I took an open stool and watched her in the mirror.

She was in her element here, gabbing and tossing her hair. The men on either side of her looked like fishermen. One was wearing a white T-shirt that showed off his powerful shoulders and bronze biceps. The other was older, in khaki work clothes but clean. They both seemed to be competing for her attention. Her white teeth flashed when she threw back her head and laughed. She was swaying from side to side, and in one sway she caught sight of me in the glass.

I saw the recognition, but she ignored me for a minute. Then she stood up gracefully holding her high-ball and did a little tail-spin before setting off in my direction.

"You seem to be following me," she said. The little pink sweater was still an attention-getter, and not a smudge on it. Juanita was a careful flapper.

"That's right, I am," I admitted. "And you're not making it any easier for me coming all the way down here. Did you drive yourself?"

"Is a girl supposed to do that?" she asked. Her voice was almost foreign.

"Where are you from, Juanita?"

"New Orleans, dahlin'. That's where I met Whitey." She emptied her glass. "You going to offer me a drink?"

"You talk funny."

"That's just the way I am. How about a drink?"

"Why not?" I waved for service and the bartender set us up with a smile. Everywhere I went I was buying drinks and knocking them back. I suppose I could handle it, couldn't I?

"Am I right that you came from New Orleans with Whitey?" I asked, taking a sip.

"True enough," she said. "Why am I standing up?"

She had me there. I gave her my stool and enjoyed the sight of her legs sliding into my seat.

"This is much better," she sighed. A look down the bar told me the other guys weren't pleased but were seeing the humor in the situation. "I came with Whitey to Florida because he said we could be safe here, but he got himself in a fix right away and abandoned me in this

Never Land."

"Where's that?" I asked.

"It's from a film, dummy. Don't you go to the movies?"

"I've been to a couple. The fact is, you came to Florida because Donny and Whitey robbed a bank in New Orleans and were on the run, right?"

"How did you know that?" she asked.

"Because Whitey told me."

"I don't know anything about that," she lied, avoiding my eyes. "After Whitey and Donny got into that shootout at the ladies' house here, they ran back to Louisiana. And Donny got killed by the cops."

"And Whitey pled guilty to robbing a bank hoping not to be brought back to Sarasota on a murder charge."

"Maybe. But you can see how well that worked out. He's in jail."

"So now you are all by yourself in Sarasota. It's not much like New Orleans, is it, Juanita?"

That got a laugh. She thought it was so funny she whistled. "No it's not, cowboy! It's not like New Orleans or anywhere else I've ever been." That made her sad, and she stared at her drink. She had ordered a Cuba Libre.

"After the shootout at the cathouse," I said to bring her back to reality, "Whitey and Donny only made it about a week before they got cornered in . . . what was the name of that town?"

"Slidell," she said softly.

"So you know it?"

"Yeah. Fish and crabs."

"Where Donny was killed by the police and Whitey was taken to New Orleans for the bank robbery charge."

"Like I said, he was innocent of that, but he pleaded guilty." She ran a hand over her forehead to push her hair away. "It's not important."

"No, not important at all. Because they sent Whitey right back to Sarasota charged with killing two women. He's locked up, but why are you still here, Juanita? How come you're not on the next train to New Orleans?"

"Other than wanting to see things done right for Whitey?" She spat it out, like she was mad at me and everything else.

"Do you care that much for him? I don't see you doing much on his behalf. Why are you still here?"

He mood changed. "You're not bad looking," she said and put an arm around my waist. She pulled me closer, thigh to thigh. "Maybe I'll tell you a secret." She was drinking rum and smelled sweet. I was tired and liked feeling her warm fingers along my belt, and, of course, I was getting a buzz from the booze. She leaned back against me, her head resting on my shoulder. "Such a nice night," she said dreamily. "It is pretty down here, the palm trees, the dark sky, all the stars. I'm getting sleepy."

"Don't go to sleep yet. Whitey said you can get some cash together for him, and for me. My services aren't free."

"Do you have a car? A place to stay?" Juanita asked.

"Pay attention, ma'am. I'm trying to make a professional arrangement."

She put a finger on her cheek and looked at me slyly. "Whitey has something just as good as money," she said. "And I know right where it is. I can pay you, though it might take just a little-bitty while."

"See you later, doll," I said and pushed away my half-empty glass.

"I could use a ride," she said and tugged at my belt.

"How did you get here?"

"I took a taxi. That nice fellow down there," she pointed, "brought me all the way. And he didn't charge me a dime." That nice fellow had laid his face onto the bar and was taking a nap.

I sighed. "Would you like me to drive you back to Sarasota?" I asked.

She nodded, against my neck.

I helped Juanita outside, though maybe she didn't really need much help. She was steady enough on her feet but seemed to be attached to my side. Her taxi-driver friend didn't care. I don't think he noticed us leaving.

Juanita slept on the way back to Sarasota. Slumped against me part of the way; then she shifted over to lean against the window, her palms together made a small cushion against the glass. At the Bee Ridge turn-off, I pulled to the side of the road in the gravel beside a closed fruit stand and shook her awake. She came around groggy and suspicious. "Where are we?" she asked.

"Almost back in the big city of Sarasota," I told her. "I live a few miles off the road. Where do you want to go?"

"Is it too late to get a drink?"

"It is for me. But I can get you home."

"Let me consider my options," she said. After doing that for a few seconds in silence, she asked, "What about I stay at your place?"

"You could do that. You could have my son's old room, though the sheets haven't been changed in a while."

"That's the offer?"

"That's it."

She sighed. "It's better than being in jail."

I laughed at that. I thought she was talking about Whitey, but as it turned out the next morning, in our conversation over fresh bacon and country eggs, she was talking about herself.

She accepted the accommodations I offered, and I barely made it into my own bed before falling asleep.

KELLY BUCKS CLOSES UP

Back at Whiskey Corners, the owner of the establishment, one Kelly Bucks, had locked up for the night. The crowd was gone; the staff had left, save Sandy, the old man who lived in a trailer at the back of the parking lot and kept an eye on things. It was a moment for reflection, and after reflecting Bucks re-opened his safe, where he had secured the night's receipts. He studied the two bags resting side-by-side on the bottom shelf, next to his money. One was a duffle bag, courtesy of the ill-fated Whitey Jarvis by way of the fresh face of Juanita Ropollo. The other was a grainy leather satchel which had been dropped off by an old acquaintance. These obviously related treasures had been delivered to him by two different clients, each probably aware of the other's business, but who wanted to keep their affairs separate. Their distrust of each other, but trust in him, could only be because Kelly Bucks had an unparalleled reputation for discretion second to none, and a history of producing results. He was also widely regarded as an independent businessman, blessedly free of the yokes of the mobsters who were building their kingdoms of vice in cities just a few miles to the north. Bucks ran a clean operation, a rural operation beside the seashore. He was a community leader.

It would be an interesting challenge disposing of these two collections Tomorrow he would have to make some calls to special friends.

Waking up with a woman in the house again was strange. Since Clarinda had left, I had gotten used to having the place to myself. I'd never invited Germaine to sleep over, for lots of reasons, but, really, Germaine had made it clear she had no interest in my farming life.

I found it agreeable having Juanita here, while I boiled up coffee and grits and fried some meat I'd salt-cured and smoked myself. The smells lured my disheveled guest out of her bed. I pointed her to the bathroom where I'd set out my one clean towel for her. I poured her a mug of java. She looked better when she came out, black hair combed out and last night's lipstick gone, and she accepted the coffee greedily. Her tight pink sweater didn't have a wrinkle in it so she must have washed it and laid it out before she passed out.

"How'd you sleep?" I asked.

"I don't remember, so I guess it was good. Scrambled with pepper," she added, scraping back a chair to sit at the table where I'd laid her out a fork and knife.

"So, this is where you live," she said, taking in my country cottage.

"More than thirty years," I told her.

"Is that you?" She pointed at a framed photograph on the wall, a younger me posing on a horse, rifle across the saddle, wearing a brown flat-brimmed hat. I liked that photo.

I nodded, and handed her a plate of eggs and bacon.

"You were a sheriff, or something?"

"Something. I'm retired from that. I'm a private detective now. And I work at Ringling sometimes."

"But you're asking a lot of questions about Whitey." She looked at me skeptically while reaching for the can of pepper. She shook it until everything on her plate was black. "I like some eggs with my pepper," she commented, to me I guess, since no one else was around.

Fascinated, I watched her take a mouthful and swallow it down. "What?" she asked.

"Nothing. Whitey's sister Germaine and I are friends. She asked me to look into the matter, but not as a lawman. Germaine thinks he's innocent, naturally."

"I wouldn't know," Juanita said. "I wasn't there."

"No, you stayed at the bar."

Snapping a piece of bacon in half, she said, "Whitey's not the type to shoot people. He's too much of a dandy. And he's clumsy."

"Well, there was a gun left at the scene."

She laughed.

"What?" I asked.

"I'll tell you a secret. Whitey's gun wasn't even loaded. He was so fucking drunk at the bar I pulled the gun out of his pants and unloaded it into the palm of my hand. He grabbed for it back and got the gun, but the bullets went right into my purse where he couldn't get 'em. He yelled bloody murder but off he went."

"You're saying it was empty! Really? I think the sheriff might have noticed that."

She shrugged and continued to break her bacon into little bits to mix with her pepper and grits.

"Donny was seen with cash at the bar," I said, "and Whitey had a duffle bag. He took it along when they went over to the cat house. What was in it?"

"You tell me."

"It could have been money. Donny was seen holding a wad of cash."

"That's an interesting theory," she said, coyly. "It would take a lot of money to fill a bag."

"Yeah, it would. Where would they get it?"

She looked up from her plate and grinned at me. "Okay, we robbed a bank." She laughed. "You going to turn us in?"

I sat back, surprised. Not surprised that Whitey Jarvis was a bank robber, he'd told me as much, but surprised that she'd admitted it was "we."

"It wouldn't do you any good to turn me in anyway," she explained. "There's already been a trial."

"At which Whitey pleaded guilty."

"There were five people who robbed the Canal Bank and Trust on Dryades Street," she said proudly. "Two ran in. Two stood guard outside. It didn't take but a few minutes. I drove us away. And nobody got hurt."

"You drove?"

She nodded.

"All the way to Florida?"

"We took turns. I'd never been outside of Orleans Parish in my life. It was a thrill."

"How in the world did you get involved in this?"

"Donny Ropollo is my cousin. He introduced me to Whitey, and we had this romantic thing."

"Donny is the one the police shot in Slidell, Louisiana, right?" I asked. "When they captured Whitey?"

"Donny was always pig-headed," Juanita explained. "He was in love with guns." She wiped a tear from her eye. Maybe it was from the pepper.

"You must have gotten away with a share of the haul, Juanita. I'd like to get paid for my time. I no longer do this for fun."

"Yeah, I heard you say that about six times. You're wrong about the money. I didn't get a penny. But there is a way." She had a very precise way of speaking.

"Where's the bank dough now?"

"I wish I knew," she said. "Our cut of the bank loot left here with Whitey and Donny and never came back. My guess is the cops kept it."

"Whitey told me you could lay your hands on some cash."

"He has some deal working," she said enigmatically.

I pressed her a bit. "What's the deal, and when's it going to work?"

"I can't tell you what it is, but the payoff should come very soon."

I let the matter drop, not to be forgotten.

"Who were the other two guys at the bank?" I asked.

"They were just some goons Donny knew. They planned the whole thing."

"But you must have got to know them pretty well, too, on that long drive to Florida. What were their names?"

"You think I'm stupid? I'd have to be to tell you that."

"Was it them who broke into that cat house to boost Donny and Whitey's money?"

"Could have been them. I don't know for sure. I'm not a witness. But I doubt it. I heard they went down to Palm Beach to spend their shares. I wouldn't be surprised if they tried to stick up another bank on the way."

"Whitey didn't leave his cash with you, Juanita, did he?" I asked.

"No," she cried. "Donny took it and now he's dead! Those two floozies are dead! And Whitey is facing a murder rap!" She raised an angry fist, but with nowhere to land it she just shook it in the air.

I gave her a minute to calm down. I wasn't sure I believed her about the money or the "deal" she had working. When she took a big swallow of coffee I asked, "Why didn't you flee with Donny and Whitey when they hot-footed back to Louisiana?"

"I could have gone. Whitey asked me to when he ran back to the bar for the car. I had to make a quick decision, but, you know…"

"What?"

She looked at me like I was an idiot. "Bank robbery? Murder? Getting chased by the cops? This girl wanted to slide, Mister. Slide away from all that."

It was a point I could understand. We each sipped our coffee. "At the bank," I resumed, "what was Whitey's job? Was he one of the robbers who went inside, or. . ."

"You don't know Whitey," she whispered. "There's not a vicious bone in his body. He may talk tough sometimes, but he ain't got the stuff for it. They didn't want him inside where he could screw things up. His job was to stand outside, try to look natural, and stay out of trouble. Whitey was only there because of me. Donny needed me to drive."

After breakfast I drove Juanita Ropollo back to Sarasota. She directed me to the Bay Haven Hotel on the Tamiami Trail. It was a solid three-story establishment that had seen happier days. She said a friend of hers had a room there, and she was invited to stay. I didn't ask any more questions, just let her out of the car and watched her walk in the front door like she owned the place – a girl in a pink sweater with no luggage. A girl who seemed to know people with hotel rooms.

I checked the mailbox when I went home to see if Clarinda had dropped me a line, but the only thing in there was a *Progressive Farmer.*

CHAPTER ELEVEN

WHITE MEN ARE TARRED AND FEATHERED

Thinking that my son Mack might have heard from his mother, and wanting to let him know I'd be coming his way soon, I rang him up. The conversation was short since I was paying for long-distance. He said his mother had told him we might be getting back together, which was encouraging. He also reported that things were getting "mighty rough." The Socialist Party in Tampa was running candidates in a city election and the cigar workers were going on strike again. All the newspapers were blaring headlines about the "Red Menace" non-stop. I could give a big whoop-la, but it all may help to explain what happened to Mack's good friend, Eugene Poulnot.

This part of Southwest Florida has never truly been a civilized country. We've had vagabond outlaws, greedy assassins, tough-as-nails pioneers, and mean-as-snakes crackers. Over the years I've seen it get richer but, in most ways, worse. What the experience of Eugene Poulnot showed me was that all the boundaries of respectability had been broken. Have times changed so much? Or is it just that there are so many more hateful people now?

Black folks, including the family who had given me the nearest I had to a mother and father, have been treated terribly - forever. I hate to say that, but it's a fact. But whites, to my knowledge, had never before been treated as hideously as Eugene was.

You may recall that Eugene Poulnot, my son's best man, was a union printer at the Tampa Tribune. He must have had his hands full with four kids of his own, yet he seemed to think it was his right to proclaim to anyone who was curious that he was a Socialist. Give him credit for braveness.

His job at the Tribune wasn't even covering his bills, and, according to Mack, Eugene had become bitter about the state of the world's affairs. Roosevelt had brought in a program where men on government relief could do public works for low wages. Eugene couldn't join that program, but he did see the low wages as a situation he could protest. It wasn't necessarily his business, but he was giving speeches about unionizing the unemployed.

I planned a trip up to Tampa, expecting first to see Mack and then to continue over to St. Pete, where I would drop in on Germaine to report the little I had found out about her brother's case, and then on to Seminole to visit Clarinda. I'd left a message with her mother, Lovelady, that I'd be coming.

My friend Reuben invited himself along for the ride. It had been a long time, he said, since he'd been "up North," meaning Tampa or St. Pete. But what he really wanted was to check out "this Germaine woman" I'd been dating. Of course, he also wanted to see the long-lost

Clarinda, though he promised to wait out in the car during my reunion.

"Maybe we can get to a Bolita club in Tampa," he suggested. "I'd be up for that."

On our sunny drive north, Reuben regaled me with tales about various women he'd met while working for the Pinkertons at the Ringling Circus. Two of his many stories in particular have stuck with me. The first involved a beautiful tiger-tamer named Irene Mabel who performed daring acts with a 400-pound Siberian cat while wearing a tightfitting costume of red, white, and blue seashells and white leather boots, armed only with a whip. "A long whip - like a Florida cracker," Reuben explained. Irene would stick her arms, elbows, legs, and even her head, into the tiger's mouth, and make the cat roll over, roar, and sit on a barrel. All the while Irene shouted commands that could be heard to the top of the tent.

"Irene was good at this, but she was actually terrified of that cat," Reuben continued. Before each show she would consult her friend for reassurance, a mysterious female Chinese fortune teller named Sin Sui, who would normally convince Irene that she would survive the day's performances. "However, if Sin Sui said the signs were bad on a given day," Reuben said, "Irene wouldn't go on." This, of course, did not sit well with the stage manager, and he would ream out Sin Sui for telling what she prophesied from her crystal ball.

So, one day Sin Sui saw signs of danger, menace and peril ahead for Irene, but mindful of what the manager had threatened, she lied. She told Irene that everything would be okay. And Irene went on as scheduled. But things were not all right! The tiger was nervous, paced about, and was hard to control. The crowd yelled louder and louder, and Irene's commands were drowned out. Irene had to rely on her whip, but she was frightened. Something went wrong, and she missed a snap. In the blink of an eye the tiger was upon her and sank its teeth into Irene's forearm. The crowd gasped. It was all over for Irene!

"When suddenly a tiny woman raced into the ring waving a scarf in her hand." Reuben shouted theatrically. "It was Sin Sui!" She swung her scarf above the tiger's head, higher and higher, circling the beast's snarling teeth, and the cat forgot all about its helpless trainer Irene and sprang up to snare the scarf in its claws. Irene crawled off the stage and was helped to the wings, bleeding profusely. Sin Sui abandoned her scarf to the tiger's jaws and also attempted to escape, but the tiger, crazed by what was later found to be wild catnip infused into the fabric, pounced on the fleeing fortune-teller and broke her back. "Poor Sin Sui went to her Chinese afterlife," Reuben said sadly. "The cat was sedated with a dart fired by a lion-tamer and dragged away with ropes."

I was very impressed by Reuben's story-telling abilities. "And Irene?" I asked. "What happened to her?"

"You know," he continued, "she survived. And her arm got well. And she went back to work with that same tiger in just a few weeks, without the benefit of a fortune teller."

"That's quite a story."

"Yeah." Reuben was thoughtful, which was unusual for him, though he was a sensitive soul. "I'm not sure a man would have rushed in to save

Irene like Sin Sui did. And I'm not sure that a man would have had the nerve to go back to work after something like that happened. Honestly, I don't think I would have."

"You could be right," I agreed.

"Proving that women can be a whole lot tougher than men."

We rode a few miles without talking

Reuben broke the silence. "Here's another one," he said. "A couple of gals from the commissary invited me to go with them for a picnic on the beach at Lido Key. So, we all drive out there, me and the three of them, all giggling like sisters. We parked at the Pavilion and spread out our blanket on the sand. I hiked over and rented us an umbrella. The girls went to the concession stand and bought me a chili dog. There was plenty of people-watching, a lot of young ladies, you know, men showing off with barbells and the like. Then the girls said they wanted to go swimming, and they ran off to change. And here they come back. I'm just lying there under the umbrella chowing down on my hotdog, watching the waves, sipping on the flask I'd brought along, and I notice a commotion down by the water.

"Some kid was in trouble, fell off his rubber raft or something and couldn't swim. I jump up, being a career servant of the public, and start yelling for the lifeguard, who's busy talking to some young chicks. While I'm jumping up and down, waving for help, here go the three girls racing across the beach like coon dogs on a hunt, and they charge into the water and swim out to this poor kid. And damned if they don't rescue him! And get him back ashore! While the lifeguard is still pulling his pud and I'm flapping my arms like an idiot!"

"So, that's another example?"

"That's right. Women can do things men can't. Turns out these girls also do bathing beauty gymnastics at Wekiwa Springs."

After a mile or two of thought, I admitted something. "I've never been swimming in salt water."

Reuben laughed. "You're kidding me."

"No. Swimming in the Gulf just wasn't anything we did growing up, Reuben. You remember that, don't you? Ponds, sure, but not salt. We all handled boats, and we knew salt water to be dangerous. We pulled enough sharks and stingrays out of the blue to know that it could hurt us. I never heard of anybody back then going swimming in the Gulf unless their boat tipped over and they had to tread water for their lives. Did you?"

"Well, it's been popular quite some while, Gabe," Reuben said, like an understanding uncle. "I know you're a well-rounded individual. Maybe it's time you gave salt water a try."

"Maybe you could arrange for me to try it with those three gymnasts you're talking about."

"That would be the safest," he acknowledged.

"Remember when we were kids, swimming in Miller's pond and dodging alligators?"

Reuben laughed.

"We had fun being young," I said.

"I was born young at heart," Reuben said.

I thought about telling him right then and there what I had learned about his birth parents. But I didn't.

The first stop on our trip was in Tampa to pick up Mack for lunch. We all went out to what passed for a Jewish delicatessen, where Reuben wanted to try pastrami sandwiches, a new thing for all of us. But Mack was distracted and visibly distressed about something. He suggested we carry our sandwiches outside where we could eat privately at a table in the shade, out of earshot of any local busybodies. This is the story he told.

Just the night before, Eugene Poulnot and some Yankee-transplant named Joseph Shoemaker had convened a meeting in one of those old airplane hangars in the same row where Mack lived. The meeting was for a lefty group they had formed called the "Modern Democrats," which planned to run a ticket against certain Tampa political bosses. By the Grace of God, Mack did not go to this meeting!

Some "rat-cops," Mack called them, sprang out of the shadows and broke into the hut. They arrested Eugene, Joseph Shoemaker, and the rest of the "crowd," which was three other men. It was nearly midnight. At the police station the other three men were released, but Poulnot and Shoemaker were interrogated about being Communists. Then they, too, were released out the station-house door. And, when they stepped outside Eugene Poulnot and Joseph Shoemaker were seized by a "gang of Klansmen," said Mack and taken out to the woods miles from town and tortured. "Tortured!" Mack exclaimed. My son was even angrier about the world than I was. Maybe because he'd served in the Army and expected better of his country than what he was witnessing. "Tortured with chains, hoses, and straps!"

The men were flogged until their backs were red meat and then their broken bodies and genitals were smeared with gobs of hot tar and rolled along in the sand and through a pile of chicken feathers brought for the occasion. That's how they were left, in the woods, smeared with tar and feathers to die! Mack's face was red with emotions I'd not seen since he was a child. But this wasn't child's play.

Our lunches went uneaten. Tar-and-feathering seems like such a barbaric and primitive way to damage someone.

"What you just said makes me sick." Reuben grimaced. "I've seen some crazy cruel hombres, but I've never known them to get together in one group, or gang, or klan, whatever they call themselves. And the cops who allow brutality like that, or join in themselves, that's never happened in Sarasota, has it Gabe?"

I had to admit that the conduct of the lawmen I'd known back home, corrupt grafters though some may have been, had never come close to anything like what I was learning about Tampa. There was no fun and frolic in the sun here.

This very dawn, Mack continued, his jaw knotted, a boy, hunting earthworms for bait, had found Poulnot and Shoemaker in the woods and run for his daddy. The abused pair were now in the hospital, thank God, and some trusted men were guarding their room. Joe Shoemaker had been mutilated and his privates torched. His wounds and burns on one leg were so serious that gangrene had set in, and the doctors had already cut that leg off. He was not expected to live.

"Jesus, son!" I was almost overcome. "It's a good thing you weren't there," I mumbled.

"If I had been there," he declared, "I'd be in the same shape as them. The main cop, I know him, Smitty Brown. He would have busted me in a minute just because I ride a motorcycle he thinks is too loud. And once they've got you, you're got! Maybe those Kluxers would have known me and let me go, but what good would that have that done Eugene?" Mack was distraught.

"No good at all, son. You were lucky. They would have been afraid you'd identify them and might have killed you, too. Why do you say 'Kluxers'?"

"I know who the cops were, and Eugene does, too, and we think they're in the Klan. Eugene didn't recognize all the men who worked him over, but they had the same look about them."

"What look is that?" Reuben asked.

"Lean, mean, hungry and vicious. Men who could be country preachers but who enjoy using brass knuckles and knives. They're Klansmen, and they don't care who knows it."

I had to sit back and take a breath. I remembered the story of Robert the hotel clerk. "You know," I said. "Something like that happened over in St. Pete last year. Some young man got mixed up with the wrong woman, or maybe liking men too much, and a bunch of fools took him out in the woods at Safety Harbor and cut his nuts off." That was the only way I knew how to put it.

Mack took a deep breath. "Holy . . . I sure didn't know about that!" he said.

"Very horrible," I told my son, "This boy said he knew one of the men, a cop named Luther Peacock. I'd heard about Peacock a long time ago. I don't know if he was a Klansman or not. I just thought he was a dumb piece of spit-wad."

"Peacock? Could he have been one of those who grabbed Eugene?"

"No, Peacock's dead. Apoplexy as I remember. Heart failure before he could testify."

"This city. . ." My son, who is a strong young man, looked sick.

"My advice is keep a low profile, Mack." What would any father say? "How's Eugene doing?"

"Looks like he'll make it. His wife is at the hospital keeping him clean, you know. Joe Shoemaker took the worst of it. Maybe because he's not from here. He's in a bad way."

"Well, I don't know what can be done about all this, Mack, when the public is on fire to hang all the Reds and bust the unions, and the cops are helping them do it."

"Dad, I didn't know you had that level of understanding about the state our country is in!" Mack was actually surprised.

"Thanks a lot."

"That makes it easier for me to ask you something."

Reuben shoved back his chair to show he wasn't part of this exchange. He looked off into space.

Mack had never asked much, but I knew what was coming, and I didn't want to do it.

"Help me get those fascists who tarred-and-feathered these good men, and help us get them convicted and hung."

Now it was my turn to take a deep breath. "Son, I don't know a thing about Tampa, St. Pete, the Communist Party, or the local police force. This is just not my territory. I'd like to help out Eugene, but I'd just screw everything up."

If I had expected a lot of complaints, I didn't know my son. What he said was, "I see your point, Dad." And, after a pause, "I'll take care of this myself."

"What in the Good Lord's name are you talking about, boy? How are you going to take care of this?" I was anxious.

"Lots of resources, Dad. I have lots of resources."

Had I let my son down? I guess so, but I was absolutely out of my element here. And that's the way we left it.

The three of us wrapped up our sandwiches, me paying the tab, and all said our goodbyes outside a friendly delicatessen in the rotten city by Old Tampa Bay.

"I've got this, Dad," Mack assured me, gripping my hand like we wouldn't see each other for a long time.

What the hell?

MACK'S STORY

I worked for anybody who'd hire me, but my best customers were gangsters. I wasn't raised for a career like this, but it happened. I needed to make a living.

Everybody knew there were two rival mobs in Tampa. One was led by Charlie Wall, an "old Tampa" civic leader who ran his gambling operations through Tito Rubio and an enforcer named Eduardo "Eddie" Virella. The other mob were these Sicilians from Chicago, run by Ignazio Antinori and his especially nasty lieutenant Mario Perla. This was common knowledge, and you'd often see the hoods, especially Virella or his enemy Perla, cruising around town in their chauffeur-driven Studebakers and Packards.

I did not go out of my way to meet these dangerous men, but I had been introduced to several in the course of my flying business.

When Christy and I were courting, we once splurged and had dinner at the El Dorado, a Bolita nightclub, and I was introduced very briefly to Mr. Wall, who a lot of people called "The White Shadow." That's right! He was a tall and ghostly figure, always dressed in a white suit.

Mr. Wall was royalty. Not only had his father been a Tampa mayor, but his wife's father had been, too. Charlie Wall was the black sheep of the upper crust of a sinful society. At his famous club, he made the rounds of the tables. He smiled when he shook my hand, but his eyes didn't smile. I guess I seemed like an all-right guy to him because I did get charter jobs for his "associates," once to fly Tito Rubio to Tallahassee, and twice to fly Eddie Virella and Virella's girlfriend to destinations in and out of state. On those Virella trips, my passengers were both drunk the whole time, which the girlfriend said would keep her from getting sick. On the trip to Biloxi, she tried to get into my lap and take over the cockpit. Eddie thought that was funny, but he was not too far gone to realize the danger she was causing and he wrestled her back to her seat where she was supposed to be. He nearly lost his glasses, and he glared at me even after he recovered them.

I even got work from the rival Antinori gang. They hired me to fly Mr. Antinori's right-hand man, Mario Perla, to St. Augustine one time. He slept the whole way, which suited me fine. He has a cruel face. I don't think we exchanged ten words.

Not long after Joe Shoemaker died from his whipping, and my friend Eugene Poulnot nearly died, I got a message from Mario Perla. I must have made a good impression on him, as someone who could reliably transport hoods and keep my mouth shut. The message was that I should call one Leonard Trout about a flight he needed to make.

Leonard Trout was actually the brother of a boy I had grown up with on Catfish Creek in Sarasota. I'd heard before that Leonard had advanced in life to run errands for the Antinori mob and maybe provide muscle. Was that a problem for me? Not really. Money was short. I'd fly for anybody who could afford it, and gangsters could.

Leonard wanted a quick out-and-back a day hence, a nighttime job down to Buchan Field in Englewood and back again to Tampa. But that happened to be Christmas Eve, and my wishes were to spend that night and Christmas day cozy at home with my little family. I offered him the day after Christmas, and he said, "No, it has to be tomorrow tonight." I was a businessman about it, and told him it would cost extra because I had to cancel another customer – actually I had to cancel dinner with my wife and little baby boy Gordy, and Christy was making her special meatloaf which she knew I liked – but Leonard Trout said he had anticipated that this might be a hardship and he would bring my extra fee in cash.

After our lunch with Mack, Reuben and I were mostly silent in the car as we drove over to St. Pete. Reuben unwrapped his pastrami and took a bite. He frowned and threw the rest out the window. "Your son has his work cut out for him," he said.

I was too lost in my worried thoughts to do more than just nod. My knuckles were white on the wheel. I was imagining who I could kill.

If I had ever thought about the Ku Klux Klan, it was to picture a middle-aged men's club – a watered-down version of the old Sarasota Assassination Society. Hell, the shoe salesman from whom I bought my

Red Wings had a Klan sign in his window. It didn't concern me very much. Until now!

It was only a little past noon, and one could only hope that the rest of the day would be less, uh, revealing. Less revealing about how depraved men could be. As much as you see if you are in the law enforcement business, there may still be things you encounter and hear that will shock the human being in you.

We parked, and Reuben followed me into the Sunshine City Diner, but my meeting with Germaine was blessedly short. She was working and busy. She couldn't leave the premises, so Reuben and I took an empty table by the front window and signaled for cups of coffee. The shadows from the restaurant's name, painted on the glass outside, played over the front of Reuben's shirt.: ENIHSNUS.

Two mugs came steaming and hot to the touch. Germaine stood over us waiting.

"Can you sit down?" I asked.

She looked around the room, which was almost full. "I'd better not," she said, anxiety all over her face.

"I don't have much to tell you anyway. So here's the short version. Whitey seems to be surviving the jail. He's in a cell by himself. He didn't complain to me. I met his girlfriend, Juanita Ropollo, who's from New Orleans. She helped him rob a bank there. She was at the bar with Whitey before he decided to go out to that house down the street. Juanita claims she unloaded your brother's pistol before he left, because she thought he was dangerously drunk. Even though he's in jail,

Whitey has something else in the works – probably criminal - that may yield some money, according to Juanita. That's it."

The anxious expression had not gone away. "Can you come over tonight and talk some more?" Germaine asked in a low voice.

"Excuse me," Reuben said and jumped up to use the rest room.

"No, ma'am," I told her. "I drove up here to see Clarinda."

"Well, that's it then. The coffee's on me."

Germaine turned on her heel and went back to work. I tossed some change on the table and left. It was blazing hot outside, and the coffee wasn't doing my stomach any good. Reuben caught up to me on the sidewalk.

"So?" he asked.

"I told her no. My plan is to get you and me both back to Sarasota tonight."

"And Clarinda?" Reuben asked. "Like I said, I'll wait outside for that one, too. If you change your mind about staying over you can just drop me at a bar and I'll take it from there."

We got in the car. "What'd you think of Germaine?" I asked.

"She's a nice looking woman. Hard worker. Nothing wrong with her that I could see."

"Damn right," I told him, and we didn't say any more about it.

Reuben mentioned that he was hungry, so I dropped him off at a little restaurant right where we came into Seminole. There really weren't any Seminoles left in Seminole, but this café was called the "Totem Pole Grill."

My meeting with Clarinda was even more brief than my coffee with Germaine. She wasn't at the store where she'd said she'd be. Her mother, Lovelady, was embarrassed.

"Clarinda knew you were driving in today," Lovelady said angrily, "but she hasn't had her 'see you later' talk with Alf. Maybe that's where she's gone." Lovelady saw the doubt in my eyes. She put her finger on my lips. "I know it's crazy. I know you want Clarinda back, and she wants to come. She has just been putting it off. And Alf is very busy."

"Busy sending the Klan out to kill people," I spat out.

"Oh, dear, I hope not!" Lovelady's hands shot up to her hair. "You know, Alf said he'd take her to France. I think that's the only reason she likes him."

"France!" I shouted. "What's that got to do with anything?"

"Oh, my." Lovelady was frantic. "I really thought Clarinda would be back here by now. Of course, Alf is in charge of the department store, and he has so many meetings."

What do you say? I couldn't believe Clarinda was giving me the runaround.

"Gawain, can't you wait? Please?"

I was tired of this place. Tired of Seminole and tired of St. Petersburg women. So I just swore under my breath and beat it out of there. I let the door slam behind me.

I found Reuben at the Totem Pole Grill. He was finishing his ham sandwich with a pickle, and I ordered the same to go.

"Let's get out of here," I said. "I need to be back in Sarasota where the people are more humane."

"Another new word," Reuben commented, and paid our check.

Driving back past the big city, I knew I was mightily tired of Tampa, too. In any normal person's view, it was a smoky city full of crooked cops, a city that was all about graft for hundreds of politicians all trying to get a slice of the booze and illicit slot machine business, run by gangsters and big shots who kept the common people in line with the Ku Klux Klan. And they had prostitution and heroin, too. And they kept the Cuban cigar craftsmen in debt playing Bolita. You couldn't drive a block without seeing a squad of armed police "detectives" backing some political party. And there were depressing lines of people waiting for free soup, and rabble-rousers telling the workers to demand their rights. The only orderly city blocks were downtown, after dark, where the casinos and night clubs lit up the black sky, obliterating the stars. The cops protected those blocks, knocking heads as needed, all to make ill-paid Cubans and their well-to-do masters, out for a night of slumming and Latin trumpets, feel at home. The whole town stank to me. I was sorry my son and grandson lived here.

Driving home, Reuben asked me what I thought about socialism.

"I'm not sure what it means," I replied honestly. "Isn't that where the government runs everything?"

"No, that would be Florida."

"I believe in democracy," I said. "Is that radical enough? Government by the people."

"Government by the yo-yo's?"

"Like you and me."

"True enough, but we don't have the do-ray-mi," Reuben pointed out, "and that's what it takes."

I couldn't think of a come-back to that.

I dropped Reuben off at the house he was renting near the Fairgrounds. He invited me in for a drink, but we were really both too worn out from the stresses and revelations of the day. And I still hadn't told him about his parents.

CHAPTER TWELVE

A QUESTION OF BULLETS

Whitey had maintained to me at the jail that he had shown his brave and manly side when he was attacked at the sisters' house, but the fact was that he had dropped his unloaded gun and made a run for it. That, at least, is what Juanita had led me to believe. The morning after I got home from St. Pete I went back to the Sarasota lock-up to see what the master-criminal Whitey Jarvis had to say about that.

This time Chief Tilden Davis was away on "police business," and Sheriff Pearson himself was at his desk. I had to introduce myself.

"I heard of you," the sheriff said, scratching his chin. "You were the first City Marshal here in Sarasota. You used to work for Sheriff Heinie."

"Sheriff Levi, that's right."

"Why did they call him Heinie?" Pearson was curious.

"He spoke German. I think he learned it from his family growing up. He interrogated captured German soldiers during the War."

"Ah, I always wondered. I thought maybe it was because he had a big butt." Sheriff Pearson laughed and looked at me to see if I enjoyed his wit. "He was a Jew, right?"

"To tell you the truth, Sheriff, I'm not positive about that. We all worked for Honoré Palmer before they got the county formed. None of them, Palmers included, seemed to be especially religious to me. They were mostly interested in ranching and celery farming and selling land to the Yankees."

"Right. Same then as now," Pearson said, all business again. "What can I do for you?"

"Whitey Jarvis is the brother of a friend of mine, and I visited him here last week. I'd like to visit him again."

"Your interest is?"

"He says he didn't kill those girls."

'Well, that may be what he says, but he sure enough did. You can visit him all you want, but it won't change the facts."

"I appreciate that, and so will his sister. Could I also take a look at the evidence?"

"What's that? You're not some lawyer are you?"

"No, no," I assured him. "But the man deserves to hear about the case against him from someone he trusts. Like me. If he did, he might even plead guilty and save everybody a lot of trouble."

Pearson considered my line, and finally said, "I see what you mean. By 'evidence,' what did you have in mind?"

"How about his gun? And maybe there's some statement concerning the events from the gentleman who came out of the back room and jumped through the window?" I was fishing.

"Ricky Weed? He's innocent of everything but bad judgment. He had no business being in that house, and him with a wife at home."

"So you know him?"

"You remember how it is, Gabe. I'm the sheriff, and I know everyone."

"No special relationship?"

"Now you're making me mad. Forget Ricky Weed. Lacey Bell told me at the hospital, while she was taking her last breath, that she did not know who shot her or who came through the door. On the other hand, Whitey Jarvis is a convicted bank robber, a fence for stolen goods, and he's admitted being in the room when those women were killed! Of course he killed those girls! Or he knows who did but won't say! His trial will be short and sweet. That man Weed who jumped out the window may not be as clean as the driven snow, since he's married and shouldn't have been in that cat house, but he got winged in the nether regions and necessarily must have had to make some confessions when he got home. Believe me, he's already had his punishment! Yes, it's true that he didn't identify Mister Jarvis as the guy who shot him, but he was too busy saving his own skin."

"Again, sounds to me like you know the man pretty well."

"Well, I'll be…," the sheriff snorted and slammed his palm on the desk.

I saw that his temperature was heading straight up and took a step back. "Okay, I get it," I told him. "Makes sense to me. Let me see that gun, and then I'll give Whitey a talking to." The sheriff's comment about Whitey being a fence for stolen goods was interesting enough. I hadn't known that.

The sheriff's face had now assumed its permanent frown. He raised a finger at me and shook it. But then the angry creases gave way to a grin. "All right partner," he said. "I'll let you take a look."

There was a substantial floor safe close by against the wall. He swung around and took his time opening it, shielding me from seeing the combination with his own big behind.

Out came a package wrapped in newspaper, which he placed gently on his desk.

"Colt .38 Special," he said.

I didn't dispute that. The weapon of choice for cops, criminals and varmint hunters everywhere, though I personally preferred the .45.

"Can I touch it?" I asked.

"If you want," Sheriff Pearson said. "We've already copied Whitey's prints off the handle. And anyway, he's admitted that this is his gun." The sheriff had the confident look of a man on solid footing. At trial, all he had to do was say those same words, in that same slow, resonant tone of voice, and the jury would waste no time agreeing that Whitey Jarvis was guilty as charged.

I rolled back the newspaper and picked up the gun.

"Careful, it's loaded," the sheriff said.

Juanita had told me that Whitey's gun was empty so I was surprised, but also curious. I opened the chamber. "I see three cartridges in here," I said.

"That's true," said Pearson. "He must have got off three shots. And that accounts for the girls and maybe Ricky Weed, too."

"Mind if I look at these bullets in the cylinder?" I asked.

"You mean, take 'em out?"

"Under your supervision, yes, sir."

"Okay." Pearson was frowning again, but he nodded slightly.

I extracted one, just to check it, then pulled another. I placed them both back inside the chamber.

"Okay," I told the sheriff. "That's enough for me. Now can I see the prisoner?"

Pearson glared at me for a moment, establishing his authority, then he smiled and said, "Come on."

Whitey came to the bars, sleepy-eyed. The sheriff withdrew to his office and locked the cell-block door behind him, but he could probably still hear us if we talked loudly enough, or if I called for help.

I dispensed with the greetings and got to the point.

"Juanita says she unloaded your pistol before you left the bar. You went over to the sisters' house with an empty gun."

Whitey just frowned and looked thoughtful, so I went on. "When the shooting started, you pulled out the gun, then remembered you had nothing to shoot, and threw it down. Maybe you even raised your hands to show you weren't armed."

He blinked and looked at the concrete floor of his cell. "That would make me a drunk and a coward," he said, offended.

"Better that than getting fried for murder."

The prisoner stared mournfully at his shoeless feet. "My whole life has been a waste," he said. "The only good thing I've ever had was Juanita. Maybe one day, someday, I'll get out and see her again."

"Maybe. What kind of bullets are you claiming you had in your gun, Whitey?"

"Donny favored Colt Specials. He'd buy ten boxes at a time. He was the gun expert."

"Not hollow-point?"

"No. Cost too much, and Donny said hollow-points didn't have the range."

"That ain't the way it's shaping up, Whitey. They've got your gun."

"Right. I know that 'cause I dropped it in the house."

"And it's got three cartridges in it, all hollow-point."

"That don't make sense." He rubbed his cheeks, thinking.

"That's for sure. Your gun was empty."

"Not true," Whitey insisted.

"Have it your way. The cops are going to say that you shot the two women, and maybe the guy from the back room, leaving those three cartridges in the cylinder."

Whitey lifted his head. "I gotta admit I was shit-faced drunk, but I didn't have no hollow-point bullets."

"Were you too drunk to realize that your gun wasn't loaded at all?"

"I've got my pride," was all he said.

"I've just learned that you have a sideline as a fence for stolen merchandise."

"Who says that?"

"The sheriff."

"I guess I do have a record for that, but I didn't know the merchandise was stolen."

"What merchandise are you talking about?"

"The…," and he caught himself. "Any merchandise," he continued. "I was found with a silver dining set, years back, but it was a bogus charge. I got off."

"I'm curious. Where do you sell hot goods here in Sarasota?"

"Not in Sarasota. No. People here talk too much." Whitey clamped his jaw shut.

As I left he called out, "Give my love to Germaine."

I beat on the door and Chief Davis let me out. Sheriff Pearson must have found someplace else he needed to be.

"Did he confess, yet?" the Chief asked.

"He's unlikely to," I said. "The bullets that killed the sisters, and the one that got the customer in the leg, what type were they?"

"Type? The deadly kind. They died from multiple gunshots. And they were probably buried with the bullets in 'em. Whatever hit that poor Weed boy from the neighborhood went clean through him." Chief Davis was a composed fellow with a crew cut and big black eyes that could hold mine. He didn't have a mark on any part of his skin that wasn't covered up by his gray uniform. He chewed gum. I wanted to like him, but there was something wrong with his story about the gun.

"So there was nothing to match any of those bullets with Whitey's gun?" I asked.

"There was a trail of violence and blood all the way from that house on 24th Street to that fish camp in Louisiana," he declared, tapping his fingers on the desk, "and Whitey's partner died shooting it out with the law. What you saying, Gabe? That Whitey Jarvis, who dropped his gun at the scene and drove all the way to Louisiana in an attempt to escape his crimes, didn't shoot those women? That's ridiculous, MacFarlane."

"It may be ridiculous Tilden, but those bullets in that gun. . ." I pointed to it. It was still on the sheriff's desk, ". . . aren't Whitey's. His gun wasn't even loaded when he threw it down. And, even if it had bullets, they were regular .38's, not hollow-points. He didn't use those. They cost too much. Somebody put hollow-points in that gun, but it wasn't Whitey."

"Nuts!" Davis said.

"And just being curious, what kind of cartridges do your men use?"

I wanted to hear his answer, but I knew what it would be. Every cop from the FBI on down to the dog pound was proud to arm himself with what we – they – called "Keith-style" bullets, cast with a hole in the point. They were known to be accurate and knocked a very big hole in whatever they hit.

"Hollow-points, of course," Davis said, "but that proves nothing. Are you done here?"

I was, and I left. But he had answered my question. It gave me a lot to think about as I drove home to my farm. Juanita Ropollo believed that Whitey's gun was empty. But, even if he had slid in a couple of rounds from his pocket while staggering up 24th street to the ladies' house, they wouldn't match what was in his pistol today, the one in the sheriff's safe, waiting to be presented at trial. There was no evidence showing what variety of bullets had killed Lacey and Bertie Bell, or winged the man in back, so it all led nowhere. But it made me think that Whitey Jarvis was an innocent man, or at least a crook who was innocent of murdering two nice women who entertained gentlemen in a dark Sarasota neighborhood with slow jazz music and a few drinks.

I fell out of bed the next morning to find Juanita at my farm house door. How she remembered where I lived I'll never know, but she actually had hired a taxi, and it was waiting for her fifty feet down my dirt drive. My dog Nero had loudly announced their arrival, and he was outside intimidating the car. I whistled him back, and started the water to boil for coffee.

Juanita ran past my hound and up the porch steps, and she didn't waste any time getting to the point. She laid her palm flat on my chest. "I'm out of dough, Gabe," she said, desperation in her voice. "I can't even pay the cabbie outside."

It was almost funny. She, or Whitey, or Germaine, or somebody, was supposed to be paying me, not the other way around. "You expect me to give you money?" I laughed.

"Just a loan to tide me over till Whitey gets out of jail. A hundred dollars would see me through."

"Whitey may never get out of jail, Juanita. Besides, I don't have a hundred dollars, and if I did why would I lend it to you? You'd never pay it back. Is that why you're here?"

"Yes, and that's where you're all wrong," she said. "We're going to get lots of money, and I have collateral for today." She slipped her fingers below the neckline of her blouse and from her ample bosom she extracted a gold watch, which she dangled it in front of my eyes.

I took a closer look. "What exactly is that?" I asked.

"It's an antique timepiece," she said. "I'm told it may be 200 years old."

I took the watch from her fingers and inspected it. The finish was dull, and it certainly looked very old. The case was made of what I thought might be solid gold. Etched on the back were words in a language I didn't know.

"Where did you get this?" I asked. "Is it hot?"

"Sort of, but I didn't steal it." Her face was all innocence. "I don't believe anyone has missed it. You know it's worth way more than a hundred dollars."

"Take it to a jeweler and sell it."

She lowered her eyes. "I guess I'm not that sure it's safe to do that. Maybe you could find out," she brightened up.

"I suppose you could come inside and tell me some more of this story."

Juanita grinned. With a wave of encouragement to the cabbie she waltzed inside. It was quite a story.

According to her, when Whitey and Donny tore out of the Bell sisters' house, leaving the two sisters for dead on the floor, they had run for the car they'd parked behind the Roadhouse Tavern, now the Coquettes' Club, but Whitey made a quick detour. The more alert patrons, having heard the gunshots, were quickly exiting the premises, but Whitey edged through them, far enough inside the bar to beckon Juanita to come talk to him. They met quickly in the parking lot, and Whitey gave her a duffle bag to keep for him – not a bag full of loot from the bank. Unfortunately, Donny had that. But a duffle bag full of jewelry and golden watches that he had been given to fence.

He didn't think it prudent to drive off to Louisiana with such valuables of questionable origin, especially considering that nothing inside the bag belonged to him. He hurriedly instructed Juanita to handle his incomplete transaction, since he was fleeing the state post-haste. And this, she told me, she had done. Though she admitted that her poor circumstances had forced her to purloin a few of the items, such as this gold watch, as her "commission."

"Where did the watch and the jewelry come from, Juanita? Who do they belong to! Tell me quick!" In my mind I had a very believable vision of a squad of Pinkerton detectives hot on the jewelry's trail, a trail that led straight to my farm.

"Out of a shipwreck," she said breathlessly. "Some ship that belonged to the man, what's his name, Ringling, who owns the circus."

Suddenly it became clear. The Zalophus! And I had been there when the doomed yacht went under. Nobody would be searching for the jewelry Whitey had!

"This watch doesn't look like it's been underwater," I said, and I was remembering how it had all happened.

"Strange. I noticed that, too," Juanita said. "Maybe it was in a waterproof pouch or something."

Or maybe it was filched by the last people who got off. Instead of Pinkertons chasing me, I now envisioned Charlie Ort and the boat captain, the two who had insisted on being the last to leave the sinking vessel. Now it was making sense.

"What makes you think that nobody is chasing after an obviously very valuable collection of jewelry and watches?" I asked her.

Juanita shrugged. "Whitey said so. He said that nobody knows they've been stolen – I mean salvaged. Everyone thinks they went down with the boat."

"Highly unlikely, but where is this precious treasure, now?"

"I did like Whitey told me. I took the bag to a man who knows how to sell iffy jewelry. He has foreign customers. Whitey said to trust him. They've done business together before. As soon as the jewels are sold, I'm to pick up the money. Whitey said he'd tell me how much to keep, since I get a share, and how much to pay the fence, and how much Whitey gets, and how much to turn over to the party who salvaged the haul."

"That's a lot of cuts coming out of one bag of jewelry." I was still hoping to get a fair wage for my time and expenses, including my gas for running all up and down the coast.

Juanita nodded in agreement but explained by saying, "None of that is any problem. Whitey says the right collectors will pay up to $100,000 for the lot of the jewels. Can you imagine that?"

"No! Sounds like complete bull to me."

She shrugged. "Whitey is a dreamer," Juanita agreed. "I'll give you that, but the man I handed them over to said they looked real good to him. In fact, he got very excited and bent my ear talking about his international customers from Key West and Cuba. How he'll make a quick sale, and so forth. So maybe it's real. He's taking ten percent. Whitey is also due ten percent, and I'm taking ten percent. All this is okay with the owner, according to Whitey. We can pay you out of Whitey's percent."

Not hers, I noted.

"Who is this owner, and who is this broker?" I asked.

"Now, darlin', I can't tell you that." Juanita smiled from ear to ear and asked for a cup of café au lait.

"What's that?"

"Mocha, baby. Alright, coffee to you."

"Why didn't you say so?" I heated up the pot. "If you won't explain who the jewels came from or where the jewels are going, I guess I'll have to question Whitey about it. And that could be our last conversation because I'm not working for a percent of his percent or your percent."

The reality was, I now had deep misgivings about ever getting paid. But the case had become quite interesting to me.

Juanita had not lost sight of her main issue. "What about the hundred dollars for the watch?" she asked. "I'll leave it with you as my security. A girl's got to live. And, aren't you one of the family now?"

"Hell no!" I told her.

But I took pity on her, as much from curiosity as from anything else, and fished three twenty dollar bills out of my wallet. She grabbed them gratefully, and ran out to her cab, leaving me holding the watch. She jumped in the car; the cabbie honked and backed slowly out of sight. My dog Nero followed it, barking all the way.

I had no idea if this watch was really worth sixty bucks. But Mack might want it, for himself or for Christy. Hell, maybe I'd give it to Clarinda if I ever spoke to her again. Or I could give it to Germaine as a farewell gift. She was Whitey's sister after all, but I hated to get either woman involved in anything out-of-the way. Hell, what was I doing getting involved with stolen goods, for that matter? Had my years of service to the law (and near-law) left me that jaundiced? (Jaundiced, that was Mrs. Ephram's term.) I'd have to think about it. In the meantime, I had a hiding spot out in my orange grove where the watch wouldn't be found, and it wouldn't be bothered by the weather either, unless we had a hurricane.

It was a beautiful day outside in the groves, where I went to work with a shovel. Pink feathery clouds drifted above the citrus across our great blue heavens. A swallow-tailed kite made slow loops over my orchard, and the air was full of the sweet smell of orange blossoms. After I made arrangements for the watch, however, I turned my back on this peaceful scene and made a slow return to the county jail. I hoped to make Whitey fill in a few of the details that were missing from Juanita's story.

CHAPTER THIRTEEN

A FLIGHT TO ENGLEWOOD
GOES HAYWIRE

The third time I went to see Whitey Jarvis, Sheriff Pearson was back at his desk eating a bologna sandwich. He'd shoved aside a pile of papers to accommodate his fat tube of pink meat and a bone-handled carving knife, both laid out on his blue ink-blotter. Along with a jar of mayonnaise. He wasn't overjoyed at being interrupted, though I assured him I didn't want to be a bother while he was enjoying such an elegant meal. All I needed was a couple of minutes to speak with his prisoner.

He stood up with a sigh, dusted off his shirt front and retrieved the key from a hook on the wall. "Don't be long," he said. "I'll be leaving here shortly to make my rounds, and you wouldn't want to be stuck in the cells half the day." He admitted me to the small block and locked me in. This time there was another prisoner, in a cell next to Whitey's, a flabby, tired-looking man wearing a sweat-stained gray T-shirt. He observed my entry, and we exchanged strangers' wary nods. Whitey rolled off his cot and came to the bars to greet me.

"Before I get to the interesting visit I had with Juanita, let me ask you again about your gun, Whitey. Are you certain you didn't load it with

154

'hollow-points'?"

"Yes, I'm certain. I didn't have any such cartridges to load into my gun. What's this all about?"

"That's what's in your pistol now. Who else could have put the 'hollow-points' in it? And why?"

"How many did you say were in it?"

"Three," I told him.

"I'll be truthful with you. I think when I dropped that gun there was all six bullets in it. I didn't even get off a shot. That's how agitated I was. And not one of those six was anything other than a regular .38."

"Whitey, Juanita swears your gun was empty, anyway." I reminded him. "One of you is lying."

"No, no! She's just forgotten. Why would I have an empty gun? I'm not such a chump. But I didn't shoot anyone."

He was such a chump, and he was the one lying. His story was that the gun was loaded, but he didn't shoot it. Whitey had some self-esteem issues about swaggering around with his weapon being unloaded. And he was ready to get electrocuted for it. His problem. I believed Juanita. And now I was getting suspicious of Whitey's description of all of the events leading up to the shootings.

"Whatever," I dismissed him. "Who put those three bullets in your pistol is still the question."

He paused to consider the puzzle. "I can't think of who would have planted those bullets," he said finally. "Unless it was the sheriff."

That was the logical conclusion, since when Whitey and Donny ran out of the sisters' house, and when the back-room customer jumped out of the window, there was nobody else known to be in the building except for a dead woman and her near-dead sister on the floor. Could Juanita have entered and reloaded the gun? She would have had to move fast, since the cops were there in minutes, but I couldn't imagine why she would have thought of such a ruse, and where would she have gotten the G-man-type bullets?

But why would the sheriff or his men have done it?

"Back to the original question." I said. "Who were those guys?"

"I never saw them before. If I was to guess, they looked like cops."

"Did Donny think they looked like cops? Is that why he pulled out a gun?"

"The man, that guy who came out of the backroom, he's the one who had a gun."

"Is that true, or did Donny take one look and start blazing away at everyone?"

"There was a lot of shooting," Whitey conceded, "and I was pretty drunk."

"Did Donny shoot first?"

"Jeez, Mister MacFarlane, I couldn't actually swear what happened. I just hit the floor. And I started defending myself."

"With an empty gun?"

"That wasn't it. I had a loaded gun."

"It's your life, Whitey."

With that he broke down and cried.

"So, why are there three bullets in that pistol now?" I asked. "And wrong ones, at that?"

He just shook his head.

I got up to leave.

"There was forces bigger than me involved," he said, so quietly that I almost missed it.

"What did you say?"

He closed up and stumbled back to his cot.

So, why had the sheriff and police chief, if my surmise were correct, put three rogue cartridges in an empty gun?

I could think of one answer to that. They might have done it just to close the case, to secure a conviction. If, as it seems, they were discounting the man who had jumped out of the window, and if they had no idea what had become of those two other patrons, the two strangers firing weapons according to Whitey, why not just pin it all on the one man they did have in a jail cell? And I could guess at another answer. They had had to chase Whitey and Donny three hundred miles, all the way to Louisiana - and they had gotten themselves into a gun battle to kill Donny and to arrest Whitey. In the police mind, after all that trouble, Whitey deserved everything he got.

"Listen up, Whitey," I called him. "I'm not really interested in who those men were or who fired the first gun. You'll never guess what Juanita gave me last night."

His looked up from his bunk and his eyebrows shot up.

Aware of the prisoner next door, I whispered. "An antique watch.

Made of gold. Your girl said it's part of a big stash of watches and jewels you were fencing for someone. You left them in her care to complete the deal."

"She gave it to you?" Whitey was distressed. He jumped off the cot and started hopping back and forth from one foot to the other.

"Not the whole lot! Listen up, Whitey – just one watch. Keep your voice down! And she didn't give it. She pawned it to me for sixty dollars. She said she needed money to get by."

Whitey spun around and fell back into bed. Then he was up again and hurried back to the bars – his lips to my ears.

"I gave her that loot because I didn't want to be charged with a crime I didn't commit. Juanita wasn't supposed to keep anything until the whole collection was sold. But I understand . . .," he got himself together. ". . . She needs a little bit to live on, I get it. But did she say that she delivered the rest of it to Whiskey Corners like I told her?"

Now I had something. Whiskey Corners. I remembered seeing Juanita in the bar, coming from somewhere in the back.

"Juanita didn't say where she delivered your collection," I told Whitey.

"We'd better find out," he hissed in my ear, "or I'll be in big trouble!"

"They can only hang you once, Whitey," I reminded him. This was all working his brain hard. It wasn't that hot in the cells, but he was sweating.

"I've got my reputation to think about," he whispered through gritted teeth. "And I need the money."

"I'm on board with that, brother. You haven't paid me a nickel. And what else do you need money for? To hire a lawyer? That would actually be a very good idea."

"I need money for my life plans, sir." He stood up tall. "Don't you have plans, Mister MacFarlane? There are people who'll help me once I get out of here. Juanita and me are going to have a future together. She's got a big family in Louisiana. I can get a new name. But it's very important that whatever I gave to Juanita gets sold and that the money gets paid to all the proper parties, including me."

"Good luck with all that, Whitey," my voice low. "I'm not going to turn you in for this jewel heist, or whatever it was. It wasn't you who did the stealing, right? But I'm not going to help you commit a crime either. This is probably the last time I'll see you."

"No, no! Don't say that," he cried. He was very disappointed to hear this news and sank his face into his hands, sobbing. For some reason, I still couldn't help but like the guy. He was entertaining in a sad sort of way.

"Just tell my sister Germaine what you told me," he begged, straightening up. "Please tell her I didn't kill anybody. And ask her to look after my Juanita. I truly love that woman. Sis will do what's right."

I walked out, passing the other inmate who feigned being asleep. I beat on the metal door.

Sheriff Pearson took his time, but he finally let me out. All signs of his lunch were gone.

"Did Chief Davis tell you that I raised questions about the bullets in that pistol?" I asked, nicely.

"He did." The sheriff's shoulders raised up an inch and he put his thumbs in his belt.

"Somebody planted those bullets," I said.

Pearson showed his square jaw. "Never happened, MacFarlane," he declared. "It's time you took your retirement seriously and stopped trying to pretend to be a lawman. You don't have the stomach for it anymore."

My mouth fell open. I was about to let fly all the things I had to say about him, my career in law enforcement, and what I thought about screwing with the evidence, but I could smell the bologna on his breath and thought, what's the use?

So I shut up, made my mouth turn into a smile, and left.

"Tomorrow's Christmas!" Sheriff Pearson yelled after me. "Don't come back."

Yes, tomorrow was Christmas. Nobody had invited me for the fatted goose, but I'd spend the day whittling some kind of toy, maybe a truck or a pair of pliers, for Gordy.

On this Christmas Eve, however, I didn't know for sure who had plundered the Zalophus as she was sinking and who had given the goods to Whitey Jarvis to fence. My money was on Charlie Ort. Or the boat captain. Maybe they each had their own pile. How many places were there to sell Renaissance watches and fine gold jewels in South Florida? Was Whiskey Corners the place?

Just questions, but no answers.

It was a windy afternoon in Florida. And, no surprise – it wasn't going to snow for the holidays.

MACK'S STORY (CONTINUED)

Leonard Trout, who the Antinori mob, via Mario Perla, had instructed me to fly to a destination south, met me at the Tampa airfield as scheduled, just as the sun was leaving its last orange streaks in the west. White birds floated above us in the sky. It was a beautiful Christmas Eve. I was so sorry to miss the occasion at my home, with my new family.

Trout was wearing a checkered sport coat but the shirt underneath was untucked, his belt was loose, and his blood-shot eyes were red. He was drunk. He wasn't carrying any baggage.

"Fly me away, Mack!" he said in a jolly voice. "Who would have ever thought."

"Ever thought what?" I asked as I powered my plane slowly onto the runway.

"Who would have thought that two boys from Sarasota would get this far? You a veteran airplane pilot and me working for the Tampa big shots."

"Is that what you call them?"

"I call them 'yassuh' and 'boss man.'" He laughed loudly. "Want a drink?" Leonard couldn't have been happier.

He fished a pint bottle out of his coat and pulled the cork. I gave him a sideways look and saw he had a gun holstered under his shoulder.

I told him no thanks. I should probably mention that my main memory of Leonard was him tormenting me at school, mashing dirt clods into my hair, and pushing me off the bridge over Catfish Creek, before I got big enough to defend myself. Not a man I cared to drink with. That, and the first rule of flying a little plane like mine is to stay sober. Any plane, for that matter.

"But you go right ahead," I told him and gave my engines the fuel they wanted. All conversation was drowned out. Up we went.

"Whoa," Leonard choked mid-gulp. Whiskey sloshed down his shirt. No matter, here came the sky. We wheeled around in a wide arc with the sun sailing around us until the horizon flattened out and we were pointed south.

Leonard rolled around in his seat like a sack of beans. He threw up on the floor. I'd seen that often enough to ignore it. We were on a short hop and I could clean up the mess in good time. The last of the sunset faded quickly, but the headlights of the cars running on the Tamiami Trail below my wings showed me the way.

Leonard cleaned himself up as best he could with his pocket handkerchief. "Sorry," he mumbled. "I think I'd better settle my stomach." He stared at his bottle as if challenging it, then took another deep swig.

It went on that way until we reached Buchan Field in Englewood. Good thing I knew where it was. From the air the tiny runway was almost invisible, but it was a decent enough airstrip in the midst of a wide swath of woods near Lemon Bay. The only evidence of nearby human occupation was the occasional barn light. But the moon was rising above and to the west the sun's last rays still shimmered off the coastline of Manasota Key, and veteran fly-boy that I am, I was able to bump us down properly. We rolled to a stop near the end of the soft grass runway. There was no hanger there, just a dirt road and a wire fence around the field, but there was a black car parked right inside that fence, and its headlights were pointed directly at my plane.

Leonard composed himself and gave me a lopsided smile. He quickly polished off his bottle. "That's my ride," he told me proudly. "Everything is arranged." With some effort he got himself unbuckled. I disembarked, too, and helped him down to the ground.

He said, "If I'm not back in two hours then I guess you're screwed."

No. I thought, in that case you're screwed. But he was the one laughing.

Leonard marched off the field and got into the waiting car. Its motor came to life, sounding as quiet as a whisper after the roar of the plane, and the car and its happy passenger cruised off into the night. With the darkness came silence, and I was left alone with only my airplane for company on a long and empty field. Nothing but moon.

The silence was short-lived. In a few minutes the sound of cicadas absorbed everything else. They had hung around late this year. Laughing ducks passed overhead squawking on their way home, to somewhere. A horned owl sounded in the woods bordering the field. With time to kill there was little to do except check out the plane with a flashlight and roll a cigarette or two.

I'd a whole lot rather have been at home eating a good dinner, but this wasn't so bad. The air was sweet and I could remember my family's old house, growing up in the country with mom and dad. Those were good memories. We were upright then — not like me now, working for hoods.

I cleaned up Leonard's mess in the cockpit and threw the rags in the bushes. I took a leak under the stars. That's how exciting my job is.

Two hours and a few minutes more passed that way. I dialed around my radio, and used it to check the weather. Finally, the headlights appeared through the trees again. The black car parked itself in the same place and out climbed Leonard. Now he had a leather valise in hand. He stumbled.

The driver of the car got out, too. I was close enough to see him but it was nobody I knew. Square face, high cheekbones, dungarees, dressed like a fisherman. Maybe he'd been in the war or taken a few blows in life. He didn't smile when he dragged Leonard over to the plane. "Your man is drunk," he reported angrily. "He's all yours now. Tell 'em I did my job. My ol' lady is expecting me home."

He dropped Leonard onto the grass, bowed as if to say thank you, and walked away.

Tell who? He didn't name anybody, and probably didn't know any names.

Leonard Trout was beyond being under the influence. If he hadn't been a paying customer, I would have left him in his own puddle of mess – let him wake up in the boondocks and hitchhike home.

But, that's not the way it was going to work. With a lot of encouragement, Leonard could stand. I muscled him up and into the plane. All aboard. The leather satchel came in last. It was stained and dusty, and it was heavy.

Back in my seat, turned the key, flipped and pulled the controls, and up we went again.

Our flight back to Tampa was uneventful. The skies were clear. Leonard woke up, and in his jacket he located a new bottle. He pointed it at me. I smiled, but declined. As we flew, he put a dent in it, but this time he didn't throw up.

Leonard's drink revived him. He sat back and told me some stories about his younger brother who had been in high school with me, how he had been thrashed by his father for skinny dipping with Evelyn Landwehr, stuff like that. I could care less. Trout's younger brother was alright, but I was ready to be done with Leonard.

The field at Tampa was brightly lit and easy to see. We touched down with a gentle bounce. As I taxied toward the North Hanger where I had parking privileges, Leonard opened his satchel and stowed his bottle in it. I was too busy steering to determine what else might be inside his bag.

The hanger was illuminated by four security lamps hanging from the eaves, and when I cut the engine I saw that there were two impressively large sedans parked beside the runway.

"Looks like you have an escort?" I commented.

"I suppose I do have an escort," Leonard said in a singsong voice. He popped the door open and hopped out, for that moment leaving his bag on the seat. I had my own door half-way open when the shooting started. Instinctively, I ducked behind the wheel but not before I saw one of the gunmen's faces. It was Eddie Virella, gambling and loan-sharking partner of Charlie Wall, leader of the Charlie Wall Gang, and he saw me see him. I slammed the hatch shut and got my engines fired up again. With the passenger door swinging wildly I pulled a U-turn that caused Virella to duck and hit the ground to avoid being clobbered by my wing. Lying next to him on the clay was poor Leonard, and I don't believe he was going to be telling any more stories

about us growing up together. I didn't know why Virella and the Charlie Wall gang would want to declare war on the Antinori mob by assassinating Leonard, but I didn't want to be in the middle of it.

I don't know if the welcoming party was firing at me while I gained speed and took off. If they were, my plane wasn't hit or damaged. I managed to grab the passenger door which had been slamming around while we got airborne and pulled it closed without crashing the plane. Only then I did I realize I still had Leonard's old leather bag.

CHAPTER FOURTEEN

A DEAL IS MADE

MACK'S STORY CONTINUES

Within a few minutes of watching Leonard Trout get shot, I was miles away and landing at the cornfield near my house. I didn't waste any time cleaning up the plane but I hopped on my Harley and raced back home where I could look into this peculiar valise in privacy. Christy was long since asleep, and so was Gordy. Our little Christmas tree with popcorn strung round it still made the front room smell good. I was quite sad to have missed my family on this particular night but awfully glad that I had not ended up like Leonard Trout.

I poked my head into both rooms to check on my crew. Christy raised her head off the pillow long enough to see who I was, and I gave her a wave. Gordy breathed softly. Back in the kitchen, I popped the clasp on Leonard's bag.

There was a whiskey bottle inside. I knew about that. But piled in the bottom of the case was a tangle of jewelry, gold chains and lots of glittery stones. The clear sparkling ones I took to be diamonds. The red, blue and green ones I didn't know, but they had to be valuable. I could give Christy a Christmas present to remember. Underneath that pile of treasure were at least a dozen gold watches, each wrapped in oil cloth.

It was all dazzling, but not so much that I could avoid the unmistakable reality. None of it was mine. Having this prize was a death sentence, unless I could get rid of it immediately. Mario Perla had sent Leonard Trout to pick it up. Leonard had served a bad master but he did as he was told, and now he was dead meat. Just as easily could have been me.

As I said, I had recognized one of the gunmen who ambushed Leonard, Eddie Virella. He was in the Charlie Wall Gang, a rival to the Antinori Gang, which was Leonard Trout's employer. So as far as Mario Perla would know — and he would find out - his enemy Eddie Virella had slain his courier and stolen his jewels.

But Eddie Virella would know the miserable truth: Mack MacFarlane, me, had the bag. Plain as the nose on my face, I'd better complete a deal with Virella and get myself out of the middle or I'd be as dead as Leonard.

So, I left my wife and child peacefully sleeping and hurried outside to crank up my bike again. I rode it to a bar, still open in the wee hours, where I could make a telephone call in private and, with luck, make an appointment. I had no option but to give up the bag and the jewels inside, but my plan was to exact a price.

I tried to reach Virella at his Lincoln Club but was handed off to Tito Rubio. He handled a lot of the business for Virella and for Charlie Wall, and we arranged to meet.

This is still Mack speaking. I need to get in a few words about the other pressures we were experiencing in Tampa. Because Joe Shoemaker had died from a "tar-and-feathering," his medieval ordeal made big news – far more than poor Eugene Poulnot's nightmare. Eugene was only scarred for life. Physically and maybe more. The papers could not recall any other white men ever being tarred and feathered and battered in this fashion at any point in Florida's sorry history, though I'm sure there were some that never made the news. But the gruesomeness of Eugene Poulnot's torture and Joe Shoemaker's death stirred up the better element of the Tampa community.

The six cops who had arrested "the Reds," as they were called, had no warrant and were in truth and fact accompanied by individuals they called their "special deputies," all of whom, some reporter figured out, were actually Ku Klux Klansmen from Orlando. And this story made the papers, around the country.

It also had consequences here at home. Tampa's Police Chief, R.G. Tittsworth, decided to go on an indefinite leave of absence. The mayor of Tampa, then one Robert E. Lee Chancey, thought it expedient to suspend the six policemen who had been involved. He also called up the Florida National Guard to keep the peace.

Those six, and three Klansmen from outside the area, subsequently got indicted as a single bunch, for kidnapping, murderous assault, and second degree murder.

With Shoemaker dead, Eugene Poulnot became the only witness against the cruel murderers. He lost his printing job as a result of all the publicity and was lucky to get a $30 a month wage provided to unemployed men who "enlisted" in the WPA. (Thankfully I never had to go to the WPA, or the PWA, or the CCC, or anything else the government had to offer. Neither did my Dad, which should go without saying. But people were needy in those days.)

Then Eugene even got fired from the WPA for being a "Red." His politics were apparently a big problem for the government officials of Florida, and his unfortunate firing even made more headlines for him. By the time the trial for the police and Klan lowlife who beat him up finally convened, Eugene was quite well known in Tampa. Maybe 'notorious' is the better word. Pamphlets littered the city park benches, put out by the Socialist Party, denouncing Eugene's tormentors and proclaiming him a "Workers' Hero." The newspapers thought he was making it all up.

Here's where it gets wild. Two of the defendants, a Klansman and a police sergeant, both committed "suicide" before they were called to testify, one by carbon monoxide poisoning and the other by jumping out of a window.

Eugene believed that the attorneys for the rest of the defendants were being paid by the "White Political Party" machine. At the trial these lawyers blew past the gory facts of the beatings but instead honed in on the reputation of my poor friend, tying him to other local "Reds" who were reported to have had amorous relations with Negroes. Can you believe this? Time and again Eugene was asked whether it was true that he had cursed the United States Government, the flag and the White House, and had praised the government of Russia, and each time he protested vigorously, "That's a lie!" Which it was!

Dad had told me to look out for the judge presiding at the trial, a Judge Braxton, whom Dad called a "monster" for reasons he did not explain, so it was no surprise to me that the judge threw out the assault and murder counts for insufficient evidence and let the jury consider only one charge – simple kidnapping. And, no surprise, all of the defendants were acquitted. As the jury foreman said, "Serious questions had been raised about the credibility of Poulnot," who was left poor as a church mouse and completely unemployable around this town.

The whole Poulnot clan, there were six of them, had to move back in with Eugene's parents. They got some charity from the Socialist Party up north, but that was cut off after the case was over. Christy took the family some groceries, but Eugene made it clear he resented it. He and I have been close friends for years, but something about this has cut him off, and now he doesn't want to speak to me. He may think that I smell too much of the mob, and the mob smells too much of the cops, and the cops smell too much of the Klan.

But that's just for background, to explain that Tampa was full of problems. And they were all landing on my home and my life, which I prayed I could save.

EUGENE POULNOT'S STORY

I'm not a "workers' hero." I was born and raised in Florida. And I grew up in a union family. My father always sang union songs, and my mother danced to *J'ai Deux Amours*. She dried flowers and hung copies of paintings on the walls. We were a big happy family, and everyone read books. We had a *phonograph; we even had a GE refrigerator, paying on time, and my parents had educated friends. Some taught at college. I was raised to speak my mind, in church and at home. I volunteered to go to war for Democracy. We won the war, but I can't turn a blind eye to fascism and the repression of the American Negro. Just look around you! Am I supposed to keep quiet?*

Even after what they did to me. Even after they killed brother Jospeh Shoemaker, I believe all this is going to change. And sooner than you think. We are going to win! All across the world. And, yes, all across Florida.

MACK'S STORY (CONTINUED)

My Christmas Eve call to Tito Rubio was successful. Negotiations with him and Eddie Virella commenced the day after Christ's birth, when I walked into the Lincoln Club, a grand Bolita saloon in Ybor City that had made its name during Prohibition. It was still very popular now that drink was legal, and famous for fine dining, swing bands and a packed dance floor. I'd never ventured into the place, but I knew about it from people who boasted of seeing its Latin shows, featuring blaring trumpets and colorful dancers in costumes made of tropical flowers. Of course, major events included Bolita night, when all the customers could hoot and holler, lose their money, and call it fun.

I entered the club right at opening time, 6 o'clock. Being that it was the night after Christmas, I supposed the crowd might be small, what with so many people nursing holiday hangovers, but I could not have been more wrong. There was already a long line of customers waiting to get in. I cut to the front like I was important and introduced myself to the lady who guarded the door as "Mack MacFarlane, the pilot." I stated that I had business with Mr. Rubio.

There was a little back and forth, but eventually she told me that I could wait inside at the bar while she relayed my message. I did, and took a red-upholstered stool, but I declined the bartender's offer to fix me a drink. "Maybe after my meeting," I told him.

The messenger reappeared and ordered me to follow her to the back and down a hall where we reached a door marked "Private." She knocked, the door buzzed, and I was admitted.

Tito Rubio was presiding in a tall leather chair behind a very large desk. He was a good looking, black-haired guy, a dapper dresser, with a smile about his lips and wide searching eyes. His jacket was folded on the table beside him, and he was wearing a starched white shirt and a tasteful purple tie. Standing to his right by the wall was Eddie Virella. His eyes, circled by wire-rimmed glasses, had the same ice cold expression I'd seen when he was firing his handgun into Leonard Trout's chest. For some reason he reminded me of my classroom flight instructor in the Army.

"I met you before, MacFarlane," Rubio recalled. "You flew me to Tallahassee once. I hope you had a pleasant Christmas."

"Barely," I said. "I was lucky not to get shot like Leonard Trout."

Virella stirred uneasily, but Rubio didn't even blink. "You get right to the point. That's good. It helps to avoid unnecessary unpleasantness. What are you bringing me?"

"I've got the bag of jewelry that Leonard Trout was carrying. Not with me, of course, but I want to give it to you. I'd like you to do me a favor in return."

"A favor?" Virella barked from his spot on the wall. "Why should we do you any favors? You're just a flunky!" His voice was very loud. "My favor to you is not to put you in a hole with Trout!" Rubio laughed at that, and he was the one I addressed. He seemed a lot more reasonable than Eddie Virella.

"It seems to me, Mister Rubio, that I might do better just to hand the bag over to the Antinoris. Mario Perla is the one who chartered my flight with Trout, after all. If anyone ought to have the jewels, I'm sure he would say it's him. And in gratitude, I think Mario Perla might protect me from you."

"Not a chance kid," Rubio said easily. "Nobody cares about you. If you gave Mario the satchel, he still wouldn't care if we dispatched you." I believed him but didn't admit it.

I took a brave stance. "Mr. Rubio, I fought in the War and nothing much scares me. I also know that if anything were to happen to me, my father would come after whoever did it and make them wish they hadn't."

Virella joined the conversation. "Who's your father?" he asked softly.

"Gabe MacFarlane. He used to be a Sarasota County sheriff's deputy. He knows everybody in law enforcement. And he's a good man to have on your side."

"We've got our own friends in law enforcement," Virella said, dismissing me.

Rubio interrupted. "Wait a minute, let's hear what the young man has to say. After all, he's offering to be of service to us. Go ahead, Mack. Spill it out."

So I did. They could have the jewels. No questions asked. But in return, as regards to their friends in law enforcement, I had one personal favor to ask – and it was non-negotiable.

There was surprisingly no resistance to my proposal, and when the deal was done, Tito Rubio and I actually shook on it, just two businessmen. Eddie Virella lit a cigarette with a big match and watched me leave. I walked out of their office careful of each step, and I skipped that drink at the bar. I felt fortunate just to get away from there alive.

CHAPTER FIFTEEN

I MEET KELLY BUCKS

So that was Mack. He gets to tell some of the story. He's the coming generation. But I'll get back to my own tale now. Which, of course, involves him.

Yes, Mack gave me an account about the shoot-out on the tarmac at the Tampa airport. This was back at our house in Sarasota. He related how he flew Leonard Trout to Englewood, who I remembered well as one of Mack's school mates. I'd hired the kid one season to help bring in my orange harvest, but he cared more about sleeping in the shade of the trees than picking them. He was a harmless, goofy guy, then. He didn't make much money from me.

And Mack told me about the leather satchel of jewels and watches, which I assumed was Whitey's treasure that Juanita had deposited at Whiskey Corners (though now in a satchel and not a duffle bag). Mack told me how he had escaped, and how he had the good sense to make a prompt arrangement to hand the bag over to Tito Rubio and Eddie Virella. Everybody, even an occasional visitor to Tampa like me, knew who these men were. They ran Bolita gambling for Charlie Wall, also known as "The White Ghost." He was a prominent white member

176

of the city's political machine and social scene but he needed Cuban partners to run his gambling halls, hence Tito and Eddie.

I had enjoyed those gambling halls a few times with Germaine, but I knew they were really a racket where the house took the lion's share no matter who won the prizes, sucking money from the working community. The prostitutes who hung around the clubs had to pay rent to management for their access to lubricated customers. Bettors who got into trouble had to borrow from loan sharks, who kicked back a share to the mob. Cops had to be bought to look the other way, so there were payroll expenses. And then there was the issue of liquor – illegal for a decade, now legal and taxed, but taxes could be avoided, and bottles could be watered down. Forgive me for my hostility. I've always been a cop. Gambling is a popular and entertaining vice, but it's always mired in ways to screw money out of people.

Delivering that same sermon was on the tip of my tongue when Mack said, "I used your name, Dad."

"You what?"

"When I met Rubio at the club and later gave Virella the valise in Centennial Park, I mentioned that my father was a retired Sarasota deputy sheriff. I said it partly to get his attention, and partly as insurance."

"Insurance against what?"

"I was a little afraid he might break my arms, hurt my family, blow up my airplane . . ."

"And did it help?"

"I hope so," Mack said, and gave his laugh. "I also wanted to work out a deal with them, and I thought you being in it might, I don't know, make it sound better for them."

"What the hell are you talking about, son?"

"It's nothing, Dad. But I know these guys. They don't believe in doing anything for free. They don't trust anybody who does. And whatever they can do to make a friend in law enforcement, they're for it."

"Nobody's making a friend out of me!" I was mad. "What kind of deal did you make?"

"I can't really go into that, Dad. Nothing you need to know about. You'll never hear from them, never. But maybe you should stay out of the clubs for a while." He gave me his laugh again.

"I'll tell you about 'never,' Mack. I never wanted to hear anything like this from you!"

I stood up and walked out of my own house and down the porch steps. I was so angry I came close to striking my son. He was old enough to know better than to consort with criminals. If he did, so be it. But he was never to involve me! I thought I'd raised him better than that. In Tampa, criminals were everywhere. They could show you the time of your life, rob you, beat you, kill you, and the city fathers, the cigar company owners, the gangsters, the Klansmen, made it all happen.

Getting my breathing under control, I went back inside. I couldn't truly blame Mack for getting himself into this. Everybody in his city was involved. I just wondered what kind of a deal it was that he had worked out with Tito Rubio and Eddie Virella, before he handed them the fortune that I believe was stolen from John Ringling's yacht. The sordidness of it all! I looked at my old nightstick hanging on the wall. At the photo of me riding my horse, bringing law to our community. I sent the Lord a grateful prayer that my home was in Sarasota, where the air was cleaner and the corruption more manageable.

Recognizing the thunder clouds building, Mack tipped his hat and left.

TITO RUBIO'S STORY

 *Of course I've made a lot of money. But it's impolite to talk about it.*

As soon as I cooled off, I went looking for Juanita Ropollo, Whitey's girl who liked me. I thought she ought to know that Whitey's treasure, which I deduced she had delivered to Whiskey Corners, had been taken from there and lost to Eddie Virella and his mobster pals. That, plus she owed me sixty bucks, and I had a watch to return.

The clerk at the Bay Haven Hotel claimed to know nothing about any guest named Juanita Ropollo. It was Friday. He was busy. He didn't want to fool with me and muttered something about, "No dagos here." But then I spied her sitting in one of the lobby chairs dressed up in a red shirt and black pants that flared at the ankles, like a calypso dancer. She had the attention of a gentleman on the sofa nearby, and they were deep in conversation.

"Hi," I said from behind her. "Registered under a different name?"

"Si, senor," she said and rose to take my arm. We walked to a corner where we could speak privately in the shadow of a tall Grecian urn.

"Geez, Gabe," she said flirtatiously. "You shouldn't surprise a girl like that. Want to buy a lady some dinner?"

"No thanks, Juanita. I've got to get out to my farm, but I have some news for you." She pulled closer and widened her eyes, waiting. "The . . . stuff . . . you left down at Whiskey Corners. I hate to tell you this, but that stuff isn't there anymore. I'm advised that some businessmen up in Tampa have gotten hold of it."

The merriment left her eyes. "If that's true," she spat out, "Kelly Bucks owes me."

"Who is this Kelly Bucks?"

"He owns the Whiskey Corners Bar. He's got connections in Key West and Cuba. He's the one selling the goods for Whitey."

"Juanita, I'd advise you to get busy and check on that situation."

"You're damn right. But how do you suppose I'm going to get to Whiskey Corners?"

"There's such a thing as using a telephone."

"No, that won't work." She chewed her lip. "Nobody with any brains talks on the telephone. How about you take me. It's not that far."

"It's more than an hour's drive, Juanita. Florida is a big state."

"I'll make it worth your while," she said.

I doubted that, but actually I had taken the hook and wanted to see how this whole operation worked. All my life I've wanted to fathom what seems so strange and unnatural to me – the tangled inventions of the criminal mind – and to see them unraveled. Juanita was trouble, I knew that, but to me she was a new breed of cat and certainly didn't look bad. My thoughts about women were muddled at that time needless to say. Going back to my house could wait.

After a few traffic lights we were on the Trail pointed south. The highway was fine, paved and smooth the whole way, and businesses had popped up everywhere to cater to the motoring trade, all the "tin can tourists" traveling to see the Everglades, or the lights of Miami, or just an alligator to send a postcard home about. The Depression may have crushed many a dream, but not the dream of driving through Florida. We passed gas stations, Italian restaurants, motor lodges, jewelry stands, "Indian Village" attractions, and even a drive-in movie.

Near the little fishing village of Englewood we had to turn onto a bumpy county road, a blacktop. Talk about hard times. Englewood might boast an airfield, but the town was no longer even an official town. The citizens couldn't afford to pay the price for renewing the city charter and so gave it up. The same sad thing happened in nearby Grove City, where Reuben used to run fishing expeditions. Ambitions were drying up everywhere.

Continuing south toward Placida the traffic and all the headlights disappeared, and we were cruising into darkness.

Juanita was humming to herself. Once she said, "Reminds me of New Orleans," but that made no sense.

"What's that silver ring on your finger?" I asked. I'd been curious, since it made me think of Scottish coats of arms, and I thought she might like me taking notice of it.

"It's the symbol of my hometown. It's a Fleur-de-lis. It reminds me of where I come from. Before everybody came hunting for me."

After that we didn't talk.

You saw the glare of the bar before you reached the crossroads. There had been a neon upgrade and now the big lighted sign that said WHISKEY CORNERS stood out for a mile. When you drove into the parking lot you got a sense of the crowd and could hear the music kicking within. I was awake, sensible enough of the situation by then to consider whether I should leave my pistol in the glove box or wear it inside. I decided to leave it in the car.

I let Juanita walk in first, the gentlemanly thing to do, but I doubt I could have held her back if I had tried. She was after her money, hers and Whitey's, and she was determined to confront this Kelly Bucks. Kids were running around everywhere.

Juanita knew the layout better than I did and threaded right though the tightly-packed paying customers. They were mostly mullet harvesters and sawmill hands to judge by their clothes and callouses. But, here and there, sat a blond tennis player from one of the resorts. Juanita got to the traditional door at the end of the hall marked "Office" and beat on it while announcing herself loudly.

The man who came to admit us was undoubtedly the best looking guy in the place. He was about forty and dressed nice as pie in a white shirt, unbuttoned at the collar, a loose black tie to match his curly sideburns, and a fedora cocked on his head in the style popular with local outdoorsmen - the crown left round without any pinches up front. All tied up with a red hatband.

"Juanita, honey. To what do I owe the pleasure? And who is this? Your bodyguard?" he asked, meaning me.

"Like I need a bodyguard, Kelly! This is a friend, Gabe MacFarlane."

He sized me up without offering his hand. "Weren't you a Sarasota County Deputy Sheriff?" he asked. "And then, a Pinkerton man at the Circus?"

"You know all about me, but I don't think we ever met."

"No, we never did," Kelly Bucks agreed. He pointed us to some chairs and took himself to sit behind his polished wooden desk. "Considering some of the crazy things I used to do, I can't say I'm sorry we never crossed paths. I just heard your name from time to time." On the wall behind him were some framed fishing lures and a certificate of some type issued by the Charlotte County Sheriff's Department.

Juanita launched in. "Here's the thing Kelly," she began sweetly. "I left you a big bag of valuables which Whitey gave me, before he got snatched by the cops and put in jail. Whitey promised a certain party he would sell them, and you promised to arrange the sale for us, meaning me."

Kelly just nodded. He kept his eyes on mine.

"Well, where's my money?" Juanita demanded.

"I still have your duffle bag full of goodies, honey," he said. "It hasn't sold yet, but I think it will soon. I'll give it back to you if you want."

She was momentarily taken aback. "Is that right?" she asked. Now they were both looking my way.

So, I had to lay it out there. "There was a bag picked up here on Christmas Eve last week by a man named Leonard Trout. He worked with some questionable characters in Tampa, and he got this leather satchel – so it was described to me - from you. This man, Trout, was a courier for a fellow you may know named Mario Perla, and he left by fast plane back to Tampa. Where he got himself shot to death."

I don't think this was news to Kelly, though he pretended to be shocked. He lowered his head and shook it sadly.

"I always hate to hear it when a customer leaves my establishment and gets into trouble, but shot to death, that's really terrible."

"And I also wonder whether any of this is related to two dead hookers in Sarasota."

"What's a hooker?" Bucks asked innocently.

Before I could respond Juanita cut in. "Yeah, but what about those jewels, and the watches?"

Kelly was the picture of sincerity. "Honey, what Trout took wasn't yours," he said. "I was engaged to sell two very similar packages by two different gentlemen. All legitimate, I was assured. One bag came from Whitey Jarvis, by way of you. I'd done a bit with the kid before – like moving a chess set and some silverware. Very small, but I always liked

Whitey. The other bag came from a reliable party I've known for years. It was no coincidence that the merchandise in both bags was very similar. It was obviously related. But in my mind the two transactions, coming from two different sellers, were quite separate."

He shifted his gaze to me. "The package I gave to Leonard Trout was the one I got from this other party, not the one from Whitey. There was no reason for Whitey, or you, to know about any of this.

"Anyway, the other party changed his plans and no longer wanted me to handle the sale of his bag of goods. He arranged for Leonard Trout to arrive here and retrieve that satchel. I got a small payment for my efforts to date, though I had not made the sale, and I relinquished possession as requested. I didn't ask why the other party's plans had changed. None of my business. I'm an honest broker."

"That didn't turn out very well for Mister Trout," I pointed out. "He also relinquished his possession, when he was ambushed at the airport."

Kelly spread his hands helplessly.

"Never mind all that!" Juanita yelled. "Why haven't you sold Whitey's stuff? Whitey needs his commission!"

"It will sell," Kelly assured her. "And it's the more valuable of the two – all those antique watches. I've got a collector offshore who wants to see them. It shouldn't take too much longer. He's due to be here any day now."

"Good, because Whitey goes on trial next week, and he needs money to hire a lawyer."

I interrupted. "Who else knew that there were two similar packages, as you say?"

Kelly understood the seriousness of that question. "Well, both of the owners knew about the other. One preferred to deal directly with me, and the other preferred to deal through Whitey, because they had worked together before. Whether that deal still holds since Whitey went to jail, I don't know."

"You'd better believe it still holds!" Juanita interjected.

"Yes. Okay," Bucks went on. "Both of the sellers knew I was handling the other's bag, but it certainly is my hope that neither seller has divulged the existence of two bags to anyone else, especially considering what happened to Leonard Trout."

He looked us both in the eye, in a way that was almost menacing. "I've been in this business a long time and have a sterling reputation."

"As a fence," I said.

Bucks frowned but ignored me.

"If you've still got Whitey's jewels," Juanita said. "I want to see 'em."

Bucks stood up quickly and turned to a large floor safe sitting in plain sight behind him. He spun the dials and came up with a canvas duffle bag, which Juanita clearly recognized. He hefted it up and poured the contents onto his desk.

It was a dazzling sight, a tangle of gold necklaces and colorful stones, and at least a dozen of those engraved pocket watches, unpolished, but warmly golden in the light. Juanita ran her hands through the jewelry.

"Looks like you're telling the truth," she said. "Nobody's going to miss just one." She plucked out a cluster of diamonds.

"I guess that's your business," Bucks said. "But you may have to answer to somebody."

"This is my commission," Juanita whispered. "Whitey owes me something."

The bar owner shrugged. "I meant the owner, but the last instructions I got were to deal with Whitey and you. Do you still want me to sell the lot?"

"Of course," Juanita replied. "And the sooner the better." The brooch went inside her blouse. "Now I think I'd like a drink."

"Have one, on the house," Kelly offered. "Just tell them at the bar. I hope to have good news for you soon. How do I reach you?"

Juanita took a pen from his desk and scribbled something in his address book. She slid it back to Bucks without showing it to me, her bodyguard.

"I'm having two drinks," she informed him, "and I'll be waiting to hear from you."

Kelly ushered us out of his office. "Whitey's a good man," he called to our backs. "I've known him for years. He's caught a bad break." The door closed behind us.

After two drinks, or was it four, it was a wobbly road back to Sarasota.

Juanita laid her head back on my shoulder again, and my mind, to tell the truth, was on where that brooch had gone.

I didn't ask her where she wanted to be dropped off this time. I took her up that little dirt road to my cabin in the country.

CHAPTER SIXTEEN

USELESS MEETINGS ALL AROUND

Germaine called me on the party line in the morning to tell me that Whitey's trial was on the docket of Judge Braxton's court on the coming Monday, and couldn't I do something about it? I suggested she rally her family together to raise some money to get the man a good lawyer who could beg for time. She had several reasons why none of the relatives was interested in investing another nickel in Whitey's battles with the court system. Everybody agreed he was one of the nicest guys around, but he was destined always to be in trouble. "But I promise to take care of your fee, Gabe, if I have to work two shifts for the rest of my life."

I could have told her that was nonsense, but I didn't. I had given up on ever collecting a fee, unless you counted the watch that I still held in pawn for Juanita.

"I'll try to talk to the sheriff again," I told her, "But talking to the judge might do more harm than good. Judge Braxton has long held the belief that I had an affair with his late wife."

"Did you?"

"He thought so, and I have a strong suspicion that he killed her for it."

"The judge?"

"He's not a good man, Germaine. For instance, last week he let off all of the murderers who killed that Shoemaker fellow in Tampa, and who tar-and-feathered Eugene Poulnot."

"Then I think you should threaten to shoot his ass! And make him believe it! This is my brother we're talking about!"

Her request was unreasonable any way you looked at it. Shooting a judge – even this one - was not something I was going to do. But despite breaking off our relationship, I had formed an emotional attachment with Germaine, and against my better judgment I said I'd give it a try. I regretted that promise, and the promise to approach the sheriff again, as soon as the words left my mouth. I have no excuse for my momentary loss of control. Maybe I can blame it on the sight of Juanita with a blanket around her rising from my bed and stretching in the sunlight streaming in through the window to the east. She looked at me unashamed. Rubbing her eyes, she asked, "Coffee?"

Within a minute my phone rang again. This time it was Clarinda. "I had my talk with Alf," she said. "That's all taken care of."

"Okay."

"So, we'll give it a try?" she asked.

I rubbed my own eyes.

"I still think we ought to," I told her.

"I'll be working on it, Gabe." She hung up.

CLARINDA'S STORY (CONTINUED)

*I heard Alf talking on the phone and telling someone they needed to break some heads, teach some people a lesson, run them out of town, things like that. It was clear to me that the ones he wanted to beat up and run out of town were the same people that my son, Mack, is friends with. I've stood clear of all that mess as best I can, but family comes first for me. And I've come to realize that Alf isn't man enough to do any head-busting himself. He'll pay others to do it. So my mind is made up. Goodbye, Alf.*

Later that morning, and after coffee, I drove Juanita to an apartment she now had a key for. It was right by the Rosemary Cemetery, where every city father and mother I'd ever heard about was buried. There were

Cunliffs and Whitakers. There was J. Hamilton Gillespie, a popular mayor whom I recalled as being the one who had helped lure all those unfortunate Scotsmen to Sarasota where they lost their fortunes and nearly froze to death in a scam perpetrated by his family's Florida Mortgage and Investment Company. And Carrie Abbe, cousin of the murdered postmaster. And there was Harry Higel, another mayor whose murder on Siesta Key had shocked our entire populace, which I had avenged. And there were other famous victims, like Ella Green and her three kids, murdered, every single one of them, by her husband Dabs. Sheriff Sandy Watson had buried Dabs where he shot him down on the road to Manatee.

High society had moved on from the area, however, and great numbers of our hard-working laborers in the Celery Fields had taken their place. Black businesses were opening up store-fronts in the old homes. Those houses were still in good shape, and rents were attractively cheap.

"See ya," Juanita said, and she was out of the car. A tough broad, I thought. I wondered if they were all like that in New Orleans.

"What room are you in?" I called after her.

"Eighteen," I think I heard her say as she disappeared.

The winter morning was fresh and invigorating in downtown Sarasota, and the tourists on the sidewalks all looked so relaxed and happy, buying their souvenirs and sunglasses, that I hated to go inside the police station. But I did and saw Sheriff Pearson sitting behind his desk reading a newspaper. Chief of Police Tilden Davis was also in view. Both of them tried to ignore me, hoping that the lady with the glasses at the counter would take care of my problem, but I walked around her.

"Hi, Sheriff. Hi, Chief," I said. "Whitey's trial is coming up, and we all know something's wrong with that gun. He dropped it empty and now it's loaded with police bullets."

I was loud enough that the lady behind the desk heard it, as well as a pair of people waiting in chairs for their turn to see her.

"That's a travesty and a lie!" Sheriff Pearson declared, standing up. "That gun is in evidence, and it has short bullets in it, nothing like our cartridges. Same type of bullets that killed the sisters. You're just raising a ruckus!"

"A ruckus?" I cried, but I was out of steam. They had changed the bullets, and I told them so. "Those were hollow-points last week."

Chief Davis found something to do in a filing cabinet. Pearson sat back down and said, "Bullshit!"

"I can't believe you're saying that, Sheriff."

He looked at me and spread his hands. "Look, I like the man, Whitey. I can't help that. But two women were murdered, right here in Sarasota. And Whitey Jarvis and his partner ran us all around the country before we caught up to them. His partner, Donny, shot at us first and died for it. Justice demands that somebody be tried for these deaths. And pay the ultimate price."

"That's what you believe? Even if he didn't pull the trigger?"

"Yes, I do believe it. Whitey was in the room where the shooting happened. He dropped his gun at the scene and ran. He had no compunction about those women at all." Pearson ticked these off on his fingers.

"Besides, we ain't got nobody else," Chief Davis laughed behind me and excused himself to go to the bathroom.

"It's a dirty deal," I told the sheriff.

His face was red, with self-torment or rage. "You're barking up the wrong tree!" he yelled. "You've had your day wearing the badge and now the responsibility is mine! And you can just shut the hell up and get out of my office or in one minute you'll be in a cell right next to Whitey!"

He had one hand on the pistol at his hip and the other on a ring of keys to the cell block, and he made a quick believer out of me. Nobody handy was going to come to my rescue, so I made an angry exit.

"What about Ricky Weed jumping through the window?" I mumbled while departing. The sheriff heard me, but I was out the door. So much for the first part of my last-ditch mission to help Whitey Jarvis.

Judge Braxton had jurisdiction in Tampa, Bradenton, and Sarasota and travelled from courtroom to courtroom. This week was Sarasota's turn. I walked to the courthouse to see if I could get an audience with him while I was still good and mad. The judge was off the bench at the moment, and two lawyers lounged at the defense table swapping stories.

"He's in chambers," one told me. "Till about two p.m., when we get to go first."

"You're having a trial?" I asked.

"Yep. Battery by intentional touch or strike, it is so stated. And yes, it will take a while."

Barging into the judge's chambers through the door behind his lofty bench would probably get me off to a bad start with Braxton, so I went out to the hall to enter the anteroom to his office properly. It was guarded by a clerk, a stern looking woman who wore her silver hair tight in a bun. More lawyers were sitting in there, paying her compliments while waiting to see his eminence. I gave her my name and told her my business, which was to talk to the judge about the accused murderer Whitey Jarvis, and she asked did I represent him. I told her no but I knew the judge from when I was the City Marshal and Deputy Sheriff, and I thought he would want to hear my point of view.

"Well, okay," she said, "but he's out to lunch at the moment and these gentlemen are ahead of you."

"Fine with me. I'll wait my turn." There was one more folding chair crammed against the wall and I settled into it, crowding three members of the bar who were naturally dressed better than me. We exchanged smiles. After a minute, conversation resumed, but it wasn't very interesting to me so my thoughts drifted back over the decades to when I first saw Judge Braxton's wife, Estelle, riding a fine horse on her, their, ranch, and me mounted proudly on Whisper, the best horse that ever was. Of course, Braxton wasn't a judge then, just a budding tyrant. And I was maybe nineteen or twenty, and just married to Clarinda, and for whatever reason, probably to show my disdain for her husband who had just offered me a job burning out settlers so he could steal their land, I blew her a kiss. And how some few years later that moment came back to both of our minds when we encountered one another at Jack Rudd's harness shop and the memory led us into our illicit, brief love affair.

It didn't have to happen but it did. This affair was one of the major events in my life and no doubt one of the reasons Clarinda eventually decided to leave me. Though several years passed between my infidelity and her departure. My few days of passion with Estelle had really shaped my whole future. I was thinking about that when the judge walked in picking his teeth. Another lawyer was on his heels, laughing at the conclusion of some funny story and slapping Braxton on the back.

The judge saw me, frowned, and kept going, stepping over all of our feet to get back to his office. He slammed the door in the face of his lunchtime companion, catching him in mid-laugh, who, embarrassed, shrugged at the rest of us poor supplicants. There weren't any more chairs. He started to sit down on the corner of the clerk's desk but caught her glare and thought better of it. She arose, smiling sweetly at his discomfort, and maneuvered past him to tap on the judge's door, and then disappear within.

Minutes passed while we outside stared at the floor and the Audubon sketches of birds on the wall. She emerged. "Mister MacFarlane," she announced. I maneuvered over and around the four attorneys who gave me congenial smiles as if they were used to the arbitrariness of it all. I entered chambers.

"Pull the door shut," Judge Braxton ordered. "Have a seat, but don't plan to stay long. As you can see we are very busy today." He was the same tall man with a chiseled face. It had hardened even more over the years. He commanded an expansive desk, and the chairs in front of it were upholstered in plush blue leather.

"I thought perhaps you were dead, Gawain," he said, using my true name.

"Not quite yet, Judge. And I hate to intrude on you, but you should know about an injustice."

He laughed, a dry laugh, without comment, and he beckoned me with his hands to continue.

"There's a murder trial on your docket, for Whitey Jarvis. He has no lawyer. I'd like you to appoint him one. I'd also like to say he is innocent of the murder, and furthermore that you'll find in evidence his pistol that he threw away at the scene. He did that because it was unloaded. The conclusion being he didn't shoot anyone. But Sheriff Pearson may have planted three bullets in that gun to suggest that Jarvis fired the other three into the pair of, what shall I call them . . ."

"Prostitutes," the judge filled in.

"Okay. You're familiar with the case. Whitey was there, sure, but with an unloaded gun, and when the shooting started he ran as fast as he could. He didn't kill a soul."

"I suppose you were present at the scene, of course."

"No, Judge. But I've talked to the man several times at the jail."

"How does this concern you, Gawain?" he asked.

Jasper Braxton used to be a dynamic and forceful horseman and cattle rancher, but now the steady gaze was gone, and I thought the veins running through his cheeks looked like dead vines. The skin of his neck was still sun-toasted but it had started to sag.

"I know Whitey's relatives," I said. "They have no money for a lawyer."

"Will it personally pain you if I find him guilty?"

Was there ever such a trick question? I shrugged. "Just seems unfair," I said. "Cops shouldn't plant evidence."

"Thank you very much, MacFarlane," the judge said. "Cops should always stand up for virtue and truth. Honesty and faithfulness. I'll keep that in mind when I hear the case. Now please excuse me. I have a trial."

He dismissed me to concentrate on the papers on his desk. He who used to have a mighty fine wife before he murdered her and buried her in the Myakka wilderness. Waving me goodbye before I even stood up, my meeting was over.

Unwilling to shoot the son of a bitch, I left his office and smiled at the next lawyer in line.

Both of these meetings had turned out just as productively as I had expected.

CHAPTER SEVENTEEN

ON THE TRAIL OF THE MONEY

It was with a sad heart that I called up Germaine to report my failures. I used the phone booth at the courthouse, plugging in nickels, because I knew it to be a private line. Naturally she was mad after I finished. The sheriff and the judge got roundly cursed.

"How can they claim to be upholders of the law?" she shouted. "That fucking judge!" I heard Germaine slamming things around in her living room. She might have been drinking.

"That's just the way it is, Germaine." I tried to reason with her. "Let's look at this from another angle. What if I told you that Whitey was trying to sell some jewelry that didn't belong to him?"

"Whitey's no thief," she insisted loudly.

"No, I mean fencing them for somebody."

"Well, maybe…," I realized that Germaine probably knew more about her brother's career than I did. "I was aware that he had some sort of problem about slot machines in Tampa. I think I mentioned that to you. That's why he went to New Orleans in the first place. But…" her voice trailed off.

"Do you know who his problem was with?"

"He didn't tell me that." I wasn't certain that she was telling the truth, but I moved on.

"So, supposing he was selling jewels that belonged to somebody else," I continued. "Let's say Whitey had them with him when he went to that house on 24th Street, and maybe, just maybe, his client, who gave him the jewels, would have an idea who the gunmen were who showed up and why the two sisters were killed. Can you tell me who that individual might be, Germaine? Who was the person Whitey was selling those jewels for? Germaine?"

She calmed down a bit, probably deciding how much to share with me. "Honestly, Gabe," she said. "I don't know very much. But it is just possible he was fencing the jewels for the man he called 'the Captain.'"

"The captain of what?"

"I don't know," she said, thinking it over. "I guess you'll just have to ask Whitey?"

"It's not very likely the sheriff will let me back in to see your brother again." But I had an idea of what "the Captain" meant, and I could think of one person I could grill some more.

Juanita never seemed to stay in one place too long, so I didn't really expect to find her in Room 18 of the Embassy Arms Apartments. I tried knocking anyway and a fat woman with a dirty apron answered the door. "Juanita's moved," she told me.

"Do you know where?" I asked.

"Who wants to know?" She had a square jaw and looked like she had given and taken a few punches.

"I'm a friend," I told her.

"How good a friend?" she asked.

"About two dollars' worth." I offered her the bills.

"Make it a five."

"Okay." Done deal.

It wasn't a great deal. Juanita had moved upstairs to Number 26, a room with a view.

And she was at home. "Who's there?" she called through the locked door. I told her, and she let me in.

"Nice place," I commented. She had a bed, a window with green curtains, and a dresser with a hot plate on it. Oh, yes, and a chair. I sat down on it. Juanita was in her nightgown.

"It's clean," she said, by way of an excuse. "I won't be here forever."

"Probably not. What can you tell me about 'the Captain'?"

She stood by the window and looked out at the street. "Why is it so important to know that?"

"The loot was in two halves. Somebody killed Leonard Trout to get the half belonging to the unknown 'other party'. Don't you think they might also kill to get the 'Captain's' half, the half that Whitey was fencing?"

"Kill who?"

"Maybe the two sisters on 24th Street. Or Kelly Bucks, or Whitey, or 'the Captain'. Or you, Juanita. Who knows? Somebody may be trying to find out where 'the Captain's' duffle bag is. The goal is to solve the mystery and save lives. Whitey's, if possible."

"And to get those jewels sold," she said scornfully. Scornful of herself, possibly.

"That's cold, Juanita, but it is another way to look at it."

"That way you'd get paid, too."

I shrugged it off. Honestly, I was over the private detective thing. This was now about justice and grudges.

She thought about it. "I don't know the whole story," she said pensively. "But I think he was a boat captain. I sort of met him when he first gave Whitey the jewels to sell. We were in a hotel in Sarasota, and I was made to leave the room. I can't even tell you what hotel it was. I was new to town and, you know, a little sauced. The Captain looked like a man who didn't like bullshit. He wanted Whitey to handle the sale, down at Whiskey Corners. That way, he said, he could keep his own hands clean. He chiseled Whitey down on the commission. If I'm not mistaken, the man's name is Wellesley, Wellesley Flagstead."

"That's what I figured, Juanita. I just wanted to hear it from you. He used to be the captain of the Zalophus. I was working on John Ringling's yacht the night it sank. That's where the jewelry came from. Captain Flagstead was at the helm, and he stayed behind after I left the ship. I also have a good guess about who wound up with the other half of the loot, the half that Leonard Trout was killed for."

"Who's that?"

"Nobody important," I said. That would be good ol' Charlie Ort, but I didn't share that with Juanita. "Where might this Captain Flagstead live?" I asked.

Juanita shrugged. "I told you I don't remember the hotel. But don't boat captains like to hang out with people who own boats, big boats?" she asked.

Juanita would have made a good detective when sober. I stood up and gave her a little salute. "Good thinking, babe," I congratulated her. "I'll take a drive and see what I can find out."

"Stay on the trail of the money," she urged. The thought of money acted as a stimulus to Juanita. She left the window and came over to lay her palms on my chest. "And come back to me, okay, Gabe? Just as soon as you can."

Up on tiptoes she kissed me hard. I pushed her back onto the bed. "Nothing of the kind, Juanita. It's strictly business from now on. The other night was my mistake."

"Sure," she laughed. "But don't keep me waiting too long," she said to my back.

I couldn't help thinking about the contrast between that invitation and my wife's.

The Sarasota Yacht Club had its clubhouse out on the Municipal Pier. I really wasn't dressed for such a fine joint, where fashionable attire tended toward white seersucker shirts and Navy-blue jackets. Whereas I was outfitted in worn jeans and a tan work shirt. But at least my clothes were clean. Maybe I would know the doorman.

Better than that, when I was crossing the parking lot, who should I run into but Loralie Cay, my old flame from when I was sixteen, the flame I'd never allowed to blaze up. Prettier than ever and dressed in white for tennis, with a one-piece knee-length dress, a wide belt, lace-up saddle shoes, and sunglasses. And a yellow scarf holding back her red hair. She was getting out of a fine looking Chrysler Imperial convertible, so my guess was she had married well.

I hailed her.

"Gawain MacFarlane!" she exclaimed and gave me a big smile. "A sight for these poor old eyes." She danced up and gave me a peck on the cheek. "Where on Earth have you been, and what are you doing here?"

She was a petite woman with a lot of spirit. "I've been around," I said, greeting her under the hot afternoon sun. Suddenly I wasn't tired anymore. "I'm retired, you might say. Or I could call myself a private detective."

"Ooh, sounds mysterious."

"Very. And you?"

"I don't actually work hard, but I'm not retired. You didn't know? I have a real estate agency."

"You mean Cayside Realty? I guess I never made the connection.

How's it going?"

"Kicking ass, Gawain. I'm rich. Listen," she said excitedly, taking my elbow, "how'd you work it out with your wife who ran away?"

Did everybody know this? "She is still a runaway, if you want to know, but we hope to work things out."

"Oh, that's too bad. Where are you off to now?"

"I was going into the yacht club to try to find out the address of a person who I'm betting just might be a member."

"That may be a secret," Loralie whispered. "Why don't I take you in and let's find out."

"Perfect, and how's your husband?" I was guessing. She was marching me across the parking lot toward the front door.

"Dead, I think. I haven't heard from him in years, Gawain. I got his club membership, and that was about it. One marriage was enough for me. I live one hundred percent better now, all by myself."

So, I stood corrected about who had paid for that Chrysler.

"Why don't we have a drink at the bar and you can tell me all about your life?" she said cheerfully.

"A quick one. I've got my business to attend to."

"The bar prefers not to serve unescorted ladies so you'll be doing me a favor. And I'll try to do one for you."

It might have been early in the day, but inside the clubhouse the bar was cool and expensively hopping. My town of Sarasota was an alcoholic's paradise. Surrounded by walls decorated with mounted fish and classic fishing rods, sportsmen of all description were poking each other's' ribs and telling hilarious stories. It was a manly place, and gentlemanly, too, as space was immediately offered to us at the bar.

Loralie ordered a rum and cola, same as Juanita, and I got my customary Canadian on the rocks.

I told her I was trying to learn the whereabouts of a Captain Wellesley Flagstead.

"Oh, I know who that is," she said. "He's a very seaworthy-looking fellow and about your age, too."

"Yeah, well, I met him once. And I need to speak to him as soon as possible."

"Looking for a sea voyage?"

"No, but it is a matter of importance to him and to me."

"Interesting. And you can't tell me what it is, right?" Her eyes were glittering.

I tried to ignore them. "That's right," I said.

"Don't let anybody take my stool." She hopped off and left the bar.

In just a few minutes she came back and sat beside me. "Success," she reported and handed me a sheet of club stationary. "The first address is the hotel where he likes to stay in Sarasota. The second is a house he's built in Punta Gorda. The Harbor Master thought he was staying in Sarasota this month." She smiled and lifted her glass.

I did the same and gave her a toast. She took a healthy swallow of her cocktail. Mine was the real stuff, for a change.

"I have to go looking for him," I told her.

"Not before I finish my drink," she said. "And you're not leaving here until I've heard some news. Why did you decide not to run for Sheriff? I always thought you'd look good on a campaign poster."

So, I filled her in on the years since we'd spoken last and she gave me some information about her life. She had flower gardens, dogs, and no children. She wrote down her address and her phone number. We promised to stay in touch, and I got another kiss on the cheek. I left while there was still daylight enough for a sobering walk ashore to Captain Flagstead's hotel. I was trying hard to keep Clarinda, the wife who "might" want to get back together, on my mind.

As I rounded the street corner, who should I see hurrying out of the hotel's front entrance but my old buddy Charlie Ort. He was walking speedily in the other direction. Suddenly I had a more interesting quarry even than the Captain.

I set off after Ort. Three blocks later I saw him about to go into a tavern. He was in front of the same old Cigar Store, the hangout where he'd first sold me on the job at the Ringling Circus. If he was going in there, so was I, but between my old and new girlfriends, I thought I might be developing a drinking problem.

Evidently Charlie changed his mind. He bypassed the Cigar Store and elected the sidewalk shoeshine-stand next door. He clambered up onto one of the comfortable seats and plopped himself down. After exchanging a few words with the shine-man he settled himself behind a Sarasota Herald, courtesy of the establishment. I strolled up and climbed into the chair next to him.

Ort glanced my way with a welcoming smile. His eyes registered recognition, and, theatrically, his jaw dropped. "Is this Gabe MacFarlane?" he asked in apparent awe.

"Howya doin' Charlie? Long time."

"Why, yes, it has been," he said, and folded his paper. "Not since our pleasure craft sank." He laughed, meaning the Zalophus. "What a night!"

Charlie hadn't aged so well. His robust pink countenance still glowed, but he had acquired some lines and wrinkles and gained a few pounds of girth. He didn't have much hair on top now, either. He was sizing me up at the same time, and I hoped I looked better than him in all those categories.

"Do you still get any work from the Circus?" I asked. The shine-man was singing softly and whapping his brown cloth over the glossy toes of Charlie's wingtips.

"Well, I certainly have some serious prospects for returning to the Big Show, Gabe, but I'm back into real estate now."

"How's that going? Rough market these days, I'd think. Everything is for sale, but who has the dough to buy?"

"All of my listings have been sold in record time," Charlie said proudly. "And I'm always looking for new properties. Got something you need to sell quick?"

"Yeah, about a hundred carets of precious jewels, set into necklaces, bracelets and pins, and maybe twenty gold watches, vintage Renaissance Italy, I'm thinking, but I'm just a country boy without much education."

The shine-man chimed in. "Comin' up on your shoes, boss. Just one minute to finish these." He lavished cream on Charlie's footwear, rubbed it in, and said, "How's that, sir?"

"Splendid, Jerome. Here's a tip. But if you don't mind I'll sit a moment while my friend gets his shoes done so we can talk." The tip was quite generous and made Jerome's eyes widen. It might have been Charlie's last dollar, but he wouldn't short a shine-man while I was watching. "High gloss?" the man asked. My ranch brogans hadn't been treated in quite a while, so I said, "The works."

"And you were saying," Charlie resumed.

I played with him a bit. "Before we get there, Charlie, what's been going on with you the last two or three years? How long has it been?"

"That's about right. It's like ancient history now." Ort found a fat Cuban in his vest and lit a match on the sole of his newly polished shoe.

"Not so ancient. So, you've just been buying and selling lots?"

"It's what I'm good at, Gabe. Care for a cigar?" I shook my head because he might not have had another. "Finding the best opportunities for the best investors is what I like best," Ort continued. "Naturally, some of the gleam is off the business since the Crash. But we do what we can."

A tall passer-by with wavy black hair noticed us and broke his stride. "Hello, Charlie Ort," the man said. Charlie's pink face suddenly went white. "I've been waiting for you to pay me a visit."

Charlie seemed to have lost his ability to speak.

"Make it soon, Charlie," the unintroduced gentleman patted my companion's knee. Then he left us and continued his walk.

"Friend of yours?" I asked.

Ort exhaled. "That was Mario Perla. I don't know what he's doing in Sarasota. I certainly didn't expect to see him here."

I knew who Mario Perla was – by reputation. A loan shark and drug-trafficker in Tampa who was part of the Antinori Gang. The same people who had sent Leonard Trout to Whiskey Corners on his way to a sudden and untimely death. Narrowly missing my son.

Perla's nest was in Tampa. There was no way he was in Sarasota for a lark. He was looking for Ort.

I marked Perla's face in my mind. Light-skinned, blue eyes, a neat black mustache. And wavy hair. With a name like Perla he could be Italian or Cuban. My bet was Cuban. Later, I learned I was wrong.

My shine was finished, and my shoes sparkled. I paid for the service, though not so grandly as Charlie Ort. "Let's take a walk and continue our talk," I suggested.

"That would be best. A private chat between old friends."

We climbed out our chairs and set off in the general direction of the Bay.

"What shall we talk about first?" he asked, unlit cigar in his fist.

"How about the jewels you grabbed out of the Zalophus safe? You and Captain Flagstead. Let's talk about that."

"If I had any idea what you are suggesting, Gabe, if I knew what you were talking about, I'd say that all that jewelry was salvage."

"It ain't salvage until the boat goes under, Charlie. Until then it's theft."

"A fine point. But if there was a theft, I'd have to point a finger at my chief of security."

I stopped in my tracks. "You mean me! Don't you remember you sent me off the boat early to escort 'the Mayor' and his girl to safety?"

Ort laughed, regaining his good humor, and stuck his cigar back in his mouth. "Just joking around with an old Circus pal, Gabe. Don't get too serious on me."

I laughed back at him and snatched the cigar out from his teeth. "Don't bullshit me, Charlie!" I threw his smoke into the street. "I know you and Captain Flagstead ripped off those items and split them between you. Then you must have decided to wait a couple of years, to let everything cool off. I know you were fencing your portion through Kelly Bucks at Whiskey Corners, but you changed your mind, didn't you? I know Mario Perla sent Leonard Trout to Whiskey Corners to get your leather valise, and that ended up with Trout getting shot. I know that Eddie Virella and his hoods did that, and they ended up with your satchel. That must have seriously upset Mister Perla, Charlie, which could be the reason for Perla's visit here today. What I don't know is how the mobsters got involved in the first place."

"This is offensive, Gabe," Ort sputtered. "And, if I may ask, what does any of this have to do with you?"

"Because my son was the pilot transporting Trout and your precious stash, and he could have been killed along with his passenger."

"Ah." That set him back, but he recovered. "Well, I am sorry to hear that, Gabe. But you know," he kept on, "I was on the up and up. I was trying to pay my debts, and then some. Trying to placate Perla. I'm hurt, hurt, that my part of the heist – did I say that? – did not get into Perla's hands. Is it my fault that this Virella monster blazes into the field and steals everything? I am innocent of all of that, Gabe!"

Ort calmed down.

"Same question, Charlie. How did all these mobsters get involved in the first place?

"Does your son still have my bag?"

"Of course not! And don't change the subject. I told you, Eddie Virella has it. My son surrendered it to avoid getting killed himself. So now, Mack is a witness to a murder. Tell me what's going on or I'll whip your ass right here on the street!" I grabbed a handful of his shirt. I was getting hot.

"Whoa! I was hoping to get that trove back, but, here's the deal. I'll be straight with you," Charlie began. Of course, I had never known that to happen. "I owe money to that man you just saw."

"Mario Perla," I said.

"Yes, Mario Perla. The specifics of our relationship don't matter, but it had to do with an investment that went south." My hold on his shirt must have been tight because Ort's cheeks were getting redder. "The depreciation of his investment was not my fault, of course. But Perla doesn't care whose fault it was. As far as he's concerned, I owe him money. Lacking ready cash, I decided to sell my salvage through a certain fence down at Whiskey Corners. But it was taking too long, and Perla was pressing me hard, so I told him he could have the jewels if he would just get off my back. I hated to part with them. The watches alone are worth more than what I owe him, but I need to get free of his awkward presence."

"Why was all that jewelry in the ship's safe in the first place? All those valuables?"

"Just conjecture, Gabe, but from what I've been able to piece together, Mister Ringling was secreting certain portions of his assets from other family members to whom he owed money and who might have had access to his mansion."

"So, you and Captain Flagstead relieved him of those assets?"

"The ship sank, Gabe. I'm not to blame for that, am I? We all could have drowned."

"Sure, I get it. You deserved to haul it all away, or half of it. I imagine Flagstead knew the safe's combination, and you just butted yourself in."

"Captain Flagstead knew everything about that ship, every lock, every key, every combination," Ort confirmed.

"And you got a share because you were the witness to the burglary, right?"

Ort's throat worked, but he said nothing.

"But then Eddie Virella hijacked your delivery," I continued. "So I guess you're still in the hot water with Perla. How did they find out about your shipment in time to intercept your bag at the Tampa airport?"

"I have no idea," Charlie said, "But I'd sure like to find out." For a moment he even looked mean, but I wasn't sure I believed him.

"And now the bag is gone and you still owe Perla?"

"Yeah. That's a big problem, Gabe, But I have a solution in mind." He was wheezing.

"Does it involve getting your hands on Captain Flagstead's half?"

His eyes widened. Apparently I'd hit his dirty little nail on the head.

"That would be a good result," he admitted. "I would like to explore that idea with the Captain, but he's checked out of his hotel."

"What makes you think Captain Flagstead would want to part with his stash?"

"I don't know. I haven't been able to find him, Gabe. He hasn't been to his hotel room for several days. I don't know where he's gone, but I'm confident he'll turn up."

I finally realized I was still clutching Charlie by the shirtfront and released my grip.

"Give it up, Charlie," I told him. "Captain Flagstead's duffle bag is up for sale, and I doubt that Whitey Jarvis or anybody else is going to agree to give it to you."

"I know it's for sale, Gabe. I'm not stupid. I know it's down at Whiskey Corners. Flagstead and I put it to the market at the same time. The Captain wanted to use an intermediary, this man Whitey, all well and good. But I can't reach Whitey. He's in jail. So, how can I get ahold of the rest of our treasure? I have to find Flagstead and negotiate!" Ort looked like a man in pain. "Where is Flagstead?" he shouted.

"Get lost, Charlie." I turned and walked away.

"I'll make it worth your while," he shouted at my back. "I ain't quit yet!"

I kept walking.

"Don't forget, we're still friends!" he called after me.

MARIO PERLA'S STORY

If people want heroin, why shouldn't they have it? If they want to gamble, why not? Who gets hurt? If they want to drink, Jesus and all the saints drank wine. It's in the Bible, so what's the beef? Prostitution? Hey, some people think I'm a prostitute. Some people may think you are. Don't you want money, too? Don't you exchange whatever talents God gave you for money? You need money, don't you? I ask you, whose business is it how you make it? Some things they decide to call illegal, and some things they don't. Hell, the Romans had slave girls, didn't they? And boys, right? You think they didn't have any sexual relations? What about the Turks, the Greeks, the Egyptians? Is that disgusting to you? My point is, legal, illegal, whatever. That doesn't necessarily make it bad. I'm at peace with what I do. I'm a fair man. I have a good family. God willing, I'll never have any legal problems I can't handle and will die a grandfather in my bed.

Now, this man Ort, he's never played straight a day in his life. He talks me into investing in his scheme to buy a whole Florida Key, but then he can't sell the lots. Instead of paying me back, he strings me along. A little this year, a little next year. He's a big shot at the Circus, so he has some money. But finally I had enough and let him know that my patience had ended.

So Ort tips me off that this petty thief named Whitey Jarvis was holding a bag of stolen jewels worth thousands of dollars, whatever, and that he could be found in Sarasota. So I make arrangements and send some muscular guys I know, some cops, to make a snatch from Jarvis. At this little cathouse. What Ort didn't say was that Whitey Jarvis had a partner with him who was gun-happy. He didn't say that there was another man in the backroom who was also armed – a man who maybe recognized my guys. He didn't tell me that shooting would start as soon as my guys walked through the door. I don't even know who shot the two broads. Could have been my guys. All they said was that lead was flying everywhere, and they were lucky to get out alive. Without the duffle bag of so-called jewels!

So Ort still owes me. And now he's got another bag of jewels, he says. It's at Whiskey Corners. He didn't think to mention this before. So I arrange to send Leonard Trout down there to pick it up. Then Leonard gets plugged by that rat Eddie Virella, and Virella gets the jewels. Who set that up? I don't know.

So Ort still owes me, and he owes me for Leonard. And where is the duffle bag? I don't know. Whitey Jarvis is in jail. Charlie Ort is never straight, like I said, and he is not going to die peacefully in bed.

CHAPTER EIGHTEEN

WHITEY'S FIRST DAY IN COURT

The lights were coming on in Sarasota as I left Charlie on the street. It was too late to drive all the way to Punta Gorda where the Captain's house was, two hours south at least. It had been more than thirty years since I had been near that little cow town at the head of Charlotte Harbor, chasing a murderer, another Charlie, Charley Willard. Back then there wasn't much to Punta Gorda but docks, a fish house, and pens to hold cattle awaiting shipment to Cuba. But now my map showed that the Tamiami Trail highway stretched all the way to that little city and crossed a big bridge across the wide mouth of the Peace River. I'd kind of like to see that.

Yet with darkness falling I was also looking forward to spending the night at my own house on Catfish Creek where I'd have a happy hound dog for company. That morning Juanita had said to hurry back to her at the Embassy Arms, but to be honest I had neither the energy nor the interest.

Leaving the blacktop for the shell road to my farm, with stars coming out and a Wolf Moon, I gave some thought to ringing up Loralie, but I

216

let that go, too. There were already possibly too many women in my life, none of whom seemed to be particularly happy.

At daybreak the next morning I was on the road headed south to Punta Gorda with a full tank of gas. It was a seamless drive on good pavement through pine forests and wild scrub that once had taken me days to wander across on foot and horseback. Motor courts had replaced pioneer cabins, and seashell shops had replaced the oak hammocks draped in Spanish moss.

The blacktop ran straight across that new bridge to the still-quaint village with its wonderful views of Charlotte Harbor. Where cows had once been on-boarded to Cuban trawlers, there was a tourist information center with concrete statues of porpoises out front. I inquired within about the address Loralie had given me at the yacht club, and a young woman with a nametag was delighted to provide directions for me. Along with a generous cup of fresh chilled Florida orange juice and a town brochure.

The Captain's home was nearby on a palm-lined street, and he had a mailbox fashioned out of a small boat sailing on top of a post made from an oar. It was a neat bungalow painted a crisp white. But another car was parked in the gravel drive out front, and the front door was ajar.

I approached cautiously until I heard a wail. Rushing inside I found a young woman in a back bedroom bending over a body under the covers. "He's dead!" she screamed, staring at me over her shoulders, plainly terrified. Putting one hand on the Captain's chest and another on his wrist I could confirm that. And the seaman's face was positively green.

"Jeez look at him," I grunted. Feeling ill myself, I backed up.

"Who are you?" the woman demanded wildly.

"A neighbor," I declared and beat it out of there as fast as I could. I backed my car out in a flash and drove about two miles south before I pulled over to collect my thoughts.

Those thoughts told me to leave Punta Gorda as swiftly as possible. Which I had to retrace my steps to do, and I did. North, across the harbor. At a bait shop with a breakfast joint attached, they had a sale on scrambled eggs and live shrimp. I pulled over to consider the situation over a strong cup of coffee.

The details of how Captain Flagstead had died and who had killed him would have to wait for another day. But I'd lay money that the Captain, under extreme pressure, had spilled the beans about who had his salvaged jewels. Surely he had identified Whitey Jarvis. Most probably, he had also mentioned Juanita Ropollo. But did he reveal that his treasure was at the Whiskey Corners Bar? Maybe not. In any case, whoever caused Captain Flagstead to die of unnatural causes was now mightily on the trail of his stash.

I determined that it would be wise to get all that richness out of the hands of Kelly Bucks most urgently. It was unlikely that Whiskey Corners would be open at such an early hour. Nevertheless, I drove there first to check it out. As I figured, it was locked up tight. Nobody responded to my beating on the door. Meanwhile, I was a little rattled by Captain Flagstead's green face, I admit it, and it seemed important to me to report this situation, somehow, to Whitey Jarvis. So I hurried north.

I stopped by my house on Catfish Creek to feed my dog and grab a quick lunch, a home-grown tomato and a slice of ham, which I put in a paper bag and tossed in the car. Then I drove on to the big city.

Nothing was going smoothly. By the time I got back to Sarasota, Whitey Jarvis's trial had begun - early.

I found out because I went by the jail to demand to see him, intent on delivering the news that the Captain's claim to the "salvaged" treasure was now much diminished by his demise, and the lady at the front desk told me Mr. Jarvis had been taken to the courthouse.

Sarasota County had spent quite a bit of money and constructed a well-appointed courtroom with rows of solid oak pews for spectators and a majestic bench for the judge. There were even oil paintings on the walls of half a dozen prior jurists – a gang of crooks for the most part. The current occupant of the bench, Jasper Braxton, would fit right in. It was a far cry from the rickety old courthouse in a cow pasture at Pine Level where I had watched the trial of the Sarasota Assassination Society so many years ago.

A light crowd of spectators and a man I recognized as a newspaper reporter were sitting close by the jury box. Judge Braxton was on the bench, and the lawyers were picking a jury. Whitey Jarvis sat at the defense table, and I was relieved to see that he had a lawyer for company. That would have indeed been good except I knew the young man to be Hershel Adams, the nephew of a wizened old attorney who minded the judge's real estate business while his honor was busy dispensing justice. Was this young lawyer honest? I didn't know. My bigger concern was whether he had ever been in court before. He didn't look old enough to shave. I sat right behind Whitey, in the first row. Judge Braxton noted my arrival with a raised eyebrow.

I cleared my throat softly and got Whitey's attention. He turned around, which made the judge look over at us and frown. Whitey's lawyer was too busy doodling on his note pad to notice. Silently, Whitey mouthed the words, "Get Germaine." I whispered back, "Captain Flagstead is dead." Whitey's eyes widened. He shook his head in disbelief and turned to face the front.

Judge Braxton announced that due to the late hour, with dinnertime approaching, the court would be adjourned for the day. It being a Saturday, the court would obey the Sabbath and resume at nine o'clock on Monday morning, as it had originally been scheduled. He consulted his notes and asked the lawyers to confirm that eight jurors had been selected, and both the County Attorney and the lawyer Adams did so.

"We should be able to make quick work of this on Monday," Braxton said, "and pick the remaining four jurors in an hour or two. Be prepared, gentlemen, to get your trial underway before lunchtime on Monday." With that, he rose up, gathered his black robe around him, and swooped away.

Police Chief Davis, who had stationed himself on the bench right behind me, came forward to take custody of Jarvis and escort him out of the courtroom, hobbled with chains about his ankles. "What about those bullets?" I asked Davis as he passed, but the chief marched on without answering.

I caught Hershel Adams in the hall before he slipped away and asked him whether he was aware that the bullets in the so-called murder weapon had been placed there by someone other than his client and that, actually, they were the second set of bullets that had been planted in the gun, the first set being hollow point bullets.

"Whitey mentioned something about that," Adams said, trying to step around me. "But he doesn't deny it was his gun at the scene of the murders, or that he took flight all the way to Louisiana to get away. That's what's going to matter to the jury. The bullets make no difference."

"That's crazy!" I almost shouted. "Whitey's gun was empty when he went into that house. Letting the jury know about those planted bullets could be the difference between prison time and the chair! And what about the other man on the scene? That Ricky Weed? Whitey claims Weed came out of the back room with a gun and fired first. Has anybody talked to him?"

"Well, sir, that man was produced to the victim, Lacey Bell, at the hospital right before she died, and she said he didn't shoot her. The prosecution has no need for his testimony to convict Mister Jarvis, and I see no need to call that man, either." The young lawyer kept walking.

"Why even put on a case?" I cried after him.

"You've got a point!" he called over his shoulder.

There was a telephone in the clerk of court's office, and she let me use it to make a collect call. It rang up the Sunshine City Diner in St. Pete and luckily Germaine answered.

"You know I can't accept collect calls here," she said, but before the operator could disconnect us I yelled "Emergency" into the mouthpiece and Germaine said "I'll accept."

"What is it, Gabe? I could get fired for this."

I told her that the state had pulled a fast one and that her brother's trial was already underway. It wasn't going to begin on Monday, as she thought, but would probably be concluded then.

She gasped and said she would find some way to be there. I hung up before I thought to ask her who would drive her. But no matter, I had it in my mind to track down one Ricky Weed, the gentleman in the back room at the sisters' home who had made a hasty departure out of a window when the shooting commenced. The place to start would be the Coquettes' Tavern, where this whole drama had first begun.

It was Saturday, and I got lucky. Pete Noski, my old friend, the Circus roustabout, occupied what seemed to be his regular seat at the bar. I joined him and we exchanged pleasantries. I offered to buy him a drink.

"What's the occasion?" he asked.

"I just want your wisdom," I told him. "On the night the sisters were murdered up the street, there was a man in the back room of their house who jumped out the window. His name was Ricky Weed."

"That's right."

"Do you know him?"

"I know who he is. We don't socialize, but I know him on sight."

"What can you tell me about him?"

"He's slime. He's a pimp."

I was surprised by that information. "I thought Ricky Weed was a family man. You know, with a wife. . ."

Pete laughed. "No way," he said.

"Was he the sisters' pimp?" I asked.

"I don't know about that, but I hear he pimps lots of girls. I see him around the Fairgrounds sometimes, always with some bimbo on his elbow."

"He gets away with this?"

"He's got some relatives who are on the police force. But honestly, I think he's an embarrassment to everybody, including himself."

"Enough of an embarrassment that someone would want to shoot him?"

Noski shrugged. "Dunno." I signaled the barmaid and bought him a beer.

"Do you happen to know where he lives?" I asked.

Pete did, and gave me the street and a description of the house.

"You're not the only one interested in those shootings," he confided. "Charlie Ort, who I know from the Circus, was in here last night asking about Whitey Jarvis. I told him that Juanita might help him. I probably shouldn't have given him her name."

"Too late to worry about that. Good night, Pete."

I drove to Ricky Weed's house, the one with a blue paint job and a tall dried-up cactus out front, just as Noski had described it. Nobody was home, and the door was locked. A dog barked at me from within. It sounded like a very big one.

My next destination was Room 26 at the Embassy Arms and Juanita.

Somebody had beat me to it. The door was cracked open, and the room was a mess. The drawers where Juanita's had stored her few possessions had been dumped out on the well-worn carpet. The bed had been stripped and the sheets piled up on the floor. A picture of an ocean beach at sunrise had been torn off the wall. Something glittered on the table by the window. It was her keepsake, her good luck ring from New Orleans, with the Fleur-de-lis on it. Why would she take it off? Why leave it behind if she was on the run? Was it a sign for me, who she had told to "come back soon?"

It was after nightfall when I pointed my car south to Whiskey Corners. I speculated that Kelly Bucks might already know that Captain Flagstead was dead. If so, he would certainly have realized that the murderer was looking for the Captain's half of the stolen goods and might know where to find it.

The joint was jumping. By now the bartender seemed to have gotten used to seeing me, and he raised no objection to my elbowing straight through the rowdy bunch of drinking locals to the private office in the back. It wasn't locked, though maybe it should have been. I barged in without knocking and found both Juanita and Kelly Bucks standing with their hands high in the air, facing Charlie Ort, who held a lethal looking handgun. He was at an angle to me and had to take a step back to keep us all covered.

"Stand over there with them," he motioned with the gun. Somehow it was hard to take him seriously. He had on a billowing yellow shirt and white seersucker pants with ridiculous red stripes running down the legs.

"Why?" I asked.

"Because if you don't I'll shoot the girl first." His hand was shaky. I never thought gunplay was in Charlie's bag of tricks. And it wasn't, because, having issued the threat, his knees crumpled and he went limp. His pistol clattered to the floor beside him. He was crying. I stepped forward and retrieved his gun.

"I'm a desperate man," he moaned. "If I don't come up with the goods I'll be assassinated just like Leonard Trout."

"Take it easy, Charlie," I said, grabbing him by the shoulders and hoisting him into a chair. "What's this all about?"

"I need, I need that duffle bag of jewels," he groaned, and pointed in the general direction of Kelly Bucks and Juanita. "Someone has killed Captain Flagstead and they won't stop there!"

I figured that Charlie probably had a good idea who that killer was.

"You can't have it," Juanita spat. "I'm taking what's mine. Bring it out Kelly."

She crossed her arms and stared defiantly at Charlie and me while Kelly bent over and came up with the bag. He slapped it on his desk. "It doesn't belong to me," Bucks said. "So, whatever the lady wants, she gets."

Juanita grabbed the sack. "The lady says, since the Captain is dead, we're dividing it up." She upended the bag and spilled its glittery contents over the wood surface. Out came the shiny baubles and the golden watches.

"I'll go for this!" She scooped up a big handful. "This is my commission." A pearl necklace dripped from her fingers. Kelly and I just watched the action.

Charlie revived and slammed his hand on the table. "Enough!" he shouted. "Whatever belonged to Captain Flagstead is now mine, by rights. We were partners." Juanita hopped backwards clutching her bit of the horde. I had to give Charlie credit for coming up with the "partners" bit so quickly.

Kelly Bucks looked at me, maybe thinking I knew what was going on or maybe because I was now in possession of the only visible firearm. Seeing that I was at a loss, he made up his mind quickly.

Addressing Ort, he said, "If you tell me that the Captain's pile belongs to you now, no skin off my teeth." Kelly said. "Just so long as Whitey's girlfriend gets hers, which she already has, and I get mine. I'll take a watch." And he did. It went into his vest.

I spread my hands helplessly, though in one I held Charlie's pistol.

"Mario Perla will kill me unless I pay him off," Charlie repeated, reasoning it out. "By rights, this bag is mine. Whitey Jarvis and this woman here also deserve their commission, sure, I don't dispute that. And I completely agree, Kelly, that you deserve some pay for your trouble. Not only that, but I suppose my friend Gabe MacFarlane deserves to be compensated for his time. And he is, I should add, holding the pistol. I was there when these jewels were 'salvaged.' The Captain and I were partners in crime, you might say, but you know as well as I do there was no crime since we salvaged the jewels." He wouldn't stop talking. "I'll grant you all your nice fees, no complaints," he went on, new pep in his voice. "I'll just take the rest, which I need to settle my affairs and continue among the living."

"What happened to Captain Flagstead, Charlie?" I asked.

"That wasn't me," he gasped. "Lord, no. I saw the body. Someone far meaner than me killed that man.”

“Did you trash Juanita’s room?”

They all looked at me in surprise. Charlie shook his head. Juanita slapped herself on the forehead.

“Someone trashed my room?” she shouted. Everyone ignored her.

It came to me that Juanita’s room must have been searched after Charlie forced her to go with him to Whiskey Corners. Could whoever had been in her room waited around and followed me down?

“Okay, let’s get organized,” I said, taking over. “Kelly, why don’t you put all those valuables back in the sack?”

“Good beginning,” he agreed and carefully lifted the pieces from his desktop and laid them one by one in the duffle bag.

“Take a ring for yourself,” I said.

“No,” he replied. “I already took a watch. That’s enough. And you?” he asked.

“Not me,” I told him. After all, I had been chief of security the night all this had been lifted from the Ringlings. “But in my opinion, treating this as salvage, the bag belongs as much to Charlie Ort as anyone. And with it goes any legal consequences for its possession.”

Charlie was resurrected from the dead. “That’s mighty honorable of you, Gabe,” he said brightening up. “And, as for any consequences, I don’t think there will be any. This whole situation is on the up-and-up. Jim Dandy if I say so.” He reached for the bag.

“Now you can turn it over to Mario Perla and get on with your life,” I said. It figured that Perla had killed Captain Flagstead, but the Punta

Gorda cops would have to sort that out. I didn't really want to see any harm come to Charlie Ort.

"Right you are, Gabe," he said happily and stood up. "There's enough here to cover all my debts and leave me with a handsome stake for the future!" he shouted with enthusiasm.

"Life can be good," I told him. That sentiment proved to be short-lived.

The door swung open behind him, and there was Mario Perla himself, and a pair of thugs both decked out in white suits like Chicago White Sox fans on a golfing holiday. Juanita's hands went behind her back.

"Not so fast, Charlie," Perla said. "I'll let you know when your debt is paid. Give me that bag, and we can go somewhere private to talk. Not here. We'll sort it all out in a proper setting."

Charlie wanted to protest. His mouth, always full of the right words, fell helplessly open. The two thugs shuffled around their boss and took possession of the sack of jewels and also Charlie's elbows. "We'll be leaving," Perla said, and looking at me, added, "Aren't you the retired lawman whose son is the pilot who ripped us off."

"No way was there a rip-off," I told him. "My son just did the job he was hired to do. Eddie Virella ripped you off."

"The way I see it," Perla explained, "your boy, Mack-the-pilot, was entrusted with certain items, and he gave them to Virella, with whom he probably had a deal. I'm letting you go so you can deliver a message to your son that he's a marked man."

With that, and with Charlie Ort in tow, they backed out of the office and closed the door behind them.

Kelly, Juanita and I all stared at each other. Kelly shrugged. Juanita opened her purse and poured her ample handful of goodies into it. "C'est la vie," she said, and smiled.

Kelly Bucks was in a hurry to see that all the crooks had left his establishment and so was I. He pushed past me and strode through the bar, where his well-oiled customers were enjoying themselves oblivious to the drama that had played out in the back room. He stepped quickly to the front doors and walked outside. I followed him at a short distance, and found him standing in the parking lot full of cars. The dark Florida night was penetrated by his big neon sign and a bigger moon rising. It was getting misty. A fog was rolling in.

"Sandy," Bucks called, and an elderly attendant appeared. "Did you see four men just drive off? Out-of-towners?"

"Yes, boss. You just missed them. Two cars."

I stepped forward. "They headed north, did they?" I asked. "Toward Sarasota and Tampa?"

"No, sir," Sandy said, proud to have noticed. "They drove west, toward the beach. Don't know why. They missed the sunset."

Juanita appeared behind us. "Stay here at the bar," I ordered. "For once, don't disappear on me. I've got a bad feeling about what's happening to Charlie Ort. Don't ask me why I care. Shouldn't take me long. There's only one way out to the beach and one way back." I left her and Kelly Bucks standing in the parking lot.

Passage to the Manasota key is by way of the wooden Chadwick Bridge, clunk-a-clunk over Lemon Bay. At a small island in the middle, motorists were charged a 50 cent toll. That's a lot for some folks. A sleepy young boy collected my money. There was a turn-around for those not wanting to pay. Black hair covered the boy's eyes, and he was outfitted in a sleeveless t-shirt and rubber boots halfway to his knees.

"Did you see two cars pass?" I asked.

"Yes, sir, I did. One man in the first car; three men in the second car."

"Did you know any of them?"

He just shrugged and shook his head. "None of my business, I guess," he said.

The fog out here was heavy.

At the end of the bridge there was a sandy roadway running down to the beach and a network of little dead-end streets that led to mobile homes for rent by the week or month. These narrow lanes were barely visible in the mist. To the right, lights shown dimly from a few bayside houses. To the left, I knew from past experience, there was a hole-in-the-wall tavern, but on this night it was blanketed in a pillowy fog. Straight ahead, a row of tall Australian pines defined were the wide beach began. The tree tops were lost in the clouds, and the waterline was invisible. But two black cars had parked there in the sand. I cut my lights and carefully pulled in next to them, worried about getting stuck.

A man and a woman walking along the road appeared like ghosts from nowhere. Arm in arm they passed behind my car, going in the direction of the bar. I was startled and slumped down, but they didn't even notice me sitting in the car. The fog was that dense. In two seconds they had disappeared.

My gun was in the glove box. I stuck it in my pants and got out of the safety of my car. Why did I feel protective of Charlie Ort? I owed nothing to the man. But I just liked him.

If anyone was near me, I couldn't tell it. I heard the Gulf's waves crashing rhythmically directly ahead, but I couldn't see the surf. It was intensely lonely. I didn't make a move. The wind whipped by, creating swirling figures in the vapors. The sensation of isolation and lurking danger took me back through the years to the "Blackjack" – those dark woods rising from an empty prairie under a bleak night sky. A fearsome place, encountered decades ago, when there was a murderer named Willard close by and a cannibal hiding in the bushes. The memory made me shiver.

I snapped out of it and walked slowly and sightlessly toward the sound of the pounding water. Sea breeze dried the sweat from my shirt. I imagined I saw a footprint in the sand, but it blew away. Then I heard what might be a voice somewhere to the right. Or did I make it up? I picked my way warily in that direction, flinching at apparitions that weren't there.

The crack of a gunshot sent me face-down in the sand, followed by a second one. Out of the fog here came Charlie Ort rushing right at me.

He went past and then caught himself. He saw who I was and dove into the sand beside me for cover.

I rose up on a knee. "Stop! Law!" I yelled through the fog in the direction of the shots, spitting grit out of my mouth and beating my gun against the palm of my hand, hoping to dislodge any sand that might have fouled it.

Two more shots followed, and this time I saw flashes through the opaqueness. They were firing in my direction. On my belly I fired back at the spot where I thought the shots had come from. Charlie was flat beside me, huddled for his own protection.

Then there was nothing to hear but the wind. I rolled over to change my position and make it harder on them to come at us. Charlie crawfished to keep up. I could see his eyes, and they were terrified.

Still nothing but wind. I listened to my own breathing, and to his, for a full minute, then scampered, hunkered over, in a wide arc intending to catch the shooters from the back. Ort sensibly stayed put.

And about where I thought they could be I found lots of footprints, and I was near certain that some were beating a path back toward the cars. I hustled over the beach to find Charlie still curled up in the sand.

"Are you hurt?" I whispered.

"No, Gabe. I thought I was a goner. They punched me, and I ran."

"I think they've left," I told him, peering around into the nothingness. "I guess they took all of the jewels with them, right?"

"Every single one," Charlie sighed. "Easy come, easy go." To listen to him was uplifting.

"All of them? You mean to tell me, Charlie, that you didn't keep a bracelet or two, weeks ago, before you brought your bag to Whiskey Corners to sell?"

"Now Gabe, you know me too well." He stood up to a crouch and dusted the sand off his striped pants.

"Another question, Charlie. I don't suppose you pointed Mario Perla to the Captain's treasure, before you mentioned yours. I don't suppose you told Perla that Whitey Jarvis had the Captain's treasure, a duffle bag of gems. I don't suppose Perla then sent his gunmen to grab Whitey. And they spotted him at the bar. They followed Whitey and Donny to that little house on 24th Street."

"I've got a big mouth, Gabe. I may have said something I shouldn't have. But I didn't want anybody to get hurt. I'll be honest, I never heard a peep about any shooting on 24th Street until yesterday when Pete Noski filled me in at the Coquettes' Lounge, I swear."

Charlie was an accomplished liar, no doubt about it. I was sure, however, that he had heard about the shooting; everyone in Sarasota had. And I was sure that he had tipped Mario Perla that Whitey Jarvis was holding gems, not Charlie's gems, but the Captain's. Charlie planned to satisfy his debt to Perla with the Captain's portion. That was wicked of Charlie. But his game didn't succeed. Of course, because of his wickedness, two innocent women died and Whitey Jarvis was on trial for his life. I wondered how much of that bothered Charlie, if at all.

Slowly, we walked back to where I had left my car. It was all by itself.

"They even stole my car," Ort complained. "What a night."

I drove us out of there. There was no toll going back to the mainland, so I cruised past the kid's outpost at a good clip. It was too foggy to catch my tag number, I hoped.

Back at Whiskey Corners the next surprise was that Juanita was still there. Not so surprising, she was having a drink and chaming the bartender.

I sat on a stool beside her and ordered a double shot of bourbon and ice while Ort got a Krueger in a can, which I had never heard of before. The bartender apologized that he was out of ice, but no matter. Juanita watched me belt my whiskey back.

"Who'd you kill?" she asked, amused.

"Nobody, probably," I said, hoping it was true. "Who said anything about killing?" I took her elbow. "Come on. We're leaving."

"I haven't finished my drink," a half-hearted protest.

"Yeah you have. Unless you want to take a chance on getting back to Sarasota with one of these jokers." A quick look around was all she needed. The family guys, out for dinner with the wife and kids, had gone on home. What was left was the salt of the earth, the local boys out on a Saturday night hoot. They were as reliable as rain; they could be counted on not to get her to her destination before dawn.

"What about me?" Charlie protested.

"Just get in the car."

Juanita collected her purse. "I owe a dollar," she informed me.

"You need to get a boyfriend," I said and tossed a couple of bucks on the bar. She gave me an evil eye, started to make some smart remark but caught my mood. We headed out. It had been a long day.

Driving northward the road kept dissolving into the fog, so I went at a snail's pace. As I weaved back and forth across the white lines, Juanita said something like, "Is this where it all ends?" Charlie hummed to himself in the back seat. Very annoying. But I kept my thoughts to myself until we cleared the worst of the haze, about where the road widens through the busted tourist town of Venice. It had been a dream of Bertha Palmer's once, but the Depression did it in. Traffic picked up, and finally I could see oncoming headlights.

"So, now you have no jewels and no money, right?" Juanita said over her shoulder, addressing Ort.

"No jewels, no money and no car. But I have a good story to tell."

"A story won't help Whitey much, and I don't have enough left to help him either," she said thoughtfully.

"Seems to me, Juanita, that you might have plenty hidden in your little purse," I pointed out. "but it's probably too late to save your boyfriend anyway. I don't know if there's any lawyer in Sarasota County who could get Whitey off, but if there is, he'd want cash. You've run out of time to turn your baubles into currency, Juanita. Whitey's trial starts on Monday morning. I'm afraid that train has left the station." It was bitter medicine for both of us.

Conversation died out after that, until we passed Osprey.

"My house is right by the Fairgrounds," Ort said.

"I guess you can drop me at the Embassy Arms," Juanita chimed in. "Even if my room was messed up, it's still my place."

"You can both forget that," I told them. "I'm tired, and this car is going to my farm. You can call a cab from there, or I'll find you someplace to sleep and run you into Sarasota in the morning."

"Not a problem," Juanita said. "Thanks for the invitation."

"Might be safer for me, anyway." Charlie liked the plan.

When I finally bumped into my driveway what should I see but Clarinda's car parked under the porch light. The house was dark.

"My wife is here," I muttered. And to Juanita, "Watch what you say."

My dog started barking, and a light came on inside. I led the way up the steps. Opening the door, I was calming down Nero when Clarinda appeared from our bedroom wearing her nightgown. She saw the woman behind me first.

"What the hell, Gabe?" she demanded.

I quickly outlined the crucial parts of the situation, including introducing Ort as an old acquaintance and Juanita as a "client involved with Charlie" – two people in trouble – and Clarinda jumped into being a good hostess.

"You can have my son's room," she told the lady. Juanita was about to say, "I know," but she remembered herself in time.

Charlie got a couch, a blanket and a pillow. We were all worn out and turned in quickly. There I was, sleeping with my wife for the first time in a year. And that's what we did, sleep.

In a way it was good that it happened like this. We didn't have to try to talk the whole thing out. We just started to fit back together.

In the morning I made them all breakfast. I set the big pepper shaker out for Juanita. Clarinda watched fascinated while her female guest blackened her scrambled eggs.

"As I told you, I mean as I've said before, I like eggs with my pepper."

"Pepper is good for your digestion," Charlie Ort commented. He gave his own plate a light dusting and dug in.

"What's on your program this morning, Gabe?" Clarinda asked innocently.

"Taking these folks both back to Sarasota. That will take the morning."

"Very good. I'll be cleaning up around here." Just like old times.

I prayed that the old feelings would also soon come back:

Till a' the seas gang dry, my Dear,
And the rocks melt wi' the sun;
And I will luve thee still, my Dear,
While the sands o' life shall run.

I dropped Charlie Ort off first. We had been acquainted for several years, but I'd never known where he lived. He directed us to a nice little white house on a quiet street with lemon trees out front. It didn't seem to fit the flamboyant character he made himself out to be.

"I'm going to miss my car," he said wistfully. "But no matter. I'm sure this will all work out. Always has." He smiled and hopped out.

When we pulled up in front of the Embassy Arms, Juanita asked me if I'd like to come up. I told her no. "We can't go there anymore," I said.

It was Sunday morning but I didn't expect Ricky Weed to be in church. This time he answered my knock on the door. He was a big man with a flat face and acne scars. He was holding tight to the collar of an angry German Shepherd.

"I don't want any," Weed said.

"I'm not selling anything, Mister Weed. My name is Gabe MacFarlane, former City Marshal and now a private investigator. I'd like to ask you a few questions about the night you got shot at the sisters' house."

"Sheriff Pearson knows everything about that. I've been cleared." He started to close the door but ran up against my shoe and my shoulder.

"That's not it, Mister Weed. My job is to see that all the facts line up. I want to be sure you're saying what everybody else is saying."

Intrigued, he took the pressure off the door. "I think I may have heard of you," he said. "What kind of facts are we talking about?"

"Mainly how many weapons you saw and what kind of bullets were used. Can I come in for just a few minutes?"

"I suppose, but the place is a mess." He stood aside to let me in. He ordered his intimidating pet to stand down, which it obediently did. In the living room a pair of armchairs faced the sofa where he'd been drinking coffee. After removing a pile of men's magazines from one of the chairs, I took a seat while he got settled back on the couch. I didn't see any signs of a wife being there.

"Shoot," he said, and let out a loud laugh.

I laughed back. "Here's the story," I said. "You were in the back room with Bertie. You hear a disturbance up front and run out. You get shot in the leg by perfect strangers and bailed out the window. Smart move, right?"

"Seemed to be at the time. Lead was flying everywhere."

"There were two men sitting in the front room with Lacey. And you didn't know them."

Weed nodded.

"And you didn't recognize any of the men who had come in the front door."

He nodded again.

"You were lucky you only took one slug, with all that shooting going on."

"You're damn right. You know what one of those bullets can do? They make a smooth hole going in but tear a big hole on the inside. See?" He rolled up his pants leg. A chunk was missing from his left calf muscle. You could see the white cross-hatching where a line of stiches had put him back together. The wound was still pink.

"Nasty," I agreed.

"And that's just from the doctor digging it out of me."

"The bullet?"

"You bet, the bullet. I made the doctor give it to me as a souvenir."

"Really. Can I see it?"

"Sure." He got up and plucked a match box from the mantle. "Just take a gander."

He slid open the box and dropped the bullet into my outstretched palm.

It was a little mashed, but the forefront had started to flare open like a little windmill.

"That's a hollow point," I said.

"Damn right!"

"Was it a policeman that shot you?"

Weed's face went dark as mahogany. "What do you mean by that?"

"Police use hollow-points."

"I don't know who the hell they were! That's the story, right?" He was angry now.

"Yeah, that's the story, but the question is whether it's believable in light of your criminal background. No open charges, mind you, but the jury may wonder. Do you know anything about a bag of jewels, Weed? Did you recognize the two men who came through the door?"

"What the hell are you talking about? That ain't the story! I'm not going down for this, or anything else." He was agitated and stood up. I did, too. "Tell that to that goddamn Sheriff Pearson and Police Chief Tilden Davis! I didn't recognize a soul. That's the story! Hey! I'm the one that got shot!"

"You came out of that back room with a gun. You were ready to defend yourself. From whom?"

"Defend myself? Damn right! Get the fuck out of my house! Get the fuck out now!" He was shaking his fist. When he started fishing under the sofa cushion I moved fast for the door.

I wanted to say - your story is full of holes. You know who shot you! Those were cops who came through the door. They were intent on heisting a bag full of jewels. You never saw Whitey Jarvis shoot anyone. The whole thing was a robbery. Maybe the sisters knew who everybody was, too. Donny probably started shooting as soon as the guys showed up, certainly as soon as you showed up, Weed. Probably the cops shot the girls, by mistake or intentionally. They were witnesses. Whitey lied about the whole thing. He didn't have a clue. And you ain't married! These were among many farewells racing through my head as I beat it pronto and hopped into my car.

I peeled rubber in reverse. Ricky Weed kicked his own door open and out came his dog. The snarling hound hopped against my car. The liar waved his pistol in my direction. "So long, fool!" I yelled to myself, or to him, and pressed the gas pedal hard. No shots were fired. A successful interview. I had the slug that had been extracted from Ricky's leg in the palm of my hand.

I didn't know where to go with these questions or with the obvious significance of the hollow-pointed bullet, which proved to me, at least, that policeman had been involved and that the invasion of the sisters' home had everything to do with Charlie Ort tipping Mario Perla that Whitey Jarvis had a duffle bag of stones. The gunmen, some kind of cops the way it seemed to me, didn't plan to do Ricky Weed any harm. He wasn't in their plans at all. Assuming they were cops, they were undoubtedly Mario Perla's cops. Who started firing first? Could have been the pimping and violent Ricky Weed himself, or it could have been Donny Ropollo, surprised at a moment when his only thought had been the joys of a relaxing warm Florida night with jazz music and a couple of friendly girls. But whoever fired first or fatally, it surely wasn't Whitey Jarvis, not with his empty gun.

Out of ideas, I pointed my car toward home, where I would share some of this with my new/old wife. If memory served me right, she often could make sense out of the things when I couldn't.

CHAPTER NINETEEN

WE ARE ALL ON TRIAL

At eight o'clock on Monday morning, the day of the Jarvis trial, the door to the Landau Camper hooked to Hershel Adams' car, which served as Whitey's lawyer's office, was locked. There was nothing to do but wait for him to appear, so I sat down in the café across the street from the courthouse and bided my time having a second cup of coffee. Clarinda had already fixed me one for breakfast. Our conversations were getting off to a slow start, but at least we were talking and under the same roof. So far so good.

I overheard the chatter from the other diners. Politics, of course. Disagreements about whether FDR was doing enough, or too much. Agreement that times were hard and getting harder. Lively arguments about the murders of the two sisters. Their occupation alone would have made the topic titillating even if they hadn't both been murdered. The consensus seemed to be that Whitey Jarvis had been in the wrong, killing those ladies, no matter what they did for a living. One man said he was going into the courthouse as soon as it opened to watch the trial. Another said his car was in the shop getting plugs, so he'd have to miss it.

As nine o'clock approached I paid for my muddy brew and went

245

on stake-out in the courthouse parking lot to grab lawyer Adams. Right before court was to start, I saw him drive in and park his fancy Studebaker, minus the trailer, and I was standing in front of him by the time he got his briefcase out from the back seat.

"MacFarlane," he acknowledged without enthusiasm.

"I interviewed Ricky Weed yesterday, that man who jumped out of the window. Here is the bullet he was hit with." I displayed the hunk of lead I had in my pocket. "It's a police-type, not the kind that Donny had. Not the kind that Whitey would have had if his pistol was loaded. What this means is that the guys who broke into the house were doing a lot of shooting, not Donny. And not your client, whose gun was empty. Their target was a duffle bag of jewels, but they didn't get it. Ricky Weed came out of the back room, Donny got confused, the intruders probably started firing at Donny, and the whole thing went to Hell, and the sisters got killed. Nobody would have thought the sisters mattered much anyway. That's the way it went down."

"Ricky Weed gave you this slug, did he?" young lawyer Adams asked. "And you are an expert on ballistics?"

"I know a hollow-point from a regular .38, and a hollow-point is a police bullet."

"But my client's gun has regular .38's in the cylinder?"

"Ding Dong! That's because the sheriff put them there. It was a hollow-point that lodged in Ricky Weed's leg, the pimp who nobody likes. But they have to protect him so he doesn't confess who the 'unknown' strangers were, who showed up and started shooting. Who is looking for those guys, anyway?"

"A stretch MacFarlane," Adams said. "But here, I'll take that bullet. Maybe I can get it into evidence." He reached for it, but I pulled back my hand.

"I'll be right there in the courtroom. I'll supply the bullet whenever you call me or Ricky Weed to testify."

"Neither of you is under subpoena."

"I'll be in the pews, waiting to testify, and Ricky Weed can be quickly found. By me."

"Considering the posture of this case," the lawyer said, "your testimony may not be possible." He turned abruptly and I watched him go up the courthouse steps.

Just then, Juanita arrived in a taxi out front. I saw her pay the man and run inside. I followed her.

I was not surprised to see that a crowd was lined up for seats and that the courtroom was getting packed. A murder trial, especially one involving women, was pretty hot stuff around Sarasota. There were even newspaper reporters hanging out in close proximity to the phone booths in the corridor. Germaine must have arrived while I wasn't looking. She was on the bench across the room from Juanita. Both of them caught my eye to indicate they had both saved me a seat. This was a minor personal difficulty.

I nodded solemnly at each of them and took my own spot standing along the back wall with some other cops. I was firmly planted there for the "O Yeas's, All Stand," when Judge Braxton took the bench.

It had the smell of a trial, that courtroom. Musty like aged wood, freshened with Old Dutch Cleanser. A scent left by the rags used by the night maids, maids who, because of their race, could not sit in the jury box. And it smelled of the moth balls that preserved the Sunday suits the defendants wore, and of the sweat of the hard working people who came here hoping for justice. All of those smells had sunk into the paint.

A whack of the gavel signaled the start of this session of court. It took less than half an hour to empanel the rest of the jury. Without any recess, the twelve selected citizens were all arranged in their seats and welcomed by the honorable Braxton.

Whitey Jarvis was made to stand and hear the charges read against him. Belatedly, his public lawyer Adams stood beside him, dusting crumbs off his misbuttoned vest. Sheriff Pearson was the prosecutor's first witness. The jurors shook their heads awake. I'd seen it a thousand times.

Yes, the sheriff said, I found the dead women, spread out on the floor. It was a terrible crime. I found the gun laying on the floor between their bodies. Investigating, I went to the bar right down the street. Patrons inside suggested that the shooters could have been Donny Ropollo and Whitey Jarvis, since they had walked out of the premises a short time before the shootings. We put out a bulletin, and the suspects' car was spotted two days later, crossing out of Florida somewhere near Baldwin County, Alabama; that's past Pensacola, quite some distance away. Then word came back they were seen crossing the state line and entering Louisiana. "We pursued them, night and day."

I could picture the sheriff and chief Davis making a grand chase across three state lines in their spacious police Hupmobile. Sirens all the way.

Pearson continued. "On a tip, we found them in a fishing camp in Slidell, Louisiana, on the shore of Lake Pontchartrain. Our tip came from a reliable source. But, whatever the source, there they were, and we surrounded the shack. We announced our presence. Donny Ropollo came out shooting. The officers did what they had to do and took him down. We called for Whitey Jarvis to come out, and in a few minutes, aware of the futility of resistance, he came forth with his hands in the air. He was placed under arrest, taken into my custody. After a brief detour to New Orleans, where there was a bank robbery charge against Mister Jarvis, we returned the defendant to Sarasota for this trial that we are having today. And here he sits." Pearson pointed a long crooked finger at the defendant.

"So, he's a murderer?" the prosecutor persisted.

"Objection," Adams said softly.

"Overruled," murmured the judge.

"Well, sir, I'd say, yes, I guess," the sheriff continued. "But, he's a nice enough fellow."

The prosecutor pressed it. "But he killed those women, yes?"

There was no objection, and the sheriff naturally answered in his deep voice, "Yes. That's sure the way it looked to me."

The Chief of Police, Tilden Davis, was called to identify the gun that Whitey had left behind. "We found three bullets that had been fired into the walls of that house. The ones that killed the victims might have drilled straight through their bodies. They were all .38's, same as the defendant's gun. When he dropped it at the scene, there were three rounds left in the chamber, making it obvious that he had fired three." The chief reported his conclusion sadly. "Just enough to kill those ladies," he said.

"Wait!" I wanted to shout. Those three bullets had been planted in Whitey's gun! He didn't shoot anyone! No objection came from the defense counsel.

Unfair. What about Ricky Weed, who jumped out of the window? What about his bullets? Who shot him? With a police bullet? And who the hell were those two strangers?

"How do you know that the gun you found at the scene belonged to the defendant?" the prosecutor asked.

"Well, Mister Jarvis never denied it, and in fact he signed a statement to that effect."

This may have been news to lawyer Hershel Adams. In any case, something made him remember that he ought to cross examine the Police Chief.

Rising slowly, Adams walked in front of the defense table, then leaned his butt against it. "What became of those bullets, Chief? The ones you dug out of the wall and which you say killed the women?"

"I don't know if they killed the women, but I sent them off to the state lab. They never sent them back."

"So, you don't know for sure what caliber they were or what gun fired them?"

"I could tell they were .38's based on twenty years' experience in law enforcement, and I'll also say they was so flattened by the wall that tracing them to a particular weapon would be impossible. But, one thing is as clear as day. The defendant admitted it was his gun."

"Alright, Chief," the young lawyer continued. "What do we know about the two men who entered the house and started the shooting?" I thought lawyer Adams might finally be starting to wake up!

"We don't know a thing about them, or even if they existed. Only Whitey Jarvis saw them."

"Is that true?" Adams demanded. "Weren't they seen by another fellow who was in the house, a local man who jumped out the window?"

"Before she died, Lacey Bell said he wasn't the killer."

"But maybe he knows something about who the killer was."

The district attorney jumped to his feet and yelled, "Objection! We saw no need to call that man to testify! Why? Because Whitey Jarvis confessed he was there, and he left his firearm at the house!"

"Well. . ." Adams began.

The judge cut him off. "Sustained!" he ruled.

Adams protested, "Then I'll have to call that man myself." He sat down in a huff.

The coroner was summoned to attest to the deaths by gunshot. The cause of both was .38 caliber bullets, two in both women.

Whoa! You say Whitey shot three? Now there were four holes in the bodies? No objection from defense counsel.

The prosecution rested, and Hershel Adams called his client, the defendant Whitey Jarvis, to the stand.

The courthouse regular seated next to me muttered, "He should never call that poor man to testify. He looks defeated already." I wasn't too sure myself about this strategy. A more forlorn and hangdog look than the one on Whitey's miserable face would be hard to imagine.

Whitey took his seat and crossed himself. Then he admitted to being at the roadhouse bar. To walking with Donny Ropollo to the ladies' house on 24th Street, and to going inside with the intention of socializing and having a few drinks. They were greeted by one Lacey Bell. All was friendly, very friendly, until two men, total strangers to him, came in. Then another man he did not know, pulling up his pants, and some woman, he did not know, barged in from the back room screaming about something. That man had a gun, Whitey said. Addressing the strangers at the door, Lacey Bell asked, "Are you guys cops?" When they said no, she laughed in their faces. One of the women slapped one of the intruders, and he slapped her back. Everybody was yelling "Shut Up!" And suddenly that man from the back and the strangers were all popping off shots.

"Those men who came in shot both of those poor women in cold blood," he cried, "and the man who barged in from the back room fired his gun, too! My partner Donny had a pistol, and defended himself with it, causing them all to duck and run outside. I didn't have time to do anything but stand there. Those two nice women were both shot down and were bleeding at my feet. The man from the back room leaped out the window and ran away. I didn't kill anyone!"

The prosecutor stood up to cross-examine. "This will be brief, Your Honor. Mister Jarvis, when you were in New Orleans, before you returned to Florida and got involved in these murders, did you rob a bank?"

"Uh, sir, I did plead guilty to that."

The state attorney faced the jury, spread out his arms and laughed. "I don't think any more needs to be said." He sat down. Now I knew for certain that young Hershel Adams was in way over his head. But to his credit he persevered.

"My next witness, Judge, will be the man who jumped out of the window. I'm not entirely sure of his name. . . "

"Ricky Weed," I whispered loudly, earning a scowl from the bench.

". . . But I need time to locate him," Adams continued, "and would ask for a recess, perhaps an hour or two."

The prosecutor jumped up, but before he could object Judge Braxton shut this whole line of inquiry down, "Sir," he said to Whitey's lawyer, "you have had more than a month since your client was arrested to locate your witness, not to mention this long weekend since the trial began, and I am not going to delay these proceedings any further. We are not going to recess for a couple of hours or for ten minutes. Please proceed with your case."

"That missing man must be a friend of the judge," the onlooker by my shoulder whispered. I thought he was dead-on right.

Whitey's young lawyer took a loop around his table to regroup. Composing himself, he announced, "I'm going to call one Juanita Ropollo."

"For what?" the judge asked.

"To prove, Your Honor, that my client's gun wasn't loaded."

The prosecutor was back on his feet. "Judge, I believe that woman to be the cousin of Donny Ropollo, who was killed in a shootout with the police. I object to her testifying about anything because she's not credible. And even if you were to believe a word she'd say, the defendant himself has never claimed to this Court that his gun was empty or that his gun wasn't fired. So, I object!"

"Your objection is sustained," ruled Judge Braxton.

"Hell, no!" I shouted and bolted from the wall, ready to charge the bench.

"Bailiff, remove that man from my courtroom and don't let him return!" The bailiff hurried my way, and so did two Sarasota policeman who were posted near me in the back of the courtroom. In a jiffy I was hustled out of the room. I walked stiffly but didn't struggle, not wishing to end up in the cell vacated by Whitey.

After I was ejected I waited outside in the parking lot. I heard about it when the defense rested and the jury retired for lunch, sandwiches delivered from the Hotel Watrous. That afternoon at about 1:30 they returned to find Whitey Jarvis guilty, without a finding of mercy. The judge sentenced him to die in the electric chair.

Whitey's girl, Juanita, bolted from the courtroom, crashing past me like I wasn't there. The crowd slowly cleared. Germaine, weeping silently into a tissue, was one of the last to come out. She walked over to meet me, and I put an arm around her shoulder. She clutched her purse to her breast with both hands, like a shield.

"They didn't even care," she sobbed.

"No," was all I could say.

"He's only thirty-five."

Whitey didn't shoot anybody, true enough, but any jury would have found him guilty of something. Yet he didn't deserve to be fried in the electric chair. He wasn't a bad man. And with all his larceny, I couldn't say he had ever hurt anybody. I didn't express that to Germaine exactly, or most else of what I felt, as we walked out of the courthouse in the direction of my car.

"Where can I take you?" I asked her. "Back to St. Pete? Or do you want a cup of coffee? Or I'll buy you a real drink?"

She found a hanky and blew her nose, but she shook it off. "No, Gabe. I want to go back inside. I'm going to appeal to that black-hearted son-of-a bitch judge to show some compassion."

"That's not likely to happen, baby," I told her. "He's stone cold."

"Maybe I can persuade him," she said. "I have to try." She rubbed her eyes and straightened her satin blouse.

I said, "Okay," but what she expected to accomplish with her feminine wiles with old Judge Braxton I couldn't begin to imagine. "I'll wait here if you want."

She gave me a quick kiss on the forehead, and said, "Thank you, Gabe. You're a solid guy."

I watched her walk back into the courthouse. It was a pretty afternoon despite our being downtown with all the traffic. Sarasota's tall new buildings, shading the sun, almost made me forget how beautiful it used to be. But it was still one of the prettiest places in Florida, all told. A few buildings couldn't hide that. I wondered if I'd ever see Juanita or Whitey again. There was the loud pop, probably a car backfire, which made me jump. It blended right in with the toots of the vehicles trying to forge their way onto the city's newly refurbished bridge to St. Armands Circle.

Germaine hurried out of the courthouse and jumped into the passenger seat before I could even get behind the wheel.

"Let's put the pedal to the metal, Gabe," she said.

"Good enough, ma'am." I backed out and made a quick exit through an alley to put us on a back street. At least Germaine had stopped crying. "Any luck?" I asked her. "You weren't gone very long."

"Just drive!" After a quick look over her shoulder to check the street behind us she sank down in her seat and closed her eyes. "I need to rest for a moment," she said. And in that moment she was softly snoring.

I had got us all the way back to St. Petersburg before she woke up. Germaine unlocked the door to her house, flicked on the outside light, and beckoned me inside.

"Will you have some whiskey," she asked when she lit up her kitchen.

I shook my head. "Then fix me one," she told me. I cracked open her ice trays, uncorked the bottle, changed my mind and poured us both a drink. "Wait while I wash up." She took her glass and drifted out of the room.

The apartment was familiar to me, and the booze made it feel good to be here. I flipped on the radio, the one she kept on her dining room table, hoping for some mellow big band from Miami, New York, Baltimore, anywhere less violent than Florida felt right now. But what came out of the box was, "Judge Shot and Murdered in Sarasota Courtroom! Assailant is described as a young woman. Motive as yet unknown. No arrests yet, but investigation is ongoing, says . . ."

What about that! A young woman! And I was reminded of a poem from the book of Robert Burns poems that my dad had left for me before he died nearly a half century ago:

And they hae taen his very heart's blood,
And drank it round and round;
And still the more and more they drank,
Their joy did more abound.

I waited till well after dark to depart my St. Petersburg hideaway. Me, my car and my Sarasota license tag drove the long way north and around to Tampa and my son Mack's house. Traffic was sparse, and it made me hope that I would find him at home before he went to bed. I was in no hurry to drive home to Sarasota while a hunt was on for Judge Braxton's killer.

At Mack's hut by the small airfield he was outside, wiping the dew off his new Indian Chief under the moonlight.

We shook hands. "Always good to see you, Dad. But I've got to go to work soon," he said. "Night job." I held him back long enough to deliver the message I'd been given for him.

"I know you've had business with those hoods, Tito Rubio and Eddie Virella," I said somberly. "But no matter I've, uh, had an encounter with one of their Antinori competitors, as in Mario Perla, and I'm sorry to say he is convinced that you stole a valise full of rare jewels from them. He believes that you must have had a deal with Eddie Virella all along, and you gave the loot to his mob, and therefore they are going to . . ."

"What?"

"I don't know. Punish you? Kill you? I don't know. Mario Perla said you were marked."

Mack chewed his lip, his mother's frailty. "Well, I can't quit working, Dad. But I may have to leave for a while. Will you take care of Christy and little Gordy?"

We shook on it.

Mack kick-started his bike and it roared into life, blasting its loud way through the misty night winds toward his airplane.

I went inside to see if all was well. Turned out, the house was asleep, and I fixed a little dinner of Spam, mayonnaise, and white bread for myself. Then I crashed on the couch. When I closed my eyes, visions of Mario Perla, Charlie Ort, Germaine Doré , Juanita Ropollo, and all the miscreants floated through my mind.

I should call my wife, I thought, and fell asleep.

In the morning I did call her, and got the operator, a woman named Sue Ingle, but no one picked up at my house. I had to drive through Sarasota on my way home, so I stopped in at the Executive Arms to look for Juanita. There was no answer at her door. A man passing in the hall said, "She checked out yesterday. Took her suitcase and walked out."

I tried the knob anyway, and the door swung open. The apartment was empty of everything except the simple furniture it came with. No special ring for me to find this time. I'd never know if Juanita was a likeable hoodlum's sidekick or the mastermind of all these crimes. Now, possibly, she was on her way back to New Orleans, to her den of Ropollos. No telling what mayhem she might still create.

"Did you see where she went?" I asked the man. "Or if she got in a cab with anyone?"

"Naw. Didn't notice." He moved on.

I never saw or heard from Juanita again. She must have figured that there was nothing more she could do for Whitey, or for me. Maybe she'd heard about Judge Braxton getting shot and was spooked. Rightfully so! She might be implicated. But at least, with her handbag of jewelry, she got something out of the deal.

My son Mack prudently left the area, quickly. He got a job working for the Ringling Circus travelling as a stunt pilot.

It was always a big deal when the Circus left Sarasota, just as it was when it arrived in late fall. Everyone tried to go to the Fairgrounds to see the elephants and tigers getting on the train. The Pinkertons called me, and I picked up a couple of days' work as added "security."

If you can picture it, the travelling Circus loaded more than 150 huge wagons, containing everything from groceries to the planks of the grandstand seats, from giraffes and seals to the trapeze artists and their ropes. Magnificent teams of horses were required to pull all of it onto train flatcars. There were caged leopards, polar bears, lions and chimpanzees, more creatures than you could name. The train itself was more than a hundred cars long, and it included sleepers for more than 2,000 employees with berths of varying size depending on one's status. Can you conceive the cost? You would expect such an undertaking to be total chaos, but the opposite was true. There was a deafening chorus of yelling and swearing, to be sure, but people knew their jobs. They'd have to, to do this at every city they visited.

Mack MacFarlane, needless to say, did not take the train. He flew.

And wife Christy and little grandson Gordy came to stay with Clarinda and me. That arrangement has been good, and it's still continuing. We've loved having Christy around, she has been good company for Clarinda, and me, too. We are all raising Gordy. From the male standpoint, I'd say the little lad has kept me feeling young.

Now I don't know what the future might bring. None of us do, but we expect it might be rough. There may be another war coming!

Or not. We are seeing Adolph Hitler on the newsreels, and Emperor Hirohito's generals pointing their swords toward where thousands of grainy gray men with helmets and bayonets are invading Manchuria. And in Italy, well . . we're in enough trouble here in Florida. Or all of this may all blow over. Nobody knows. But I'll keep my personal weapons handy.

However all of this might come out, and rough as it may be, however bad it turns out, I think my family and others like us will find our way out of the woods and we'll probably start cooking supper. And we'll wake up the next morning and start securing what's ours.

About a year after these events, by which I mean my son's evacuation from Sarasota, I got word that Beatrice Flower, who people called "Footsie," was "on her deathbed." She was being cared for by her daughter at their house behind the bar-b-que and rib joint that Footsie operated out on Cattlemen Road. Footsie and I went way back, to the days when I was a deputy sheriff and had to order her, nicely, to shut down what was then an illegal honky-tonk saloon in the woods.

We weren't close, but what hit me hard about this news was that I had been told by Cordelia Ephram that Footsie, Beatrice, was the true mother of my close-as-kin friend, Reuben Ephram. In fact, I had an old piece of paper showing where the Love Feast Baptist Church had paid the Ephrams to raise a foundling child. Why? Because the father of the baby was the church pastor, one Caleb Dawes, whom I had encountered, after he went mad, in a place called the Blackjack. I won't go into all that now because I've written that story before. But I'd never told it to the person who most needed to know it – Reuben.

It couldn't be avoided any longer, so I manned up and drove out to his place. I can't go into all that was said. It was private, between brothers. I felt so bad about keeping these facts to myself all these years that he ended up consoling me, instead of the other way around.

"Do you know who my father is?" he whispered.

I stumbled on this one. "I believe," I said, "that your father was the hermit I met in the Blackjack when I was hunting Charley Willard. I don't know for certain if I'm right." (I was certain.) "And I don't know if he is still alive, or not."

"I'll search him out," Reuben said.

"Then you're doing more than he ever did. You're a good man, Reuben. Thank the Ephrams for that. Thank yourself."

"Oh, well," he mumbled.

"I'll run you over to Cattlemen if you want to see her," I told Reuben.

"That won't be necessary, Gawain," he said. "I'd like to visit with her by myself."

"Well, give Miss Beatrice my regards."

"Sure enough," he nodded, and that was that.

Later that spring, after the Circus left, I was at our house with Christy and young Gordy, spending a pleasurable time listening to the Grand ol' Opry from Nashville on WSM radio, when a news bulletin came on. It reported that four Tampa policemen had been killed "gangland style," coming out of a political rally being held for the White People's Party. A bystander had been slightly wounded, but his wounds were apparently not too bad. The announcer made a quick note that these were the same four policemen who had once been acquitted of kidnapping two "Communist subversives," one of whom had died.

"Hey! Are they talking about the cops who killed Joe Shoemaker and tortured Eugene Poulnot?" I asked Christy.

"I certainly hope so," she said. She still kept up with Eugene and his wife, or she tried to. They were depressed, marked as Reds, and barely making ends meet. Somehow the extended Poulnot clan seemed to be holding things together, but it wasn't easy street for them. "I wonder how those cops got themselves on the wrong side of the mob," Christy said, a twinkle in her eye.

"Do you reckon that has anything to do with the deal Mack made with Tito Rubio and Eddie Virella when he turned over the bag of jewels to them?" I asked.

"I wouldn't know any of those details, my favorite old man," she said, addressing me. "But like father, like son." She hadn't called me her "favorite" before, and I took it as a sign of affection and respect. And, as for "like father like son" I took to mean – well, you can draw your own conclusions.

On April 10, 1935, Sheriff Pearson drove to Raiford, and early the next morning he escorted Whitey Jarvis, shackled, from his cell to the death chamber. When Whitey was strapped to the chair he told Pearson, "God bless you. I'll see you over there." The sheriff pulled the switch himself, according to the custom, which required this honor from the chief lawman of the jurisdiction where the crime had been committed.

I guess Pearson didn't feel very honored. He committed suicide shortly thereafter, and people said it was because he felt guilty about that electrocution. As I said, everybody liked Whitey.

It was like a family again, having Christy and Gordy around, and Clarinda and I rekindled our affection. I taught the boy about fishing and hunting, and about raising oranges, and I'm sure he profited from it. He grew a lot in those days, and I did even more. Christy got a job as a legal secretary in Venice. She and Mack wrote to each other every day the whole time they were apart.

Judge Braxton's slayer was never identified. It turned out that no one had gotten a very good look at the "young woman" who shot him.

Germaine, I hear, has found a new job, selling her beach jewelry out of my mother-in-law's thimble shop in Seminole.

You may recall my explanation that the Tampa underworld, which was also southwest Florida's underworld, was run by two competitors. The whole world knew this. "The White Shadow," Charlie Wall, ran one gang, and Ignazio Antinori ran the other. Old, white and Cuban money versus Chicago and European immigrant money. Tito Rubio operated the El Dorado for Charlie Wall, and his business partner, Eddie Virella, ran Wall's Lincoln Club.

Driving home one rainy night, after a late shift at that club, Virella was gunned down at a traffic light by persons unknown. Soon thereafter Tito Rubio, driven by his bodyguard, went home from the El Dorado to his affluent palm-lined community. When they arrived, Rubio walked to his front door, illuminated by his own car's headlights. Two gunmen leapt from the bushes and blasted him in the belly. They ran away, while Rubio's bodyguard cowered behind the steering wheel. By the time an ambulance arrived, Rubio had bled to death. The bodyguard refused to say anything at the inquest and was given six months for contempt of court.

Eight truckloads of flowers and 250 cars followed Tito Rubio to the Tampa cemetery. The crime was never solved, but Charlie Wall apparently blamed Ignazio Antinori and his henchman Mario Perla. Ignazio was sipping coffee at the Palm Garden Inn in Tampa with a young female companion when suddenly a lone gunman appeared and fired a shotgun blast, blowing off the back of Antinori's head. A few weeks later, Mario Perla, minus his head, was found floating in Tampa Bay. None of these murders were ever solved either.

Finally, Northern crime families moved into Tampa to settle the peace, which they did by taking over every corrupt thing in sight. Santo Trafficante became the new head man. Like Ignazio Antinori, he had been born in Santo Quisquinol, Sicily, and in short order he put Charlie Wall out of business. That ended the rule of the "White Shadow" and all the other local boys.

To me, it was just another case of rich Yankees taking over Florida.

For all my efforts, I couldn't see how I had helped Whitey Jarvis in the slightest degree. Nor had I apprehended the two men who broke into the two Bell sisters' house and started the terrible fusillade of bullets that took the women's lives. I hadn't done a thing to help Eugene Poulnot or expose his torturers. But, I guess my son took care of that.

Two mysteries had bothered me. One was, how those hoods knew that Whitey Jarvis was carrying a duffle bag of baubles? That one was now solved: Charlie Ort had tipped off Mario Perla, in hopes that Captain Flagstead's half would satisfy Charlie's debts. That didn't work out so well. Two women died and Whitey Jarvis went to the chair. And it didn't help Charlie any because Whitey, before he left on his ill-fated attempt to outrun the law, managed to give the Captain's share to Juanita, who took it Kelly Bucks at Whiskey Corners to fence.

In the meantime, Charlie Ort was forced to tender his half to Mario Perla. Perla sent Leonard Trout to Englewood, flown there by my son, to pick up Charlie's share from the very same Kelly Bucks. Confusing enough, but here's the other mystery. How did Eddie Virella learn, in time to arrange an ambush, that Leonard Trout was flying Charlie Ort's bag from Whiskey Corners back to Tampa?

That question deserved an answer.

I took my question back to Whiskey Corners early on an afternoon before the orange harvest, intending to return home before it got too late so as not to worry Clarinda. It was a hot day without a breeze – even the palms couldn't manage a wave or even a little sway. The doors of Whiskey Corners were open to allow clean air to flush the place, and the bartender waved as I walked past.

Kelly Bucks was in the back, boots up on his desk and reading a Racing Form. He grinned at me in a sociable way, and I posed my question to him.

"This still bothers me. How did Eddie Virella find out about Leonard Trout flying in here? You were the only person who would have known." I sounded friendly, but I wasn't.

"Not the only person, Gabe MacFarlane." Bucks tossed his Racing Form aside. "My other customer, Captain Flagstead, was here that night.

I thought maybe you had figured this out. You see, Flagstead had found out that his agent, Whitey Jarvis, had gotten involved in a murder and was in jail in Sarasota. The Captain wanted to be sure that I knew he was the owner of that duffle bag and that, to quote him, 'property rights would be respected.' I assured him that all was well with his property rights." Bucks rolled his chair back enough to get his boots on the floor. "Just as we were ending that conversation, the unfortunate Mister Trout appeared, intoxicated, and he blabbed about his business in front of the Captain. I asked the Captain to leave my office, and he did, but he was a shrewd man, may he rest in peace. He went out to the bar. You know we have a pay phone there."

"And he…"

"The Captain had an idea that Charlie Ort had tipped Mario Perla that Whitey would have a duffle bag of jewels at that bar on 24th Street. Was that true, about Ort?"

I shrugged. No comment.

"Anyway, the Captain may have decided to screw Ort the same way that Ort tried to screw him. So maybe he called Virella. You know that the Captain ran fishing charters for Virella and his friends. They were acquainted."

I hadn't known that.

Bucks smiled, "They didn't really like each other, the Captain and Charlie. Too bad. C'est la vie, yes?"

Well, there it is. People get obsessed by riches. They get greedy and then they try to do each other in. That's a bad fact, but a lesson in human nature.

Every year, late in November when the Circus rolled back to Florida, I hoped Mack would come back to stay. But in this one particular year, who should come along with the Circus but Charlie Ort. He was employed again and in the pink, and he called me up to offer me a job.

"We're riding again, Gabe. I got my concessions back, and I've got a spot for you, a good man who knows the business."

Cash was hard to come by, so I told him sure, I'd come over for a talk.

As it happened, Mack blew back into town at the same time. With the elimination of certain mobsters, things had started to feel safer here. Baby steps, we said.

He had been working at the Circus, but always in the winter, up north. When he came home, all of us, Clarinda, Christy and Gordy, we all rejoiced. Mack's first stop, of course, was our house to see his wife and young son. Mack was a full grown man, and full of himself. It made me proud to think he would carry on the MacFarlane name – just so long as he would stay out of law enforcement. We all had a great reunion dinner, then Clarinda and I went out on the porch to watch the sunset and give the young people time to get reacquainted. It was all good. Clarinda and I were falling back in love. I reflected about how satisfied it made me feel, having my whole family around me, all together, all safe for the moment. I suppose I had found the loving community the preacher once talked about.

Except for the nagging grief that I had failed miserably as an upholder of justice in my last case - the defense of Whitey Jarvis - these were the very best of times. Clarinda listened to my reciting these misgivings, and she reminded me of the many highlights of my career. I was happy, but I would soon find out that sometimes a chance encounter will reaffirms a man's belief in himself and make him even happier.

I took Mack along when I went to meet with Charlie Ort about the maybe job at the Circus.

Or Mack took me, in his pick-up. By then he had actually been a Ringling stunt-man longer than I had ever worked there, and he had the credibility of going with the Circus on its tour up North. He had a glamorous job. He had no part in the great labor of setting up and taking down the show. I'm saying he was more official than me.

The evening we drove over together couldn't have been nicer.

Thanksgiving was in the air, and warm breezes blessed Sarasota with "the fragrant birch and hawthorn hoar," as the poet says, not to mention shrimp being boiled and fish being fried.

MACK WAS THERE

Dad wanted to make a visit to the Circus, and it involved a man he knew, Charlie Ort, one of many Circus regulars I'd never met. But Dad said we needed to remedy that. We parked at the Fairgrounds and joined the line buying tickets for a dime apiece. Twenty-five feet away from us was the "Colored Entrance," and there was a long line there, too. I had seen signs around town advertising a pair of savage albino Ethiopians who were proclaimed to have come from Mars and landed in the African jungle. Their pictures on posters all over Sarasota County certainly made them look like space aliens, and probably that accounted for the big crowd. Dad took the lead. Before I could pull out my employee identification, he flashed his Pinkerton badge, which he had never turned in when he left the job, and we were admitted for free.

The weather was beautiful and attendance was high, almost shoulder to shoulder. We pushed through crowds of people, working our way down the colorful midway. All manner of attractions and games of chance, with flashing lights and ringing bells, and rides with merry music, lined the many paths, all of which eventually would take you to the Big Tent. Dad had told me that our destination was a trailer parked way back near the stables, but a most memorable event occurred well before we got there.

Some sort of dust-up was in high fever right in the middle of our route, and it seemed to be centered around the "Strong Man Contest." That's the game where a fellow can pay a dime or more and swing a great wooden mallet, its keg-shaped head encircled by steel bands to keep it from splitting apart. You slam that big hammer down onto a wide circular steel plate which works a lever, and if the plate is struck hard enough, the lever will fire a bullet-shaped projectile up the tall pole, the object being to ring the bell on top. Success brings a prize doll, the size depending on the price wagered. Play at this attraction had stopped, and the onlookers were all jeering and cheering, because the proprietor of the game, a strong man himself, had tackled two young colored men and wrestled them to the ground.

"Thieves!" he yelled repeatedly, pounding his meaty fist into one head, then the other. The men, boys really, were screaming and begging for mercy, but they weren't getting any. A prize doll lay in the dirt. Was it the stolen property?

"Hey, enough of that," Dad said, pushing through the spectators. "Knock it off, man, you're killing them!" He put a restraining hand on the assailant's sweaty shoulder, which bulged with muscles, and he tried to arrest the man's arm in mid-swing. The boys' faces were covered in blood from their noses, and their white shirts were fouled with the red dust of the midway.

The giant was not having any interference. Instead of calling it quits he raised himself off the ground, showing what an awesomely strong man he truly was, and he picked my father several feet up in the air and flung him crashing against the bell pole.

I jumped on this enormous fool, but he swatted me away like I was a pesky bug. I landed hard on some poor woman and both of us were knocked flat to the ground. The lady's escort rushed to her defense and angrily tore at my collar while screaming at me to get off his wife. As I was trying to escape I saw my father rise up and charge forward, clutching that heavy mallet in both hands. He raised it high and took a mighty swing that landed square on the back of the ogre's head. He, who had taken to kicking the boys as they tried to crawl away, rotated slowly. He raised a fist. But then his eyes rolled up, and he pitched forward and collapsed on his face.

My father dropped the hammer, and fast as a rattle snake strikes, he had a pair of handcuffs out of his trousers. He pulled the big man's wrists back and secured them together, all without missing a beat. The boys got up and ran. I thought I heard Dad whisper to the bruiser, "Keep that stuff out of here, fella!"

Dad was still kneeling on the ground when some other big gentleman put a grip on his shoulder. "Let's go, dude," he commanded.

My father straightened up and dusted off his hands. "Pete Noski," he said. "Good to see you." Pete smiled and released his grip.

"Let's skedaddle, son," Dad said to me. He shook the straw out of his hair. "This will take care of itself." He led the way, pushing through the gawkers. I followed as close behind as I could get, and in a few minutes we were well away from the scene. My father paused and signaled me to one side. He bought us a pair of hotdogs with kraut and mustard.

"Are you just going to leave that man like that?" I asked.

"What man?" he replied.

"And your cuffs?"

"I've got more," he told me. "Let's go see Ort."

That's my Dad.

So you know what? I felt a whole lot better after that little fracas. It put some gas in my tank, you might say. But I wonder, where do all these sons-of-bitches come from? Do they have a camp, on a lake, in a woods, somewhere? Maybe I should hunt 'em down. I could take Mack with me. He's got a better grip on the world we're living in now.

I'll pass the lead to him, but I ain't dead yet. I'm thinking about taking Clarinda on a real trip. Maybe a cruise. Maybe we'll go to France.

We all have to carry the hope within us that better days are coming. The poet's verses, the way I remember them, suggest it may be so.

You see that fellow called 'a lord',

Who struts, and stares, and all that?

Though hundreds worship at his word,

He is but a dolt for all that.

The man of independent mind,

He looks and laughs at all that.

Then let us pray that come it may

(As come it will for a' that)

That Sense and Worth over all the earth

Shall take the prize and all that!

That man to man the world over

Shall brothers be for all that.

And in Some Future Eccentric Planet

Where Wit may sparkle all its rays,

Not cursed with Caution's fears;

Pleasure basking in the blaze,

Shall rejoice for endless years!

THE END

Tony Dunbar has managed a deft blend of fact and fiction in his latest novel, The Story of the Sarasota Assassination Society. He paints a fascinating portrait of the good, the bad, and the ugly of Sarasota during its pioneer days, and it makes for a great read.

Jeff LaHurd, author of *Hidden History of Sarasota & Gulf Coast Chronicles*

The illimitable Tony Dunbar charges forward with another spectacular work, this time a historical fiction—a Southern, as this new genre is being called--about the most alluring of places, Old Florida. Lovingly researched and beautifully imagined, Dunbar brings to life a history that cannot stay buried, a moving and explosive story of murder, love, and redemption in the bizarre and rich landscape of the frontier. This fateful and gripping story is about the dramatic entanglements that kill us and those that save our lives.

Janisse Ray, author of *Ecology of a Cracker Childhood & Wild Spectacle*

Ever the consummate storyteller, Tony Dunbar power-dives into Florida history to produce a crime thriller that makes you want to say, "Wow! That really happened here?" Can't wait to see how the series unfolds!

Julie Smith, Edgar Award winning author of bestselling mystery series featuring *Skip Langdon* and *Rebecca Schwartz*.

Tony Dunbar is a Georgia-born Louisiana lawyer who lives in Southwest Florida on a tidal creek rich with leaping fish, herons, manatees and passing alligators. He is an award-winning author and, in addition to the *Florida Fables* series he has written extensively about Southern history and civil rights and is the creator of the *Tubby Dubonnet* mysteries set in New Orleans.